PRAISE F

Will End in Fire

"A page-turning mystery, a suspenseful domestic drama, a deep psychological character study of warring siblings, and a heartbreaking addiction saga all rolled into one poignant, powerful novel. Unputdownable."

—Susan Shapiro, *New York Times* best-selling author of *Unhooked, Lighting Up,* and *The Forgiveness Tour*

"Nicole Bokat has once again weaved together scintillating storytelling with gorgeous prose. . . . a haunting, poetic thriller."

—Judy Batalion, *New York Times* best-selling author of *The Light of Days*

"I blazed through Bokat's fiery, fast-paced new thriller in a single sitting. Navigating the perilous terrain of sibling rivalry, arson, addiction, rape culture, climate change, and a pandemic, the novel's riveting twists are driven by the questions: Who can Ellie Stone trust? What will it take for her to trust herself? What is the price if she doesn't? You'll turn these stunning pages with your heart pounding and your hands on fire."

—Tess Callahan, author of *April & Oliver* and *Dawnland*

"This novel will grab you from the first sentence and won't let you go until the last. A riveting story of love, loss, and fear that raises questions about how childhood events and family dynamics shape us, influencing what we remember, who we believe, and whether we can change the patterns of our lives."

—Anastasia Zadeik, author of *Blurred Fates* and *The Other Side of Nothing*

WILL END IN FIRE

WILL
END
IN
FIRE

A Novel

Nicole Bokat

SHE WRITES PRESS

Published 2024
Printed in the United States of America
Print ISBN: 978-1-64742-804-4
E-ISBN: 978-1-64742-805-1
Library of Congress Control Number: 2024909068

For information, address:
She Writes Press
1569 Solano Ave #546
Berkeley, CA 94707

Interior design by Stacey Aaronson

She Writes Press is a division of SparkPoint Studio, LLC.

For Jay

FIRE AND ICE

Some say the world will end in fire,
Some say in ice.
From what I've tasted of desire
I hold with those who favor fire.
But if it had to perish twice,
I think I know enough of hate
To say that for destruction ice
Is also great
And would suffice.

—ROBERT FROST

prologue

I didn't start the fire.

That was the one fact I needed everyone to know—everyone who mattered and even those who didn't. Yes, I'd smoked a cigarette that night, but only *one*, out of frustration from being stuck at my family home: after a long commute from my job below downtown Manhattan to my apartment in Washington Heights to pick up my car and drive to our suburban New Jersey town. I'd been summoned to babysit my younger brother, Josh, the week before he was to start another round of treatment for addiction to both the Adderall he claimed he needed and the Ativan he took to counteract it. That wasn't how my dad had worded this favor, of course, since Josh was a twenty-four-year-old former midfielder at a Division 1 college. Our family's golden-legged Hermes who'd lost his footing since graduation. The brother who used to be the boy of my heart, my companion in navigating both our parents' expectations and our escapist adventures in the wooded nature reserve near our house. I'd been the fearless guide, dragging his sled on a snowy path, or hopping from rock to rock in a shallow stream, cocky even when I lost my way.

"Keep an eye on him," Dad had said. "I need to take Mom away for our anniversary."

Later, rumors of what happened spread as quickly as those flames that crackled in our front hall. It wasn't the sound of camp and roasted marshmallows but of land scorched by the enemy. That enemy was me. The last words I'd spoken to Josh had been: "Drop dead."

chapter one

Early September 2019

I t was after midnight when the ball hitting the garage door woke me. That thump was the sound of my childhood. The sound hadn't changed—not even now, when practicing no longer mattered—but Josh had.

As a boy, he'd ask me to quiz him on his vocabulary words and to check his math sheet answers because I was a wonder girl, pulling in all As and glowing evaluations from teachers. We'd giggle when Mom drove us to school until, suddenly, when Josh turned twelve, he sprang up and grew muscles and became his own kind of golden. One coach after another singled him out as special. Special in a way I'd never be, in a way that demanded attention and budgeting and alterations in our parents' schedules. My brother would position his gym bag between us and stick in his earbuds and only talk to Mom about which away game was when, or could she pick up some extra protein bars for him at ShopRite. It wasn't the withdrawal of affection that stung the most. It was how he treated me like I was a random passenger, along for his life's ride.

When I began confronting him about how he ignored me, he claimed to be busy and that I was just jealous—which was true. But still, I missed him. I thought I'd become hardened to the loss, but then I was rarely in his company for such long stretches anymore.

This weekend, I'd asked him to keep the noise to a minimum. I had two articles to finish copyediting by Monday, so I couldn't just slog through the weekend bleary, thick with fatigue.

I traipsed down the stairs into the dining room.

The table was dorm-dirty: his dinner of take-out pasta with meat sauce in its aluminum container, topped by two browned banana peels, a pair of filthy workout socks, the morning's fried eggs, rivulets of yolk congealed on a paper plate—to avoid the strenuous act of loading the dishwasher—empty bottles of sports drinks. Whales would choke to death on plastic as a sacrifice to the gods of Goal Scoring. I'd left my vegan leather backpack on the floor—the high-end one I'd splurged on when I'd gotten my new job last year. One of the bottles was knocked on its side, dripping onto my bag.

Josh slid open the glass door to the deck, letting himself back into the house, phone pressed against his ear.

"You're such a dick!" I shouted.

Josh fierce-whispered, "Auds, hold on, okay? One minute." He held the cell to his chest to keep our conversation private.

Auds. Short for Audrey, his girlfriend of several years, a Celtic beauty with slightly freckled skin and long, brown eyelashes. Audrey had maybe spoken one full sentence to me in all this time. I wasn't sure if her silence was due to introversion or possessiveness. The way she grasped onto Josh, as if she'd fractured her foot and he were her crutch, made me wonder about their relationship. Josh was so happy around her—at least until he started using again and his life stalled— always smiling in her presence, as if he'd scored the winning point. But her clinginess wasn't good for someone who was sinking.

Josh's gaze was steady and cold. "What's your problem?"

"Ever think about anyone else?" I grabbed my backpack, now speckled with Gatorade marks. "First you wake me up, then you ruin my stuff!"

"And?"

"Look at this place. You treat the house like a dump."

"Are you the clean-up crew?" he asked, as he squatted down to untie his sneakers.

"Don't confuse me with your former stalker fans." Okay, that was cruel. While in college, Josh always had an entourage, being tall and lanky with tousled hair and big hazel eyes, that quirk of a smile. Now, he slept past when my parents left for work and holed up in his room in the evenings, even eating dinner alone. "I'm only here for Dad, making sure you don't OD."

"Are you planning to scoop out my pee from the bowl for Dad to test?"

"You're disgusting."

"At least I'm not pathetic," he said. "Stay the fuck out of my business."

"Drop dead," I told him.

"You wish," he said, and then to Audrey, "I'll call you right back." He took off his dirt-encrusted sneakers and plopped them on a dining room chair before he left the room.

Was Josh's animosity pharmaceutically induced? Mine, at least, had merit.

My parents had discovered Josh's drug paraphernalia when he came home sophomore year of college and confronted him. "Victory at any cost," was the excuse Josh gave. "Coach would spike the Gatorade if it ensured a win against Maryland." My dad reported this to me: the Adderall for focus, the pills to relax. But I was living in the city by then, and, for a long time, not part of the triangular construction my family had become. "He'll grow out of it, Dad," I said. *Or he won't.* I didn't chase that thought down and examine the outcome. My parents' obsession with my brother intensified and nothing they did seemed to help, not even the first stint in rehab last summer, not the expensive shrinks, not the threat of losing his college scholarship, which he'd managed to avert, not the two years of unemployment since graduation.

I was tired of it. And tired of squelching my anger.

In my bedroom, I lit a cigarette. I was down to three a day but would make an exception this weekend. Although my mom used the space as an office, my shelves still displayed my chipped plastic trophies for academic achievements, the poster board with pictures from prom—one with Alexander Liu, another AP kid, the rest of me and Nora, in our black dresses and never-before-or-again spiked heels. For so long, we'd been all drive and hustle. Once we'd received the congratulatory emails from our first-choice schools, we vowed to loosen up, party on weekends, like normal teens. Prom was not about our lab partner dates but about us, the pact we'd made to succeed. Here we were—on the same path, still best friends and now roommates—nearly a decade later.

After stuffing my clothes into my bag, I texted Nora. She'd be binge-watching her baking show, taking notes on how to recreate the chocolate mirror cakes and the ginger biscuits. Which I got to sample.

Sick to death of Josh. Let him OD.

I didn't mean that, of course. I just wanted this version of Josh to vanish, not the brother I'd grown up with, the boy who watched the Cartoon Network with me before the pink streaks of dawn, who taught me how to do chin-ups on the bar in the garage, stood in line with me outside the bookstore for the final Harry Potter book, even though he never read the series, and convinced my parents to adopt our black shepherd on my behalf. When the vet euthanized Merlin, a few weeks before the dog's fourteenth birthday and my departure for college, Josh was the one to sob until his nose ran into the corners of his mouth.

WHAT happened?

Tell you mañana. Don't wait up!

Thumbs-up emoji from Nora.

In the car, on I-95 to the Washington Bridge, listening to Sia swing from the chandelier, I cast around my bag for cigarettes. Without a caffeine kick, nicotine would have to do. My hand toured the contents—wallet, T-shirts, cotton sweatpants, copy of *The Perishable World*, which I'd ordered after editing a Q&A with the author for my relatively low-paying but challenging job, which I loved. Where were my Marlboros? Bigger question: Where was my laptop?

Shitshitshit.

All those gas emissions and outrage for nothing. I exited south and headed north again, cursing my way back to the suburbs. By the time I arrived on our cul-de-sac, all I wanted to do was crawl onto the thin-cushioned couch and sleep. That's when I saw the sun bursting low in the sky. It took me a moment to realize that it wasn't the sun at all.

The house was on fire.

It was enormous, blasting out of the first-floor window. Josh was inside.

My fingers searched for my phone, keys, and a pair of underwear I wore as a glove. *Call 911!* I thought of an article I'd written for my college newspaper on school shootings, how the average response time for police was eighteen minutes. No one was coming to rescue Josh any faster than I could.

I raced across the lawn. The door was locked, the keyhole furnace-hot, as were the shale stones of the entranceway, which were cold in all seasons. Hyperventilating, I edged my way forward. The fumes pushed at me with such purpose, the heat like no other, a crematorium. I pulled my T-shirt over my mouth and nose, as my dad had taught me to do ages ago.

Good to be prepared, Ellie. In case.

"Josh?" I screamed into my shirt. Why wasn't he tearing from the living room, the way he did across a field, fleet and sure?

I blinked against the haze. The odor was a mixture of singed carpet, cigarettes, and chemistry lab gasses. I started coughing, then couldn't stop. How would I make my way up one flight, then another?

I had to get him. I couldn't get him. *Oh God, oh God, oh God.* Tears blocked my vision. The rush in my ears built.

There was no choice.

That's what I'd later tell my parents. I was practicing my defense even as I begged my brother to emerge from the vapors.

Turning back, I fought the fog, scorching my arm on the doorknob. Across the way, the Petersons' Colonial sat placidly, the porch light winking. I scrambled onto the street, hacking and thirsty for the fresh air.

"Ellie!" Mrs. Peterson waved at me. She was in a nightgown, her face bright and shiny from lotion. "Hurry!"

There was a bellow. A gray-and-orange lion's head of flames smashed through glass. My hands over my head, I ducked. One side of our roof caved in, crashing into the dormer window. The crush in my gut: the reach of the danger now, all the way to the third floor, Josh's room.

When my brother didn't appear, I reeled backward. I could feel myself falling, close to fainting—but not quite.

"Let's go," Mrs. Peterson said, lifting me up, her touch firm. "I've called the fire department. They're on their way. They have the best chance of helping Josh."

I should have been the one to call.

"I have to get him."

"Honey, you can't. Are you dizzy? Faint?" When I nodded, she said, "Come with me. You need water, and it's not good for you to watch this."

"No. I have to stay here. I can't leave him alone in there." I was seized with trepidation. Out it came in great heaves, then, the contents of my stomach.

"Come on. Just for a minute, to get your bearings," she said firmly. "There's nothing you can do; you're in shock. Emergency services instructed me to keep you away." She coached me up her pathway and into her hallway.

I was hyperventilating and lightheaded, but I noticed her daughters' denim jackets hanging on the hall tree, a transparent umbrella with yellow dots on it, a vase of honeysuckle seated on the bench. I'd babysat for them a few times when the youngest was a toddler, the summer before my senior year of college.

What the fuck are you doing here?

"Wait one sec. Sit down and take deep breaths."

As she hurried to the kitchen, I glanced at the dark stairway, leading to her girls' rooms, stacked in their bunk beds, her ex-husband less than a mile away in his split-level condo. "Henry Peterson deserted his family," my mother once remarked.

Deserter!

Mrs. Peterson handed me a bottle of water and I drank in quick gulps, practically slurping, my chin wet.

"Where are your parents, hon?"

"At the beach."

"I'll call them." Her eyes were full of pity.

Rubbing my chin, I noticed smudges on my palm. Coughing up more phlegm and ash, I wiped my mouth with my sooty T-shirt.

"You have to be seen by a doctor," Mrs. Peterson said.

"I'll be okay." I was trembling as if stuck inside a butcher's freezer. As much as I wanted to bolt, my body wasn't obeying.

"Mommy? What's going on?" one of the girls cried out from the top of the stairs.

"It's okay, sweetie," Mrs. Peterson answered. "I'll be right there." To me, she said, "I just have to get them settled. I left a message for your mom. No details about your poor brother, just that you're here with me. They have a long drive. So, let's get them here safely."

"Thanks."

"You almost passed out. Why don't I get the girls up and we can take you to the hospital."

Then the blare of sirens jarred me into action, some clumsy acrobatic motion through the parlor. Racing and hacking. "Gotta go."

The street was a carnival: the ambulance's blue-and-red lights, the fire engine, shiny as an ornament, the men in bright yellow helmets, tanks strapped to their backs. Mrs. Goldsmith, our next-door neighbor, had bullied her way into the action, as usual. Without her glued-on eyelashes, in her lilac robe and bracelet around her veiny ankle, she seemed older. Her basset hound howled through her open window.

I ran toward my house, the sprays of water shooting into the blaze. A paramedic extended her arm to stop me. "You can't go any closer."

"I live here."

She regarded me with greater interest. "You have to be checked for inhalation."

"No, please," I cried. "I need to see my brother, make sure he got out. I was only in the house for a minute."

"Someone else will take care of him. My job is to get you on the truck." She hoisted me onto a cot, her strength a surprise. She was slight and short, but with weight-lifter biceps. "How's your breathing?" When I nodded, she asked, "Headache?"

"No."

"Hoarseness or coughing?"

"Some," I admitted. Statistics from those pieces about the never-ending California fires sprang into my mind, how toxic smoke could cause long-term health effects.

She clipped a plastic sensor to my finger hooked up to a hand-held device. "Good." She clicked a light into my eyes.

"Where's Josh, my brother?"

She squinted. "Do you know where he was in the residence?"

I pressed my hand to my chest. "Upstairs. Third floor."

Her expression didn't change, but I knew she was calculating the odds.

"Anyone else in there?"

"No. My parents are on their way."

"Let's get you strapped in." She leaned over me, fastened one belt over my waist, another just above my knees. "I'm going to slip this on. It's oxygen."

"Why?"

"A necessary precaution."

She'd tucked the tubes over my ears when the doors to the ambulance swung open and a male paramedic called out, "Cooling towels and water bottles, Ginny. Hurry!"

"Be right there," my helper said.

I shut my eyes to the shuffle and heft of the men. I tasted vomit.

"Hang in there, buddy," one said. "We're on our way."

Turning over, I saw what I could never un-see. Two paramedics were carrying Josh out on a gurney. His face was bubbling, volcanic. His hands were charred, shedding skin onto his sheet. A fist was in my throat causing me to gag until I bent over, tore the mask away, and heaved onto the floor.

"I'll take care of it," Ginny reassured me.

I couldn't stop shivering.

"How are you feeling?" a voice asked.

"Where am I?" Another slim mattress, this time in a narrow room. Ahead of me were glass doors and, by my side, a monitor that beeped an alarm.

"You're in our most luxurious ER accommodations. I got you out of the fray."

I stared at this woman—twenty-five, tops—dark-skinned with her hair braided around her head like a wreath.

"I'm Mia, your own private nurse," she said, smiling. "I just need to draw some blood and get these suckers attached. Now that you're up, let's get you into this lovely gown." She handed me a cotton garment the color of canned string beans. "You can keep on your underwear."

"Where is he?"

"Who's that, honey?" she asked.

I struggled to sit up. "My brother. Where is he?"

"Let's wait until the doctor comes, then we can figure out what's what."

"I just need to know he's okay."

"We'll do that, as quickly as possible." Nurse Mia helped me undress. As she pushed metal buttons onto my bare chest, one after the other, she bent over me. "EKG to measure your heart activity. No worries. Standard stuff." She adjusted the tentacles of wire.

The cuff around my arm was too tight as she stuck a needle deep into my vein. Watching the tubes fill made me queasy again.

"Easy, partner," Mia said, snapping off the rubber band from my arm. "You can release your fist. Let me get you another blanket."

"When did I get here?"

"Just a few minutes ago. You fell asleep on the ride."

Picturing the seared pit of my brother's face, his ashy, peeling hand, I started to sweat. "That's impossible, with Josh in that shape."

"Trauma can do that. Nothing to be ashamed of. Here you go." She gently laid a cotton sheath over the one covering me.

The glass door slid open, and a blonde with seashell earrings walked in. Her clogs made a clopping sound. "Hi, Eleanor. I'm Dr. Berry." She lifted her stethoscope and placed it—so cold—above my breast. She lifted my gown. "Any pain?"

"There's some superficial scalding on the right hand," Mia said, "wrapped in transport."

Shaking my head, I said, "I'm not hurt. It's my brother you should help."

"I'm sure he's getting the best care. I'm going to roll you over on your left side to take a look at your back, then your feet and hands," the doctor said. Her touch was light and quick.

"Please, where is he?" I repeated. Someone had to locate him, to communicate with me.

Dr. Berry exchanged a cautionary glance with Mia. "If you mean the young man in the house fire, he's being treated in the burn unit. We are the top facility in the state."

"Is he going to be . . . okay?" The only thing that mattered was returning my brother to himself, the person he was only hours ago.

Dr. Berry glanced at my palms. "Let's get you a chest X-ray."

"I just ran into the house for a minute. They already checked me for smoke inhalation in the ambulance."

"It's standard procedure. I'm sure you'll be fine."

"I need information on Josh, please."

"I'll do my best. For now, try to relax."

"What about my parents?" I asked. "Are they here?"

"I don't know their status."

The walls were empty, no pictures, no clock. I had no sense of how much time had passed. "They're driving from the shore, but there can't be much traffic this late."

She moved closer to me. "I'll ask if they've arrived." She patted my leg, then pulled Mia aside. She spoke in a low voice, but I caught, "They need to be made aware . . ."

Mia curled the loose strands that had broken free of her braids on the back of her neck. I couldn't hear her response.

"I'll call the desk," Dr. Berry told me.

"I already told the paramedic about them," I said.

"I'll make sure that the message was received. We need to do a few tests. Mia can take care of that and Carla will be here shortly with the X-ray machine to take images, so you don't even have to leave your room."

When she was gone, I exhaled. "Can I use my phone? Pants pocket. I need to reach my roommate. She'll be really worried."

"Two minutes." Mia fished out my cell for me. "I'll give you some privacy."

Hoisting the thin blanket around my shoulders, I thanked her. But my thoughts had drifted elsewhere, envisioning Josh as a boy. All that incessant thwacking of the soccer ball, the running laps around the block, that dopamine rush that caused him to fidget on long car rides, crack his knuckles and roll his head from side to side. "It's gonna fall off if you keep that up," I used to joke. "Doesn't that make you dizzy?" He'd poke my thigh with his index finger. "Nope." I'd call him "freak," and he'd challenge me to a race, "once we get there"—wherever the destination might be. I'd counter with a "sitting still" contest. Although never discussed, we envied the other's innate skills.

My mother singled out my brother as the star, the tale of his kicking in the womb, his footprint pushed against her belly, recited to whomever would listen. Josh balked at her attention, used his anxiety as fuel to train harder. Shrugged it off when I complained to him. "Double-edged sword, Elle." Then, in his second year of high school, I was gone and his responses to my frequent texts were monosyllabic or nonexistent. First came Audrey, then drugs—and I never was certain which one dragged him from his path into some dank, twilight forest. Away from me.

Now, he might never emerge again. I trembled as I called Nora, who picked up on the second ring.

"Where the hell are you? I've tried you ten times."

"Sorry." I started to sob.

"Jesus! Elle," she said when I told her what had happened. "Okay, the train schedule . . . The first one is at 5:06 a.m. I'll make it."

"Nora, listen," I whispered, "what if it's my fault?" I grabbed my phone closer to my ear and saw what I'd done in my mind's eye. The scarred face and hand, the accusations on the bathroom wall: *Ellie Stone is an arsonist.*

"What if it's my fault *again*?"

chapter two

March 2008

The first fire happened when I was sixteen. I was a pity pick for two popular girls, Anna Nuñez and Claudia Adler, who needed to sign up others for extra credit community work, digging through rich people's clothes to distribute to charity. Anna had told me, "This could get you on the list for a college scholarship, plus at least one expensive item to keep. We're doing it at my place." I figured the deal would include forking over homework in the two classes we had together, but it seemed worth it so I agreed to go.

I bypassed Anna's ginormous house and multiple-level deck to reach the garage, which was free of cars. There was one folding table set up, on top of which was a bottle of Grey Goose and a stack of plastic cups. Anna was smoking while her bestie moved a few cans of paint thinner that were lined up on the floor, tossing aside the oily rags on top of them in the process.

I pointed to the cloth scraps. "Those should be thrown away."

Claudia rolled her eyes and said, "Chill out!"

She dragged over another table that was lying against the wall, opened it, then lifted a cardboard box filled with garments onto the makeshift furniture.

Anna poured herself a shot of vodka and then offered me a cup, which I took even though I rarely drank and then, only wine or beer. She flashed me a hooded look. She was all about the red lips and thick brows, the black lashes and long tresses to her tailbone. Anna's gig was gloss and glamour and who knew whom.

Which, as it turned out, was the reason for the invitation. "Hey, isn't Josh Stone your brother?"

"Yeah. Why?"

"My younger brother went to the same soccer camp. He told me your sib is going to be some big-shot athlete, that your parents are *super invested.*"

My oh-so-sick-of-Josh-being-the-favorite default kicked in. I took a sip of my drink, not minding the medicinal taste.

I'd been counting my grievances over the last year: how my mom taped Josh's sports schedule to the refrigerator, hiding my school flyers, how she chopped up strawberries and bananas for his breakfast smoothies while I reached inside the kitchen cabinet for a box of cold cereal, how she hunched over his French assignment with him and spoke softly, "For the *passé composé*, you conjugate like this." I worked solo unless some random question about government arose in one of my classes. Mostly I used Google, but occasionally I consulted my dad.

"Can we get going here?" Claudia asked, though she wasn't moving to do anything else, and both girls were looking at me. "I have a date with Jake Thompson later."

"Are we the only ones here?" I asked. "Where is everyone?"

Claudia shrugged in that listless way of hers; she wore the persona of indifference like the sheerest of wings. "No-shows. So, more to do. Here's the deal: Only box the 'gently used' stuff. Nothing ripped or stained. Hats and scarves are okay, shoes are out."

Anna said, "If there's anything you want to keep, I mean that you absolutely can't live without . . ." She stomped out her cigarette underfoot. "You can keep it if you do the work for us."

"Sure," I said, oh-so-casual.

I started to sort through merino tops, pleated pants, velvet leggings, a *Girl Power* T-shirt, a salmon-colored tutu, and boys' polos with various designer logos on them.

I held up a pink trench coat.

Anna sighed wistfully. "That was mine."

Even I, who knew little about fashion, recognized the Burberry label and that the price tag had to have been ludicrous. I had the snarky privileged thought that some kid in faded cords and scuffed sneakers was going to wear this coat to her free school breakfast. *Don't be an asshole*, I scolded myself. Never had I worried about paying for cafeteria food. True, my mom skimped on retail, taking me to the outlet mall for blowout sales. She was saving for Josh's future: travel costs, hotels, tutors in case he still struggled in math and French. I'd overheard her talking to my father about "his potential," about university scholarships for her thirteen-year-old. I put the trench coat on the side to keep for myself.

But owning designer garb wasn't my main concern. No matter how stellar my academic record, in order for me to attend a top college, I'd have to take out loans that would follow behind me like the longest, most expensive dress train in history. Which made me wonder: Would I find things worth serious cash on eBay?

A few minutes later, I felt this cool, smooth object tucked into the front pocket of a pair of pants. It was a cigarette lighter, lacquered blue with a scripted name on the gold trim, a diamond chip on one corner. Sleek and expensive.

I flipped open the lid and turned it on. The sparks shot out, low but steady.

Anna whipped around. "Hey, that's my mom's. Where'd you get it?"

I closed the lid. "In these." I shook out the crinkled linen trousers.

"Give it to me," Anna said, her hand out.

"You said that I could take what I want. This is what I want."

"You don't even smoke."

"Maybe I'm planning to start."

Claudia clucked, her arms crossed. "Really, Stone? You're suddenly this party girl 'cause we grace you with one invite?"

"My mother obviously didn't realize she'd left it there," Anna said. "Do you know how much that costs?"

That's the point.

I clutched this prize harder. "You made a deal. I'm doing all the work here."

Anna peered at me as if reassessing a bad investment. "Everyone knows you're a total grind. But a thief—that's news!"

I chugged the rest of the peppery liquid, warmth spreading through my chest like a layer of insulation. "You steal my trig answers all the time."

"Are you fucking kidding me?"

"Well, technically, I *let* you. You can let me 'steal' this."

"That's not the same thing."

Anna blocked my way, so I'd have to shuffle sideways to leave. She fanned out her hand.

There was that thwacking sound in my head, my brother kicking the ball over and over, afternoon into evening, a sound I used to associate with comfort, with comradery. Anger rose in me, the anger of my role in the family, of never winning that first-place trophy. Oh, how I yearned to keep this prize. Right then I decided, I'd earned that right.

I played with the lighter again, at the same time that Anna lunged at me, grabbing my wrist. "Ow!" I said, as her nails tore into my skin, knocking the prize out of my hand. I saw, then, the sleeve of her cardigan was glowing.

"Shit!" she shouted.

Claudia tore the sweater off Anna's shoulders and flung it to the ground.

Instantly, I realized the magnitude of her mistake. Ignited by the rags, a blaze burst forth. It rushed up, kissing Anna's cheek like a treacherous lover, just missing Claudia, who quickly stepped aside.

I grabbed my phone out of my pants pocket to call 911. All I could get out was the word "help." And then I saw how the flames were burgeoning like orange ghosts. They were climbing up the wood wall of the garage. Soon they would reach the roof, then the vine-covered trees close by.

"We have to get out of here!" I shouted.

Claudia led her whimpering friend, the awful odors of singed hair and fried flesh emanating off Anna.

We huddled together outside, Anna weeping and cradling the side of her face, shushing herself. Nobody even glanced at me. I knew Anna's wound needed to be treated immediately but was afraid to move, as if one wrong step could cause another catastrophe. Within minutes, the first responders arrived one after the other. My head felt heavy, and my vision glazed over. I watched as the firemen hosed down the garage until it was filled with soot, gray fog, and the pieces of collapsed roof—a pile of tar-colored slates on the soaking cement. The shell remained and two men stepped inside, one taking photographs, the other surveying the damage. The paramedics insisted on examining Claudia and me before whisking Anna away in their ambulance.

A beaky fireman holding a clipboard approached us in the driveway, where we'd been directed to wait. He was carrying a charred object, no longer that lovely, varnished blue, and held it out in his thick-gloved hand. "Who does this belong to?"

"Ellie," Claudia said.

I stared at Claudia, her blonde hair covered with ash, all that glow gone.

"What are you talking about? It's Anna's mom's."

"She tried to steal it!"

"Hey, Caruso!" the other man called out, Grey Goose bottle in his hand. "Someone was partying."

"Okay, Keith. You girls stay here. I'm going to have to call the police to sort this out. You might want to get your parents on the phone."

"Why?" Claudia asked. "It was Ellie who did this. I saved Anna's life."

"You can explain what went down to the officers."

"Check this out, Dom!" Keith exclaimed, holding up, then sniffing a charred can. "Paint thinner. Cap's off."

I said solemnly, "I told them that was dangerous."

The police arrived, a young guy with a buzz cut and toned arms, and a Black woman, probably in her early forties, with her hair pulled back and gold studs in her ears. They separated us and, of course, the man chose to speak with Claudia.

Officer Turner's name was etched on her badge. She had me blow into a Breathalyzer tube. "It's .04 percent," she said.

"Is that bad?"

"It's under the legal limit. Still not a good idea to drive while intoxicated."

"I don't have my license yet. That's not an issue, the driving part," I said, stupidly flippant.

"No way!" Claudia cried, and I spun around. She was shaking her head, ash flying onto her shoulders. "I didn't do anything."

"What's going on?" I asked Turner.

"You each need to have a guardian meet you at the station."

My legs felt quivery, like they might fail me. "Are you arresting us?"

"We just need to talk to you with an adult present," she stated. It was obvious Officer Turner wasn't a fan of drama.

"My dad works in the city. He comes home really late," Claudia said. "And my mom owns a café. It's open until six."

Officer Biceps—his real name was out of sight—stretched out one large hand, the knuckles callused. He moved closer to Claudia.

He wants to touch her.

Turner noticed but didn't react. Maybe it was a habit of his: re-sisting the urge to hit on pretty, teenage girls. Maybe his partner was used to ignoring his perversion.

"What about *your* folks?" Turner asked. Her eyes on me were steady, the brows as arched as boomerangs.

"No problem."

My mother's schedule changed daily, but it didn't matter if she was showing a house or driving Josh to an away game. My dad had finished teaching his jurisprudence seminar and was probably heading home. Better a law professor than a realtor, better my tender, philo-sophical dad than my determined, exacting mom.

"I'll call my dad," I said.

He was listed under "Favorites" on my phone, and as soon as he answered, I spoke quickly. "There's this problem at, um, a friend's house. The police are here. I swear, it was an accident."

"Don't say a word more about what happened," he said, his voice the same quiet timbre as always. "I'm leaving now. Tell them I'll meet you there."

He had to believe me, the good, steady, hardworking daughter who never before had gotten into trouble, not at school and, certainly, not with the law.

At the station, seated on a tottering chair, I recounted the series of events while Officer Turner wrote in a notepad.

"Why didn't you return her possession back to Ms. Nuñez?"

I didn't dare glimpse in his direction. What he must have thought. "She promised me I could take what I wanted. It was a misunderstanding."

"So, you weren't threatening her?"

My father's hand, on my knee, rested more heavily.

"Of course not," I said.

"Captain Keith O'Brien reported you saying"—she glanced at the notepad—"'I told them that was dangerous.'"

"Claudia wasn't concerned," I answered, lamely. "Anna was smoking in there."

"But you knew better and stayed in an unsafe environment."

"We were there to pack clothes for charity and just started fooling around."

"Ms. Adler claims you were fighting with Ms. Nuñez, that the two of you had a history of a combative relationship. Have you wanted to harm Ms. Nuñez before?"

"No, of course not. And we didn't have any, um, relationship. We just know each other through school."

Turner's dispassionate expression met my glance. "Can you clarify the sequence of events?"

I squeezed my eyes shut, willing the tears not to escape. And they didn't. "We were just fooling around. I'm not used to, um, drinking."

I heard my father's loud exhale.

Wrong thing to say.

"I'd never intentionally hurt Anna. Why would I do that?"

On the way home, my dad didn't grill me. As I predicted, his first concern wasn't my culpability or motivation or even the cost he would incur from the damages to the Nuñezes' garage and Anna's injuries. It was how we would present the information to my mother. To protect her or me or himself or all of us at once—he didn't say. What he did say was, "Let me talk to Mom first."

"Peri," he said into his cell, which was on speaker. "I'm with Ellie. I'm going to pick up Chinese. What do you guys want?"

"Fried dumplings," Josh chimed in.

"Steamed," my mother corrected him. "Why is Ellie with you?"

I sucked in air, waiting for his reply.

"It's a bit of a long story. Nothing to worry about."

My father dispatched the news over dinner in his best low-key voice. "Ellie acted foolishly, but so did the others."

My mom's fork clattered onto her plate, only ever half filled. "Anna is in the hospital, possibly injured. That's beyond foolish, Dan."

"Yes, of course, the outcome is—"

She interrupted him and focused on me. "What got into you, Ellie?"

I stared at my chicken with mushrooms and snow peas, the rice soaked in sauce. A moment before, I'd been gobbling the meal as if famished, as if I'd run track for miles instead of setting fire to a girl. I repeated the reason for my decision, but it rang hollow with my mother as judge.

"How could you insist on taking something that didn't belong to you?" she asked.

"You wouldn't understand."

"That's a cop-out. You'll have to do better."

"Peri," my dad said. "You should discuss this in private."

Josh elbowed the spoon in his soup bowl, so the liquid splashed, drops landing on the tablecloth. "I've already heard and I'm on Ellie's side. That girl lied to her."

"That's not the point," my mother said, reaching across the table to pat dry the tablecloth as if my brother were incapable of cleaning up after himself.

"Yeah, it is, Mom. Anyone would take it. Anna Nuñez sounds like a spoiled bitch."

"Watch your language, please."

"Thanks, Josh," I said softly, shifting toward him. His face was scrunched up, his forehead furrowed like my dad's.

At school the next day, girls jutted their shoulders forward and glared as they passed me in the halls. The popular boys arm-pumped and called me "Firestarter," as if I were a comic-book villain.

Overnight, I'd morphed from blissfully invisible to reviled pariah. Anna posted pictures of herself in the hospital, her hand bandaged, her face in profile. Her status: *Ellie Stone did this to me. Will need surgery and still never be the same.*

Her friends responded with sad and mad emojis, dozens of comments. *WTF? How? You're still beautiful. Who? Who is Ellie Stone? That girl should have stayed invisible! She'll be sorry!* A stack of *OMGs*.

Between second and third period, Nora texted me: *Don't pee until you get home.*

I couldn't hold it in. Sitting on the toilet, I read the graffiti. *Ellie*

Stone is an arsonist. She has to pay! Get that bitch locked up in juvie!

Working on it!

My breathing became wild.

I raced to the downstairs bathroom, then the one on the top floor. Someone had written that same message in all the girls' bathrooms throughout the building. Maybe more than one person. A campaign against me had formed. Someone scribbled that she overheard me say I wished Anna were dead. Another student claimed that she'd seen me throwing a cigarette into the bushes of the school, with a crazy look on my face!

At lunch, I unsealed my yogurt, watery whey on top. I'd thrown the container and an apple in a paper bag this morning, nabbing a ride with Nora's mom to make it to zero period. Nora had early gymnastics practice—which meant nothing for me to do for forty minutes—but all I wanted was to avoid the bus. I shoved the gross food across my tray.

"Everyone hates me," I said. "They are making all kinds of shit up about me."

Nora cracked her knuckle. "Maybe lay low for a while. You could, like, homeschool. You learn everything yourself, especially in Snider's class. You're basically self-taught in World History."

"My mom would never allow that. Anyway, I have bigger things to worry about, like going to jail."

"Kids don't go to jail, do they?" Nora looked even more like an anime character than usual: tiny features other than those round, shining eyes.

"They could take me to court, be tried as a delinquent," I told her. "Worst case, I could be put in juvie or some residential program."

Another knuckle crack. "The Nuñezes aren't going to press charges."

As if she had a clue about these people she'd never met. "I love you, Nor, but that's not how it works. The district attorney's office presses criminal charges if they think there's intent, not the victim." At my urging, my dad had laid out the facts. Unable to sleep last night, I'd joined him in the living room, after eleven, where he was reading in the dim lamp light. "You saw what Anna said, the pictures she posted. Claudia verified her story. It's their word against mine, two against one."

"What did your dad say about that?"

I'd written it down in the journal I kept for English class to refer to like a study guide. I read, "Normally, prosecutors don't press charges unless they think they can prove, beyond a reasonable doubt, that the person acted recklessly or deliberately."

"Which you didn't."

"No, but . . . I looked this part up. 'A person is guilty of aggravated arson, a crime of the second degree, if he purposely or knowingly places another person in danger of death or bodily injury.'"

"You'd never do that."

"Not purposely but *knowingly*. Which that police sergeant said. I should run away."

"You won't get into Harvard if you run away."

"Don't be ridiculous. I'm never getting into Harvard."

"Why not? You're one of the smartest kids in our class."

"Like five percent of the people who apply get in. Anyway, I have a low emotional IQ." I tore the top of my pinky nail off, the one that had grown a ragged edge. "My mom thinks I need to see a shrink."

"For what? There's nothing wrong with you."

Just then, a gang of boys knocked into our table. Jake Thompson, six foot two with a chin like a knife, smacked my apple to the ground. He hissed, "Firestarter!"

chapter three

"All set," Nurse Mia said, her hand on my shoulder. "You're being released. Consider yourself very lucky."

Curled on one side, I felt a crick in my neck as I turned my head. "Are my parents here?"

"Not yet. But your sister is."

Sister?

Nora was in one of her several "Stay Calm and Breathe" T-shirts and yoga pants. Her dot of a nose was pierced with a small silver ring. She smiled at me, that pixie-round face, her ears poking out of her spiky hair.

"You came," I said.

"Bearing gifts." She handed me her tote bag, also used for her job as a Vinyasa instructor, which she balanced with her gigs as a production assistant. "Clean clothes."

"Thank you." I swallowed, thirsty again. "Is he . . . ?"

Nora shook her head, her bell earrings tingling. "Don't know anything."

"He's in the burn center," Mia spoke up. "Your sister can take you there for a while. But try to get home soon and rest. You're going to have to pace yourself."

Wobbly, I stood on the cool floor. Mia grabbed my arm so I

could slip into a pair of shorts. "Did you guys give me something, like an Ativan?"

"Nope," Mia said. "You've had a rough night. It's normal for your body to react."

"I've never even taken *that*." I sounded like a high school kid swearing that I didn't know how the weed got into my book bag.

Nora widened her anime-sized eyes at me: *TMI*.

"Could you get me some water?" I asked Mia.

"Sure thing."

Once she'd slipped out, Nora said, "She's nice."

"She is, sis!"

"I wasn't sure of the visitor policy. Family seemed a safe bet."

I slid the peasant blouse over my head. Even in the long sleeves, I was chilly. Sandals on next. "I have to see my parents. They need to know this wasn't like last time."

"Honey, I don't think that will be the first thing on their minds."

Mia popped in with a paper cup. "Your brother is two floors up." She touched my arm. "It's a difficult place, girls."

"Yeah," I said. "I get it."

I was thinking of Anna, patched up and sent home the same day.

"It's great that you guys have each other."

Nora bowed her head.

"You can either go visit him, briefly, or wait for your folks in the room down the hall."

"I don't think . . ." A vertiginous slide, room atilt, my legs buckling.

"Steady now," Mia said. "Take a minute."

I did as instructed until blood flowed back through my limbs and the spinning stopped. "I'm not ready."

Nora said, "She needs more time."

"Perfectly okay. Up you go." She held onto my elbow as I got back on my feet. "He's not awake now, so give yourself until tomorrow. But don't wait longer."

After Mia left, her ominous warning filled the silence.

"You okay?" Nora asked. "Do you need to lean on me?"

"No, I'm good."

As we walked into the hall, I stared down at the industrial white rectangles. Hustling men and women in scrubs and masks, bodies laid out on gurneys, a few battlefield groans. People flashed by me on both sides. Everyone had a sense of purpose, of urgency. "Thanks for being a shitty sister with me."

"You're not."

"I'm a coward."

"Lighten up on yourself. You've been through a trauma. You'll come back and visit Josh as soon as you get some sleep."

"If he's not dead," I said, trying to make sense of the word.

I imagined my mother conjugating verbs with Josh, so close she would have inhaled his sweat and sugary breath from his soccer drink: "*Il mourra. Il est mort. Il etait mort.*"

"He won't be, Elle," Nora said.

"I can't process this . . ."

"Of course not. You don't have to."

"They'll make me talk about it. They'll send me back to Dr. Elliot."

The Nuñezes had ended up filing a civil lawsuit with the judge but agreed on a settlement: a monetary fee and mandatory therapy for me—so no one else's child would have to suffer the way theirs did from my actions. (Anna was left with two scaly scars: the one on her hand like the underside of baked salmon, the other, a fat eel slithering down her cheek.)

Dr. Elliot, the court-ordered psychologist I saw for six months, was a tiny-boned woman with pipe-cleaner flexibility; she'd twist one leg around the other until her feet overlapped. Watching her, I'd fantasize that she'd once been a pole dancer. She was never without her silver necklace with the filigree whistle pendant. She didn't speak much but made a smacking sound with her lips—a tell—when I demonstrated "good insight."

"They can't make you; you're not a child," Nora said. She hooked my elbow in hers, guiding me to the elevator. "And you were on the highway when it broke out. I can attest to that."

In the elevator, I tugged on the ends of my hair, sniffed a few strands. It smelled like I'd been dunked in a vat of cigarette smoke. But not that fetid odor coming from Anna, not those sulfur strands. When the doors opened, I walked slowly. The waiting room was empty. The only voice was coming from a suspended TV, tuned to CNN. The president was at some campaign rally, yelling.

Nora seized the remote from one of the wooden chairs. "Where is the mute button on this thing?" She lowered the volume.

"Should I text my dad? He's probably talking to doctors . . ."

Nora clamped my wrist. "I'll give someone the message you're in here. Switch to the quadruplet and hoarder channel."

I laughed, despite myself. Even at this moment, Nora could impress me with her repository of media trivia.

Alone, I hunched over in my chair, my arms and head dangling. My body was liquid exhaustion, but my brain was lit up with snapshots of Josh on that cot. Incinerated like a dead animal, like trash. My intestines roiled.

"Elle?"

"Dad?"

He scooped me up off the chair. "My poor Elle-Belle," he said. "It must have been awful."

"Yeah," I mumbled. As he hugged me, I became lightweight as a scarecrow, unable to stand without his support. My dad's scent was the usual mix of tea, and spearmint mints, and a hint of tobacco from his one-cigarette-a-day allowance. The tears came.

"We just spoke with the doctors," he said softly.

Even as I sank into the comfort of my dad, the sight of my mother, behind him, terrified me.

She stood next to Nora, holding her glasses in one hand, her eyes sunken and dark as if they were retreating into her skull. She was five feet, seven inches but looked so much smaller, an old lady version of herself. All her sharp edges—elbows, hip bones, knees— were accentuated in her cotton dress that left her legs bare. Her festive red espadrilles were a throwback to who she'd been yesterday.

"Let's sit down," my dad suggested.

After my mother briefly embraced me—"Thank God, you're okay"—the three of us made a circle out of chairs. Nora hung back, then motioned to me as she left to wait in the hall.

"They haven't given us percentages." My father's voice shook. "But Mom read about it on the ride up here. Fifty-fifty."

This was the shock talking. This was not the man who took his worries out for a run rather than discuss them with us.

"Stop, Dan," my mother demanded. "You heard what they said. Josh is young and in excellent physical shape."

"Is he awake yet?" I asked.

Dad made a choking sound. "No, honey. He's in a medically induced coma. They're giving him IV fluids and painkillers. He has something called burn shock."

My mind begged for a respite. But that was unacceptable. I needed to bear the brunt of what I'd done. "Did you see him?"

"Yes. It was . . ."

"I know. Horrible."

My mom touched my father's hand. "This is what happens at first. It's the body's response to severe injuries like this, the swelling. He will get better."

Dad squeezed her fingers white.

My mother jumped out of her seat. "Be right back. Just need to get some water."

Even after she was gone, my father still spoke so faintly, I had to lean toward him. "The situation is worse than Mom will admit. Proteins can leak out, veins can collapse from inflammation, clots can form and kill him."

"They said all that?"

"No. Mom read about it on the way up here. But she wants to stay positive."

"Can't the doctors . . . prevent those things?" I rubbed my knuckles against my achy jaw.

"They're doing their best."

When my mother returned, she swiveled in my direction. "How do you know how he looks, Ellie?"

"What?"

"You didn't feel ready to see him. So, how do you know?"

"The ambulance."

"Yes, right. Were you downstairs when it started?"

"I tried to help him." A plea more than a declaration. "I ran into the house but couldn't get upstairs."

"*Into* the house?"

Caught.

"From where, Elle?" Dad scratched a chapped sore spot on his mouth.

"From outside, that's all."

"Smoking?" Mom asked.

"No." The miasma in the hallway, hot and greedy as death. My throat and eyes were searing, feverous. "It happened so fast."

"Could you have forgotten to put out your cigarette?"

"I wasn't smoking!" I spat tears. Crying for myself as much as for the wreckage of my brother. "We had a fight, and I started to drive to the city. I forgot my computer, so . . .When I got back, the stairs were blocked by smoke."

My mother gasped. "How could you have left him alone? We never would have gone away if you hadn't agreed to stay with him."

"Peri." My father laid his hand on her pale knee. "That's enough."

"Josh didn't want me there, watching him," I said.

"Mom just means was the fight about drugs?"

She dabbed a tissue under her nose. "Don't put words into my mouth, Dan."

"No, it was . . . He woke me up kicking the ball against the house. He trashed the place, refused to wash the dishes, and wrecked my backpack with his sports drink."

My mother seethed, "The dishes?"

"He was arguing with Audrey on the phone and didn't want me there. All I did was drive away. I didn't do *this.*"

"Your brother's face is the size of a beach ball. His kidneys could fail in the next seventy-two hours. He has a breathing tube down his throat." She was weeping, messy tears that ran to her chin. "The doctors warned us to brace ourselves because tomorrow he'll look even worse. These are just the things they're telling us."

"Mom, I . . ." A thread had come lose on my sleeve, which I picked at like a wound. "I'm sorry."

"I'm trying to put the pieces together. If you'd been there, Elle—you were awake—maybe . . ."

I was crying now and apologizing over and over.

My father said, "Ellie should never have been left with this responsibility in the first place. We should go home, get some rest for a few hours."

"We don't have a home anymore."

He pressed on one eye, so that his glasses popped up. "A hotel room, then."

My mother rose and, for a moment, peered at the television screen. "I can't leave until I know Josh will survive." Slowly, she turned to me. "I'm sorry, Ellie. Of course, this isn't your fault. It's ours."

"We're all in shock," Dad said, gently. "Elle, does the hospital want to see you again to follow up?"

"I'm supposed to make an appointment with my doctor."

Never mind that I didn't have one.

"Good," my mom said. "You have to do that."

"Yeah," I said, doubting I would.

When I explained that my Hyundai was parked on our street, my dad offered to pay for an Uber for Nora and me.

Nora clutched my hand as the driver barreled into Upper Manhattan. The sky throbbed with an impending downpour, and I thought about how rainfall in this area was the highest ever recorded since tracking began at the end of the nineteenth century. But last night had been California clear and dry, bad luck for Josh.

The thump against the garage. The cleated sneakers under the coat rack, the bin filled with balls of all kinds. Ever since he could walk, Josh had been in motion. Ten months old was so early, my mother often noted, especially for a boy. By the time he was three, he was riding a two-wheeled bike; by four, he was in a T-ball league. My dad set up a plastic basketball hoop in the driveway with an adjustable pole. Later, he replaced it with a more expensive, sturdier version. Summer vacation meant miniature golf and a run at dusk for Josh.

How would he adjust?

"She'll never forgive me," I said.

"Of course she will," my friend vowed.

"She hates me. I don't blame her."

"Of course she doesn't."

"Did I leave a lit cigarette?" I asked. "Was she right?"

"Elle, you've been through so much; you're just confused."

But I caught it then, for just a second, the flicker of doubt on Nora's face.

At our apartment, she cupped my elbow and led me to my room. As I dropped into bed, the grime of the fire still on my skin, I asked, "What if he dies?"

"They'll call you," was all Nora could say, laying my phone next to my pillow and petting it like a cat. "Wake me if you hear anything."

Sleep felt like desertion and there was nothing worse than that. But sleep pulled me into its depths and made me a traitor anyway. At some point, I had one of those dreams that have the stripped-down, visceral quality of life. Josh straggled into my room in his footsie pajamas, blanket trailing behind him. He laid it on the floor and asked for my extra pillow. Wrapped in his bedding, he told me it was too "noisy" in his room. This was not unusual; my air conditioner was quiet and powerful. His would hum and drone. Not always, but loud enough to frighten him.

"Elle, I'm burning," he said.

I turned to see him, flailing his arms, his mouth open, hair like red streamers. And I screamed. I couldn't stop screaming.

"Ellie," Nora said, shaking my shoulder. "You're having a nightmare."

I jolted up, my mouth so dry it felt as if my tongue were sticking to the palate.

"Your phone is buzzing."

"Oh, no!"

The text read: *Josh survived the first twelve hours. They'll let you see him. Come when you can. Love, Dad.*

"What?" She squeezed my arm.

"He's still alive. I have to get back to Jersey."

"We should pick up your car."

"Don't you have to teach a class?" I glanced at the time on my phone: 1:16 p.m.

She shrugged. "Got a sub."

When I hugged her, she said, "I love you, but you reek. Go bathe."

On the train, I arranged for an Uber to the hospital. The second ride—the one to retrieve my Hyundai—I'd charge on the credit card my dad and I shared. But I needed to pay it off soon, before the slew of medical bills arrived. My mind churned. Even with insurance, the expense could crush my dad. What about our house? Were we covered? I turned to Nora, whose head was heavy on my shoulder, her eyes closed. Crazy to consider asking her how anyone stayed solvent. "Hedge funds, baby," she'd say, and laugh because we were both so broke.

I checked the bank balance on my phone as if somehow the $261 in my account could save my family.

Better to stare out the window at the smattering of gray and brown-brick buildings, at the overcast sky over Newark, than at that sad number on my screen. My Starbucks cold brew was causing my gut to knot up. Still, I drank it down. Stomach cramps were *nothing*. What punishment was sufficient for destroying everything: our home, our finances, my brother's life?

I pictured Josh on the field, his leg extended as he raised his foot and his arms pumped, one in the air and one behind him, all that power put to use. Would that person be gone now?

Outside the hospital, Nora placed her hand in the middle of my spine, as if checking my pose in yoga class. "Slow, deep breaths," she said.

"This place . . ."

"Yeah," she said, "it's awful."

"He doesn't belong here," I said.

As we approached the burn unit, a part of me split off, observing myself. This must be the sensation people who claimed near-death experiences had, this floating away from their bodies.

My father stood outside a room with the door closed, staring at his chukka boots. He was flanked on either side by Audrey and Josh's best friend, Drew Colins, who'd been a fixture in our house from the summer before they started third grade to their senior year of high school. As a preteen, Drew had joined Josh in ridiculing me for my studiousness. Chubby in his oversized jeans and scuffed sneakers, he'd snicker when I ran into him in our kitchen with Josh, whisper, "Geek Girl," even as he rounded his shoulders, averted his eyes. Now, he was transformed. He'd lost weight since his first year of college— the last time I'd seen him—maybe twenty pounds, and acquired a jawline and a flat belly. He'd chopped his loose-coiled hair into a slick-backed, textured cut.

Under the fluorescent lights, Audrey was paler than usual. She was wearing a faded cotton shirt with kimono sleeves that flared when she moved her arms to wipe away tears. In all my encounters with Audrey, I'd never picked up a hint of irony, her earnestness irritating. Her shy-girl artist presentation, all those self-made clothes—drapey shirts, lantern pants, and oversized jackets that hid her tiny frame—seemed performative to me. Even washed out, her hair in a haphazard ponytail, with loose strands running down her neck and over her face, she looked like a beautiful mess. The day of the fire, she and Josh had been arguing on the phone for what seemed like hours. I stared at her, but she wouldn't meet my gaze.

"What's going on?" I asked my dad. "Where's Mom?"

The furrows in my father's forehead were deeper; his eyelids and cheeks were patchy where his eczema had erupted. "She's in there with Josh."

"Did he . . . wake up?"

"No. He's . . ."

Dread knocked me forward, my hands on my thighs.

"Unrecognizable," Drew said.

Nora cradled me. "It's okay, honey."

When the dizziness passed, again, I stood up and turned toward Drew. "You're different."

"Good different, I hope."

"For Christ's sake, Josh is wrapped up like a mummy," Audrey said in a pious tone, as if we'd been caught laughing in church. "I'm sorry, Mr. Stone."

My dad waved away the apology. "I explained to them, Ellie, that the doctors wrapped Josh in gauze as protection. The tissues with the richest blood supply swell the most. It's awful to see. He'll need to get his wounds scrubbed to prevent infection, minimize scarring, which—I don't know—seems impossible."

"Dad," I said, reaching for his hand.

"That process, 'debridement' it's called, is going to be the worst part for Josh."

"I thought they put him in a coma."

Dad's tongue found the sore spot on his lip. "He's in a drug-induced one. In some cases, patients show signs that they feel this . . . debridement. I did some research last night once Mom finally fell asleep."

"Dad, please," I repeated, as if to restore him to his former, soft-spoken self.

Audrey's face was talcum-powder white. "What's the point of the coma then?"

"It must be to make it more tolerable," Drew said.

"How did you two even find out . . . what happened?"

"*CafeEssex*." Drew was referring to the local news site. "My mom reads it every morning online. She called me."

The spinning sensation was back and so was Nora, her arm a ballast.

"The fire's online? Is that how you knew?" I asked Audrey.

"We were supposed to meet at the Indian place for lunch. Josh didn't show, so I called your mom."

"My mom answered?"

"I kept calling."

Audrey is so intense; she can get too intense, you know? Like OCD-ish.

I'd overheard Josh say that years ago, to someone.

My father interrupted, "I'm going back in his room." To Audrey and Drew, he nodded. "It was so nice of you to come. But I think it's better if we wait for Josh to have visitors."

It sounded so odd, as if my brother just needed to shower, to clean the gunk out of his eyes.

Once my dad had closed the door behind him, Drew handed me his phone.

On the screen was a close-up photo taken at dusk: the wood shell above Josh's room, his burnt-out window frame with the screen hanging on like a loose Band-Aid to wet skin. The story headline was innocuous, factual. I swallowed, thirsty—even though I had to pee from the large coffee. I skimmed to see if my name was mentioned. It wasn't.

"Is it anywhere else?"

Audrey said, "Yeah, on Facebook."

"Facebook? Did you post about . . . this?"

"Are you kidding? You think I'd do something like that? I didn't even know if Josh was alive."

Drew said, "It was some girl from high school, someone with nothing better to do."

"Who was it? What did she say?"

Nora said, "Forget it."

What had my friend seen while I slept? "I want to know if it will hurt my parents."

Audrey stared at me with those green-tea eyes of hers. "Josh could die. You think a stupid girl's status on Facebook will matter to them?"

Of course she was right. My brother's survival was the urgent center of their universe, a slip of fate that felt like a hoax. Ghoulish as he appeared on that stretcher, he would survive. He *had* to survive.

"Was it Anna Nuñez?" I asked.

Audrey tapped her finger on her cell screen, then held it out to me. "Here. See for yourself."

My body swayed, Nora caught me, and I made myself look. Every few months, I'd checked Anna's social media photos to see if the slash mark had faded. It had—but only a bit. While in college, she'd posted overhearing other students remark how her scar ruined her looks, how sad that was, what a pretty girl she might be without it. Anna determined, then, she'd never be considered attractive again. "Had to deal with that shit. Hit hard." Her new profile picture showed the thick arrow-sliver, still there, the pink covered up by makeup. Anna's smile was genuine and lipstick free. Her eyebrows were their natural light-brown color. Next to her stood a young, broad-shouldered man with tawny hair and glinting eyes.

Joy rose in me like a light switched on from the bottom of a dark staircase. Maybe Anna was happy.

But then I saw her most recent post. In black lettering on a red background: *Isn't this the Firestarter's house? Another "accident"?*

chapter four

"It's routine," my dad said for the second time. He was hunched over the steering wheel, the cuticle of his thumbnail chewed to bits. Other than a repetition of these two words, my father had been quiet on the ride over.

"Yeah," I said, again.

As we rounded the corner, I counted four American flags jutting out of telephone poles. Once inside the parking lot of the police station, two more waved on either side of the brick box of a building. There could be no confusion about allegiance to country here. I wondered if my job with a liberal news site would prejudice the officers' opinion of me.

"I wish I could be in the room with you," my dad said.

"As my lawyer?"

I waited for him to correct me, "professor," as usual. "Elle, no one is accusing you of anything."

The words in Anna Nuñez's FB post rose in my mind as they had on the screen: *Isn't this the Firestarter's house? Another "accident"?*

"I'm okay," I said: anything but.

Didn't I *need* a lawyer with me?

I couldn't ask for anything more than what I'd already received: two weeks' paid vacation time from work, another two with a flexible schedule, meaning I could write and edit from home. Family leave didn't include siblings in New York and, anyway, I wasn't my brother's caretaker. *Do you want to request a longer absence due to stress?* my boss, Rashad, had asked. His voice had been kind, but the circles under his eyes were darker than usual. The office was understaffed, running on grit and dedication.

"Two weeks is good. I'll finish the piece on coastal communities while I'm out. The thing is, my computer was destroyed in the fire."

Rashad leaned his knuckles against his cheek. "We can partial-pay for another, maybe cover half. Put in for reimbursement at the end of the month."

Now, I waited for last-minute instructions from my dad before leaving the car. Instead, he stared out the windshield, his mouth agape. "They warned us that this week would be harder than the first. Every system of Josh's body is affected; the risk is worse."

I'd been in contact with my parents every day, either in person or over the phone. But I was still the outlier, not privy to all communication, the hourly changes in my brother's condition. My dad was holding up my mother but had no one to turn to for support. In rare moments, he shared news with me in the starkest terms—as if facing the grim facts was his way of wrestling an opponent to the ground.

"What else are they saying?" I asked.

He turned toward me, the citrine sun lighting up his face, sallow with stubble on his cheeks and chin. "The doctors are cautious. This is a long-term process, multiple surgeries and skin grafts, maybe years of pain and infections, emotional trauma—if he's lucky."

The horrors he'd listed stunned me into silence. I felt the sudden stillness and imagined us as bronze figures in a museum exhibit. We could sit here for eons and be observed as the sea levels rose, droughts increased, as heat waves became more frequent, and those remaining gathered to complain about lack of electricity and food scarcity.

Finally, I said, "I better go in."

"Don't offer the police anything extra. Only answer their questions. Stick to the facts. If they ask you how you think the fire started, be honest: you don't know."

One of the investigators had told him that smoking was the leading cause of home fires. "Don't mention the cigarette?" I asked.

"Is it relevant?"

"No. I put it out."

"Then no need to say anything, unless directly asked. If they ask, tell the truth."

"Mom thinks it's like what happened to Anna Nuñez. But I swear, it's not."

My dad reached over and hugged me to him. He was thinner than ever, even than in his college pictures when he'd been on the track team. For years, he'd used the elliptical machine and lifted weights in our den. What *was* our den.

"Will our insurance pay for our house?" I asked.

"Honey, let me deal with that."

I felt compelled to say, "We had our issues, but I would never do anything to hurt Josh."

"We know that." He released me with a kiss on the top of my head.

"Maybe Josh can tell the police I wasn't responsible when he wakes up."

This last bit spilled out without my consent, the selfish beast inside me taking over.

"Josh may never remember. What matters is that he recovers."

"Right, of course. I'm sorry." I tore at a hard patch of skin on my index finger. A sting and a spot of blood. Nothing. My wound was *nothing*. Whatever suffering I felt was inconsequential.

"Let's get this part over with," he said.

Inside the station, a woman at the front desk instructed me to go into the third room on the left, a small, dim space with bone-brown walls. A fifty-something, broad-faced man with broken blood vessels on his cheeks, like road maps, introduced himself, "Sergeant Abbott," and gestured for me to sit across from him. "This is Officer Volpe."

Volpe was a younger man, probably in his thirties, with a crew cut and small eyes. He was standing when I arrived.

"Volpe," Abbott said, "get the young lady a Coke."

"Oh, no thanks," I said. "I have this." I lifted my boxed water.

"Where'd you find that?" Volpe asked.

"The city."

He smirked as if I'd brought some exotic fruit that only grew on the island of Manhattan. He pulled out the chair next to Sergeant Abbott's and sat with his elbows splayed on the metal table. He was the manspreader on the subway, the one who hogged three seats.

"Let's get this squared away," the sergeant said. "We just have to dot the i's and cross the t's." He smiled, not unkindly, and flipped open his notepad. "This shouldn't take long. What we're trying to ascertain is how the fire began. A few questions about your whereabouts."

"That's the thing," I said. "I was in my car, driving to my apartment."

He asked me what time I'd left the house but not why. After I'd answered, he followed up with, "Did you make it to your destination?"

"No. I went back to New Jersey."

"Why was that?"

"I left my computer at my parents' place." Volpe leaned forward, and I could smell his hair gel. "My work computer."

I realized how suspicious my decision sounded, as if I'd known my laptop would need rescuing. "I had an assignment to finish over the weekend."

Should I have explained how the staff at the website wasn't

unionized, that all my friends worked overtime without pay, that we all scraped by, most of us without benefits, that I was one of the luckier ones? "I'm a journalist for Terrafeed, a media company. It's just what I have to do to stay employed."

Volpe's lips curled. "Tough on you, are they? Not too happy working overtime, huh?"

Abbott raised his hand, and his partner retreated back into his chair. "So, Ms. Stone, you turned around. Can anyone confirm that you left the house, other than your brother—if that's possible at a later date?"

Would they check my car for a tracking device, or was that a step too far? I wasn't an arson suspect, not strictly speaking. Not this time. "My roommate, Nora. I told her."

The inquiry continued, specific and tedious, Volpe cracking his neck from side to side. As I recounted the events from that night, the sergeant countered with more questions. Why hadn't I called 911 instead of entering the premises? Was there any animosity between me and Josh?

Sick to death of Josh. Let him OD.

"Just the usual sibling stuff. He could be a slob," I said rapidly. "He spilled his sports drink on my leather backpack, that sort of thing."

Had he found out about the lighter, the fight in the garage, how I flicked it until the flame grew? My dad had reassured me that, since the prosecution hadn't pressed charges, I had no criminal record and there were no rap sheets for civil cases filed. But an officer could have googled my name, then researched the case's docket. My legs were crossed, my knees jerking up and down.

"Is that why you left your parents' house"—he referred to his notes—"after midnight?"

"I just wanted to go home."

They didn't inquire what I'd been doing at my parents' in the first place. Maybe, in their families, adult children hung out together in their childhood house routinely.

The sergeant tapped his pen against his thumb. "How would you categorize Josh's frame of mind? Any history of depression?"

Addiction.

"Josh wasn't suicidal, if that's what you mean. Do people actually do that, purposely try to kill themselves in a fire?"

The sergeant coughed into his fist. "It's not unheard of."

I imagined Josh as a Joker impersonator, popping Adderall and lighting matches. Yet it had been *me* who'd coveted the lacquered lighter that day at Anna's, *me* who'd flicked it on and off, so cavalier and cool. So filled with fury.

"You'd have to be crazy. Josh isn't crazy."

"People's impulsive acts can result in tragedy," Abbott said. "Anything unusual happen the day of the incident that might have upset him?"

"He'd been arguing with his girlfriend, um, over the phone."

"Yeah?" Volpe asked. "You overheard this?"

When I shrugged, Abbott asked, "Was the girlfriend in the area that night?"

"Not sure," I said, edgy. My intention hadn't been to imply that Audrey was involved. "She's in grad school in Brooklyn, but her mom lives here."

The sergeant asked for her name, and I gave it to him.

"Just a few more questions. Any recreational drug use on your brother's part that might have made him behave impulsively?"

My neck and shoulders ached, as if I'd been crouching in hiding for hours. We'd reached a crossroads: Josh or me. *No need to say anything, unless directly asked.*

After I told them that Josh had started addiction treatment, Volpe bent forward eagerly, clicked his tongue. "I'd say that's pretty significant." There was a smugness in his tone.

Hadn't my parents covered this with the police? Had I slipped up?

"Do you know if your brother owed someone a substantial amount of money for these substances?"

"You mean like a drug dealer?" My laugh was like a cough, impossible to suppress. "No way. Friends share them all the time."

Volpe stared at me as if trying to determine whether I was naive or a decent actress.

Abbott said, measured and professional, "Many are also selling them."

"Who would risk life in jail 'cause Josh owed them money for Adderall?"

Sergeant Abbott's eyes were dark, the skin ridged above and puffy below. "I admit, statistically, the odds are low. But there are disturbed individuals."

I wasn't going to argue with this man who, unlike Volpe, seemed incapable of dramatic embellishment or sarcasm.

"Does your brother smoke?" he asked.

"Not that I know."

"Not even marijuana?"

When I shook my head, he asked, "What about you?"

I ran my palms against my jeans. "Just cigarettes, sometimes. I had one earlier that day. But I put it out."

"Where was that?" I must have appeared confused because Abbott clarified, "What part of the house?"

"Upstairs, in my bedroom."

"You're certain of that location?"

My fingers pressed harder into my thighs. "Yes. I stuck the butt in a mug filled with coffee. There was no way it was still lit."

"The investigators suspect the fire started on the ground floor, in the kitchen."

Air returned to my lungs, and only then did I recognize how lightheaded I'd been. "When are they going to figure out what caused it?"

"Hard to ascertain. We can disclose that there was no accelerant involved."

I remembered the fireman inside Anna Nuñez's garage, how he had shouted, "Check out what's on the ledge! Paint thinner. Cap's off."

"You mean gasoline?" I asked the sergeant. "Or . . . paint thinner?"

"Correct. There's a lot of guesswork involved—with all the destruction."

My vision blurred from staring at my lap, the black linen shirt I'd ironed that morning. All the remnants from my childhood—pictures, yearbook, awards, stuffed animals—I'd never see again. With Josh's injuries, I hadn't considered that there was anything else to mourn.

"You all right?" Sergeant Abbott asked.

"Just tired."

"We're almost done here." He added, "For now."

I couldn't look up. If I did, Volpe would mouth my nickname.

Once the interview was over, I dashed out of the building.

The plan had been for me to visit Josh during the burn unit's evening hours. But my dad said, "You look beat. You should go home."

I agreed.

"Did it go okay, any surprises?" my dad asked.

"Just a lot of questions. The sergeant was polite, the other guy more sarcastic. At least they didn't arrest me."

"Of course not." He patted my hand.

"They asked whether Josh used drugs. And, uh, I couldn't lie."

"That's fine," he said, tersely.

"The guy in charge suggested that Josh might have owed money and that was connected to the fire. But I told him that was ridiculous. He wasn't hanging out with serious criminals."

"The police just have to rule out possibilities, even the most unlikely ones."

"Josh didn't owe anyone a fortune, did he?"

My father's eyes were weary, his voice strained. "Of course not. Listen, Elle, why don't I drive you to the train?" We were all sleep-deprived, so much so that I'd opted for public transportation rather than driving to Jersey. "You could use a night off."

"Are you sure? You and Mom don't get that."

I imagined my mother squinting her eyes in disapproval. But then I remembered something she'd said once about an acquaintance whose son had leukemia: "When your child is that sick, it consumes all your energy. You don't have any left over for other people."

"We're the parents. We're staying right near the hospital."

I nodded, the weight of the day closing down on me. Once home, though, there was still something I had to do: deal with my message from that night, which was most likely still in Nora's chat history.

Nora was in lotus pose—each foot on the opposite thigh, her arms extended in front of her, her palms facing down. Her mat was laid out in our small living room, lights dimmed, incense burning in a bronze bowl on the floor. She opened one eye and said softly, "Hey. Didn't expect you so early."

"Keep meditating. We'll talk later."

"K," she whispered.

On my bed, I unwrapped my vegetarian taco from its aluminum

foil and took a couple of mouthfuls, pieces of tomato and avocado dropping on my shirt. Outside my window, the bridge buoyed the traffic above the Hudson.

I *could* ask Nora to delete my text from that night. But she practiced the five *yamas* of yoga, which included *satya*—truthfulness. She'd raise her fingers to her mouth, stroke the scar where she'd gotten stitches in first grade when she'd fallen from the monkey bars. The conflict would flicker in her eyes: love for me versus her honesty pledge. It would be better not to force her to make that untenable choice.

I stuffed the taco back into the paper bag, took a sip of my warm, boxed water. What I wanted was a cigarette, the sharp buzz that centered my thoughts. I'd vowed to stop, had weaned myself to one a day, my daily allowance after breakfast.

In my work journal, I scribbled possible passcodes: the name of Nora's family's cat (Daphne), her favorite Sanskrit words (*sutra, ananda, dharma, prajna*), the date (day, month, year) Nora lost her virginity to her college boyfriend, and obvious ones, like her birthday and high school locker combination. Once she went to sleep, I'd try them all.

Hours later, the white lights of the bridge shone above the still black water. I stared at the series of giant Hs holding up this webbed structure. My only spiritual practice was breathing deeply as I observed the distance between the city and my former home.

My air conditioner hum couldn't block out the sloshing sounds of the cars driving in another downpour. There was always street noise, even now, at 12:16 a.m. If I listened for a while, I'd drift off. I needed to stay awake, but my eyelids felt transformed into tin.

"Don't go to sleep," Josh whispered to me.

We were watching my father's DVD of *The Wizard of Oz*. I was ten; Josh was seven. We'd seen it before, but never alone. Normally,

Josh would opt for *Shrek* or *Monsters Inc.*, but at dinner Dad reminisced about how, as a kid, this one had been his favorite film. "A classic," he'd said.

"It's great but sexist," my mother responded. "It paints women as either good witches or bad ones."

"That's not sexist. The women are the only ones with power. The wizard is impotent."

"What's impotent?" Josh asked.

My dad smiled, but my mother said, "Someone who no one is afraid of."

"I'm not afraid!"

We'd sneaked downstairs after my parents went to sleep earlier than usual. Josh's tush was at the edge of the couch, his legs splayed up in the air, bare to the thighs. He was in his pajama pants and a T-shirt with the number "1" on the back. Josh laughed when the Scarecrow and Dorothy banged on the Tin Man's chest.

"Beautiful," Scarecrow declared. "What an echo!"

"It's empty. The tinsmith forgot to give me a heart."

Josh drummed his knuckles on my clavicle.

I pushed him aside. "Wrong place, brainless!"

"Just don't go to sleep, Ellie."

"Okay, okay, Joshie. I won't."

Turned out, he *had* been afraid of us, the witches.

The floor creaked as I walked barefoot into the hall. Next door, Nora faced the wall, her back to me, a sheet draped from ankle to shoulder. The light from my phone guided me to hers, on her nightstand. My hand reached to snatch it from the wire charger.

"What are you doing?" Nora asked, as she rolled over.

"I can't find my phone," I said, stupidly, shoving it into my pocket. "Maybe I left it in here."

"That doesn't make sense."

I poked the side of my head. No brain.

"Do you want to look?" she asked, and clicked on the table lamp.

"No. That's okay. I don't know what I'm doing."

Nora scrunched her brows, so a crinkle appeared on her nose. She'd defied her *satya* philosophy by colluding with me. She knew I was lying.

chapter five

Lifting my arm up, I could smell the rank stink of my sweat. My mouth felt dry and sticky, as if I'd eaten taffy that had left tiny pieces behind. The boxed water sat on the table near my bed, warm now. I drank it anyway.

I wondered what Nora thought of my odd behavior, if she'd deduced what my motivation was for poking around her room. Would she delete what I'd written or report it to the police? She was my best friend since childhood. She would never betray me. But wouldn't she, if Sergeant Abbott and Officer Volpe confronted her in that dim room?

As a distraction, I scrolled, searching for any new, alarming messages. There weren't any, which meant that my brother was still alive, and his condition hadn't worsened. He hadn't been snatched from me—not entirely. Me, the person who would be blamed for the fire because even a suicidal Josh wouldn't choose such a cruel death for himself.

I looked for new posts about him on social media. Nothing. Instagram was dogs and friends' selfies and political ads for grass-roots change. Email was over a dozen asks for political donations, "Today's Headlines" from multiple sources, a denim sale at GAP online, and one message from Rashad with the subject heading: "File by Midweek with Changes."

I didn't click on my boss's notes, couldn't deal. I slipped under the blanket, laptop and phone by my side, and thought of how long it had been since my ex-boyfriend had been next to me instead.

"Hey, Elle, put that thing out before you torch my place."

Sam wrapped his long arms around me, snuggling close.

"Don't leave me."

"I'm already gone."

My ex winked at me, and my eyes opened. When Sam left for his doctoral program in California more than a year ago, our decision to end things had been mutual. The background picture on my phone was no longer a close-up of his oblong face, deep-set eyes, wry smile. It was one of the default wallpapers, different shades of blue blobs. The time read: 2:53 a.m.

What if I'd made a mistake?

Don't think of Sam now, for fuck's sake.

Dawn came and, with it, the sense that my skull weighed more than it had only hours before. I popped two Advil with my coffee and, in the shower, rolled my head from side to side so that the warm water could massage my neck and shoulders. I left before Nora woke up, still uncertain what she would do if called in for questioning.

On the car ride to New Jersey, my thoughts strayed from one thing to another. There was a girl who'd lived in my college dorm—not a friend or even an acquaintance—just someone I'd pass on the stairs, catch sight of in the dining hall. Her image came to me now. Red scaly patches wept from her hairline into her forehead, capped the knuckles of her hands. "Psoriasis," a friend told me, after smiling up at this girl. "Painful *and* itchy, poor thing. There's no cure."

No cure. The two words carried me into the hospital.

I figured Josh was in the tank room, as he was most mornings, having his scabs scrubbed open, his raw wounds oxidized with silver nitrate sticks. After each debridement, my mother would corner the nurses who accompanied Josh back into his room. "Did he feel anything?" she'd ask. "Is my son in pain?" They'd offer gentle reassurances, lay their hands on my mother's shoulder. No one could answer her questions with certainty.

Today, Josh was in his bed. The doctors had begun the process of removing the temporary cadaver skin from his body. They'd sliced healthy skin from his thighs and back and, after stretching it out like spandex, surgically attached it to his face, hands, and chest. Bundled in bandages from head to foot, Josh resembled a corpse that killers had wrapped in a cheaply made rug to toss into the river. Only the ventilator signaled he was alive. I grabbed onto the metal rim of his bed.

"Elle," my father said, "we need to stay strong." He nodded at my mother, who was weeping quietly on her chair next to my brother.

"I will," I said, even though I felt woozy.

This was worse than the last visit: Josh gaunt and ravaged with scar tissue, the reddish-pink flesh of his lip exposed, that ruinous, hooked-fish look. The sandy brown swatch that had fallen over his eye since childhood was missing, his forehead leathery, his brows burnt off. Eventually, he'd be ready for hair transplants, one of the many surgeries in his future. His hands were fried, as if they'd been roasting on our barbecue grill too long.

"Peri, you need to eat," my father, standing beside her, said. "I'm worried about you."

"I'm not the one you should worry about."

I yearned to pull my father aside and huddle against him; this was no longer possible. He looked depleted, stooped over, his arms hanging listlessly at his sides. "I can get you guys something," I offered, and he nodded.

My mother arched her head and clasped her hands together, as if in prayer.

I couldn't recall the last time she'd been in a synagogue—my parents were agnostics who never spoke of God or faith or anything vaguely hinting at a spiritual life. Once, at dinner, my mother complained about a place she'd been showing clients for months without an offer. The seller refused to stage her home, leaving a cross over her bed, mini Buddha figurines lining her window frame, books on astrology, tarot, and the kabbalah stacked on a bedroom table.

"Guess she's leaving her options open," I'd joked.

"People want to imagine themselves in it," my mother had said. "No one wants to see someone else's inner life on display."

I thought of that statement in the hospital elevator, how it defined my mother's philosophy about so much more than real estate.

The cafeteria was nearly empty. Eating alone was an older woman whose puffy hair sprung out of a canvas hat like a shrub of pussy willows. Two nurses carried trays with chipped white plates to the cash register.

Coffee sprayed into my cup at the drink machine. I selected the most benign-looking items from the counter, two packaged turkey-and-cheese sandwiches for my parents, a Greek yogurt and a banana for me.

There were crumbs on the floor and Styrofoam cups with liquid scumming the bottoms on the tables. I chose a seat close to the window to get a glimpse of the bright light slicing through the white sky. Five minutes, just a quick respite. I took a bite of the banana. It was too soft in the middle, on the way to rotting. Fungal diseases could wipe out the fruit in the next decade, according to one study. Another one cited change in weather patterns that produced crop failures, which would rid the planet of this food.

I squished it into a napkin.

"Hey," a male voice said. Feeling his hand on my shoulder, I balked.

"Sorry," Drew said.

"Hi."

He was standing beside my chair, polished in a dress shirt and suit pants.

"Drove from the city," he said, noticing that I was checking out his attire. "Got an extended lunch from work."

"Haven't seen you the last few days."

He lowered his eyes. "Sorry about that. This internship is intense. And with my seminar after work. That's not an excuse . . ."

"It *is*. You need to work."

Strictly speaking, he didn't. From my mother, who was friendly with his mom, Margaux, I'd learned that Drew came from money. To his credit, Josh never mentioned the difference in his friend's financial situation.

"Hard day?" he asked.

"Very. What are you doing down here?"

"Your dad told me where you were. I came to relieve you of your duties—if you need more time alone." He pointed to the paper bag filled with the sandwiches.

I peeled back the yogurt lid. "I can do it myself. I'm ambulatory."

"Also, to warn you: Audrey's here and she's upset. The police want to interview her."

"It's routine," I said, defensively. It was my doing, having mentioned her to the sergeant and Volpe. But I wasn't going to share that with Drew.

He nodded. "There's more. Let me take this up, and I'll be right back."

"Okay. Thanks."

The "there's more" grumbled in my stomach as I watched Drew walk away. I stopped eating after two spoonfuls. To distract myself, I checked in on the world: first the political rants on Twitter, then the Instagram selfies. I watched a couple of puppy videos of Hobbes, the gray-and-white Sheepadoodle with the Muppet head tilt, and Greta, the Harlequin Great Dane with the dangling jowls.

"Why is Audrey confiding in you?" I asked when Drew reappeared with a large paper cup. He'd unbuttoned his shirt at the wrists and rolled up the sleeves to his elbow.

"I guess she needed to vent. I was around."

"I thought you guys hated each other."

Every time they were in our house together, Audrey would don a sulky expression and observe the floor rugs as if searching for tears in the woven patterns. She'd play with her long-tassel earrings, the ones with the feathers or the stars. Drew hung back, away from his best friend when she was around him. Every once in a while, I'd catch her shooting Drew chilly looks full of determination. She'd marked her territory and he'd better not forget that. Josh was hers.

"I never disliked Auds." Drew placed the drink on the table. "She was the one who had an issue with me."

"What issue?"

He shrugged. "She wanted Josh's full attention; I got in the way."

"That's kind of psycho."

"She's not that bad." Drew sat next to me and poured milk from a little plastic container into his coffee. When he smiled, he looked directly at me. With his smooth shave, his skin was burnished, stamped by the sun. "I *was* around Josh a lot. You know how tight we were. Still are."

Sorrow bore into the space where my ribs met. "He stopped talking to me so long ago."

"He was ashamed, struggling."

"Josh admitted that?" I asked. It rose in me, that old yearning to understand why my brother had forsaken our relationship.

"He didn't have to."

"Then you can't say for sure. Why is Audrey even with him anymore?" I was desperate for insight into the trajectory that led to this tragedy.

"She loves him. But Josh has to get his shit together to keep her. They were arguing about that on the phone that whole day. Josh texted me a few hours before. Auds wanted to meet and talk."

"Meet?" My pulse quickened. "Did they, that night?"

"Dunno. He didn't say." Drew cocked his head. "They were both super upset, volatile. I doubt Audrey showed up and burned your house down. She's not *that* crazy."

"Everyone thinks *I* did exactly that."

"No one really does, Ellie. People need someone to blame."

"Why is Audrey flipping out about the police if she wasn't there?"

"She thinks you're framing her."

His words splashed over me, icy cold. Forget Nora, whom no officer had approached. It was Josh's girlfriend I should be worried about.

Drew rubbed his hand over his forearm. A broad white line stood out from his tan, as if from a watch band he'd forgotten to wear. "All she said was that because of you the police want to interview her."

"I wasn't throwing her under the bus."

"Look, it doesn't matter what Audrey thinks. It only matters what the police discover."

"Did she mention her theory in front of my parents?"

"No, and she won't."

"Good," I said. "They have enough to deal with."

"Agree. I love your folks. They've been great to me. I know I'm the cliché of the entitled-yet-neglected kid." He raised his palm toward me. "White male privilege. Rich but with absentee dad, stressed-out mom."

I'd overheard the essentials from my mother's phone conversations with Margaux.

His parents' divorce, when Drew was six, had been acrimonious. Drew rarely saw his father, around whom disparate rumors flew: the fallout from a Ponzi scheme, the time he'd spent in jail, the relocation to the other coast and his second marriage, the stepsiblings Drew barely knew. Margaux wasn't forthcoming about her ex but did disclose that she had sizable inherited wealth, which allowed her to raise her son without child support or alimony. Drew benefited from a full ride at NYU undergrad and now Columbia for his MBA, thanks to the education fund left to him as part of his grandparents' estate.

"You knew Josh was using again?" When he nodded, I asked, "Did he ever really stop?"

"Elle . . . he tried. He thought he could control the drugs, not the other way around."

"Did he feel guilty? The program they were sending him to was costing my dad a fortune—which we don't have." *Unlike you, we are not so lucky.* "I was really furious at his selfishness. But I'd never deliberately harm Josh. I'm not an arsonist, either."

"Of course not." With a hint of a smile, he said, "Neither is Audrey."

"People do impulsive things when they are . . . what'd you say, 'volatile.'"

For a second, he didn't reply, his jaw set. Then he said, "True."

"Unless the police are sure it's her, Audrey can escape. I never will."

How petty and cruel I was, my soul a shriveled rag. The last few evenings, I'd eaten alone in bed, with the window blinds up, staring at the bridge lights, ferociously holding onto my autonomy: the scents of Nora's curry and turmeric dishes wafting through our apartment; my workplace with its bustling energy, the cluttered space where we hunched over our devices, each in our own productive pod; my dreams of graduate school. Then the fears came in a deluge. The police would link me to the fire. Nora would report that text to them, out of a sense of duty. Josh's recovery would stall, and he'd need life-long care. Once my parents grew old and unable to attend to him, my life would be yoked to my brother's forever. How deeply selfish was I that the thought of such a future caused panic?

"What do you think is going to happen to him?" I asked. *If I do everything right from now on, will Josh recover?*

Drew reached for my hand, and I took his. "No idea."

My heart clenched like the muscle it was. Its sole purpose was to keep beating, as if allowing no room for mercy.

chapter six

Even with my noise-cancelling earphones, I could hear Jae manically tapping on her keyboard while singing the same song lyrics on repeat. Normally, I was good at ignoring the endless traffic in our open-plan office, the sneezing, sipping, sniffling, humming, shuffling. But now, toward the end of my first week back from family leave, I was having trouble focusing.

"Want a cold brew?" Jae asked, shooting up, her chair rolling behind her.

"No, thanks. I'm fully caffeinated."

"Me too. But this newsletter has to be filed in an hour."

"I thought that was tomorrow." I glanced at her bronze curls and brick-red lips. It was good to be back, even if my mind wasn't cranking at full capacity.

"Rashad changed the schedule." Jae shoved her hands into the front pockets of her skinny jeans until they slid to her hip bones, emphasizing her fat-free belly. "It's Thursdays now."

"Ugh, sorry."

"No difference. Pressure then or pressure now."

"Rashad is going to kill me if I don't get this piece done today."

Yesterday, I'd screwed up some vital information for my piece on Gen X and eco-anxiety—after finishing it after midnight. It had been due at 6 p.m. *Get it before the morning*, Rashad instructed when I'd apologized.

This looks wrong, Rashad's text woke me at 7 a.m., referring to one of the statistics in my piece.

It *was* wrong. I'd misquoted my source.

Jae jutted her chin out. "Your phone."

Dad. Three words. *Josh woke up!*

My pulse turned into a hopping frog. "I have to deal with this."

Once Jae was out of sight, I raced to the fire exit and slid to the floor. I texted my father back. *Wow! Fantastic!*

Was it? The room spun around a few times before wobbling back on its axis. What about Josh's brain function? *How does he seem?*

Just then, a message from Rashad: *Come see me 3PM.*

It wasn't even noon. A summons from my boss was never a good sign, and a scheduled "appointment," rather than an impromptu meeting, signaled trouble. Usually, if he wanted to discuss an article, he'd ping me.

My dad: *The doctors are pleased. And surprised he woke up so soon after tapering him off the medication.*

How is he?

He's in and out.

My fingers moved so quickly, like a pianist with acquired agility. *Does he remember what happened?*

Too soon to tell.

Should I visit tonight?

The light was dim in this corner, and I pitched forward to stare at the screen. "You okay there, Ellie?" someone asked, and I nodded, watching the three dots bounce in my dad's text bubble. They disappeared. My office mate walked away.

The weekend is better.

There it was, my status as the outlier in the family, the guest, the Firestarter.

Great news, Dad. Gotta go talk to Rashad.

In *four* hours. Relief was now mixed with a sense of rejection.

My dad: *Ok, honey.*

Anchored to this small patch of floor, I scrolled through my contacts, not very far, finding his name under "C" (Colins). Drew would be harried with consulting on maximizing profits, staffing, supply chain stuff—whatever it was the firm did. But he'd been kind to me in the hospital cafeteria, and he was Josh's best friend. I craved acceptance from someone connected to my brother.

Josh is out of the coma.

The world outside my purview returned: conversations, a muffled cough, the patter of feet.

Walking back to my desk, I received this response: *Fantastic! You heading there after work?*

Jae was snapping her gum. She glimpsed at me. "Crisis?"

"No, actually. Things are better."

She smiled, a person-not-in-crisis smile. "Good to hear."

"Thanks." I texted Drew: *Not tonight. This weekend.*

Talk later?

I only hesitated for a moment. *Sure.*

For a couple of hours, my writing flowed. I took a break and got a coffee and muffin at the café around the corner, a late lunch. As three o'clock approached, my attention wandered, and I glanced at Jae, who was biting down on her red lip.

The minute I sat down across from him, Rashad said, "Look, Ellie, I'm sympathetic to what's happened. I realize this is a terrible time for you."

My crossed legs started bobbing.

"It isn't fair that you can't coast for a while after what you've been through. The problem for us is the pullback from TFG and Castle."

Rashad rarely used the plural pronoun or referred to the private equity firms that funded the website. My industry's decline was one of the reasons I hoped to get my MA in environmental sciences and pivot into a government job. The other was to effect real change—if that was even possible with the inevitable political resistance.

"Are you firing me?" I asked, wobbly voiced.

He rested his fist under his chin. He had a mustache over a wide mouth, and a scruffy unshaven look that never changed; a wedge of his hair hung over one eye. "No, but I'm being straight with you. You need to step up, especially right now. I can't disclose details, but you see the trends in digital news. Facebook and Google are monopolizing advertising budgets."

"Are layoffs coming that fast?" My foot was still twitching.

"Let's talk about *you*, how we can get you back up to speed."

"Whatever it takes."

"You're an excellent editor, Ellie. And an even better journalist."

"If I'm getting another chance, I promise no more screwups."

He nodded. "I hope so. Again, I'm sorry. I hope your brother is doing better."

"Thanks, Rashad. I really appreciate the opportunity to get back on track."

Fuck. Fuck. Fuck.

I stared at the crescent moon on my iPhone, considering whether or not to activate the Do Not Disturb option. Josh was on the mend, I told myself. My mother, father, and brother were a closed circle. I tapped the icon and watched it turn purple.

It was after 8 p.m. when I left the office. Jae's departure an hour earlier was accompanied by the gift of an energy bar. Waving goodnight to the few other stragglers, I headed for the elevator. I was walking from Tenth to Eighth Avenue to catch the A uptown when I realized that Nora taught her yin yoga class until 9:30 p.m. By the time she arrived home, we'd both be too tired for anything but a quick, superficial chat. I had a strong desire to confront her, to beg her to erase the incriminating text I'd sent. To never mention it to the police, if asked. Yet the courage eluded me. *Soon*, I bargained with myself.

The subway was standing room only, and I hung onto a pole as it lurched and shuddered. A yearning for companionship rose in me like a ghost clambering to be heard. Everywhere I went—the office, the hospital, the congested city—I was surrounded by people. But, other than the times I was with Nora, I was alone. I imagined changing trains for the airport, galloping through the terminal and boarding a plane for Los Angeles, flagging down a taxi in that dry city, then showing up on Sam's doorstep like an Amazon package that he'd forgotten he'd ordered.

Outside the 181st Street station, the neighborhood was sleepy and still. I needed to reach my dad before he conked out. "You home?" I asked when he answered, "Elle." In that one word was the sound of crushing fatigue.

"At the hotel," he said.

Of course, you idiot. "How is Josh?"

"Hold on. Let me go in the other room. Mom's asleep." They were staying in a suite. A minute later, "Fuzzy. Not coherent yet."

A bearded man with a black hat and long jacket scampered past me, his wife in an ankle-length skirt and a religious wig by his side.

"Oh, is that from . . ." *His broken brain.*

"From the sedation. He can't yet retain what's going on. Dr.

Hamid talked to us about fitting him for a facial mask to help stretch his skin and shrink the scars as they form."

"He's not ready."

"The darker you are, the worse it can be."

Josh was olive-skinned.

"For how long?" I crossed the street, toward my place.

"He'll have to wear it for ten hours a day, not sure how long. It's very uncomfortable but necessary."

"Can't they wait for Josh to get better?"

"The longer we wait, the more disfigurement."

The Hunchback of Notre Dame. Phantom of the Opera. The Elephant Man. Who would my brother be without the stunning machinery of his body, its strength and beauty? I stepped up on the curb, having not watched where I was going, and fumbled, falling on my wrist and hand. "Shit!"

"I know. It's very hard."

"Tell Josh I'm rooting for him."

"Will do."

I used my key to get into the vestibule of my building, the mustard-yellow popcorn walls, the claustrophobic low ceiling. The elevator had the tight fit of a coffin for two and jolted as it stopped at each floor, a cardboard mat underfoot. The corridor smelled of onion and pork, and I realized I'd forgotten to get myself dinner. The apartment was warm but not overbearingly so, as Nora hadn't been gone more than a couple of hours. After dropping my satchel in my bedroom, I ran my hand under warm water. It was scraped and raw but not bleeding. Then I rummaged around the fridge to see if there was anything I could poach from my roommate. But the tofu, the vegan cookie dough mix, the tub of plain yogurt, didn't appeal. Jae's Clif Bar would have to do, along with a boxed water.

On my bed, I texted Drew: *Is now ok to talk? Are you home?*

Just got here.

Where do you live, btw?

Riverside, off 120.

Fancy.

I'm nothing if not fancy! As you must recall from my stylish child-hood.

A hum inside me, a loosening. What was this? Fun?

He wrote: *Facetime?*

I'd changed into cotton pajama bottoms and a tank top, no bra, my bangs pulled back in a scrunchie. The distance felt better, not being seen. I pressed on his number.

"Hey. This okay?"

"Sure. Amazing news about Josh! Did they take him out of the coma?

My tongue swept my bottom tooth, the one that was slightly higher than the others. I repeated what my father had conveyed to me. "I'm going to the hospital on Saturday."

"Want company?"

"Don't you have to work 24/7? And go to school, too?"

"I can take off, especially on the weekend. The guy I report to is a maniac but not a complete dick. He's aware that my best friend was seriously injured; he gets it."

"That's lucky. My job doesn't leave much room for personal issues."

"Is your boss a *total* asshole? Doesn't he understand what you've been through, how devastated you are?"

The word "devastated" slammed down on me. It described my mother—plunged into watery sludge, flapping to break free, barely available to speak, often lying down when I visited—her condition reported by my father for whom the world was now coated in grime and gray, his reflexes slowed. My own mood, a mix of frenzied thinking and torpid near-paralysis, was harder to define. Acute avoidance, maybe.

"It's not like that with Rashad. Terrafeed is strapped for money. Everyone has to be at the top of their game, without exceptions."

"Inhuman."

"American," I countered. "Anyway, this weekend . . ."

"If you want privacy, to be alone with him and your folks, I get it."

"No, actually. I'm pretty nervous about seeing Josh. If you come up here to the North Pole, I'll drive."

"You're not in the North Pole; you're in Reykjavik. I've been there. It's beautiful."

"Thank you."

His support felt like a bulwark. I'd gained an ally in someone who loved my brother. If he refused to blame me for the fire, wouldn't that count in my favor?

Both of us were sleepy on Saturday morning. We sipped our Starbucks drinks and listened to Billie Eilish whisper-sing while I drove up the West Side Highway. The sky was the blue of over-washed denim, a reminder that there was still beauty on this planet, even though our trip was a tour of the gray river, boxy brown buildings, and strip malls on the Jersey side. I peeked over at Drew, at his closely shaved face even on a day away from the office. He was wearing dark jeans and a burgundy polo shirt, both so crisp, I wondered if he'd ironed them. Which made me feel disheveled in my joggers, the cotton sweater on the top of a pile in my dresser drawer, and black high-top sneakers.

"So, you're nervous about talking to Josh . . ." he said.

"Yeah, I am."

"You've seen him already, so is it more about whether he's changed, his personality, his memory?"

My hands on the wheel were damp even though the car was cool inside. "It's a mix of things, I guess."

"I've read up on the possible outcomes. Have you?"

"A little. I couldn't bear much."

"Every injury is different," he said, a memorized line. "We don't know how Josh will be affected yet."

"He's going to be so depressed." I didn't turn my head, focusing, without noticing anything, on the road.

"He *might* be."

"C'mon. He was already in trouble. And now, his body . . . like this?"

"He'll probably be angry for a while," Drew conceded.

"With me. I abandoned him," I said, as I exited the bridge onto the parkway.

"I hate that you have to go through this."

A quick glance to check if Drew was humoring me. He was staring ahead, his face relaxed, his mouth slightly open. "I'm not the one who's suffering."

"Of course you are."

"Look, that's really nice of you to say . . ."

"Who taught you that, that just because yours isn't the worst situation, you don't deserve to feel bad?"

I grinned in that foolish way, as if he'd discovered a shameful secret about me. "Um, everyone?"

"They're all wrong. And, besides, things could turn out differently than you think. Josh has already defeated the odds by coming out of the coma so early. His recovery could be sooner and better than the doctors predicted."

"Thanks. For saying all that."

He draped his hand over mine.

I wanted more. To be held by him, by my brother's best friend.

.

chapter seven

One glance at my mother—the hollowing of her cheeks, the clammy skin on her neck, the trickle of sweat on her forehead—and my thoughts shifted back to what mattered. My shattered family.

"Ellie," she said, closing the door to Josh's room behind her. "Hello, Drew."

"Good to see you, Ms. Stone," he said. "Ellie was kind enough to give me a ride."

I didn't dare look at Drew. How inappropriate of me to bring him. What a miscalculation. How selfish.

My mother lifted her chin. "Josh is sleeping. Dad's in there with him. You can visit soon, when he wakes up, Elle." She bit down hard on my name. "I'm going to the cafeteria to get some coffee."

"I can get it for you. Does Dad need anything?"

"Sure, thanks. Same for Dad, with skim milk, as usual."

A nurse rode down in the elevator with Drew and me, and I stared at her narrow ankles that ended with boatlike Crocs on her feet. How did she work in this hellish place every day? I envied her commitment. I wrote about catastrophic events but did nothing of consequence to stop them. What a noble profession, I thought, working to clean up the wreckage.

Drew touched my wrist. "You all right?"

"I'm not the issue." I pulled back, put my finger to my lips, not wanting to talk in front of the nurse.

The doors lumbered open, and the nurse exited, hugging her clipboard. We followed her down the hall to the grab-n-go section of the cafeteria.

"You saw my mom," I said, once we were far away enough not to be overheard. "She's torn apart, and my dad will never be able to make it up to her, even though he did nothing wrong. None of them did. But they'll torture themselves until the day they die."

"What about you?" Drew asked.

"I'm the problem. Leaving Josh alone with me is the biggest mistake of their lives, and they'll never get over it."

"Will *you*?"

I shook my head. "That's irrelevant."

"Of course it's not. Someone has to look after you."

Was he chiding me? No. His expression was earnest. There was no sign of the tween boy who'd laughed gleefully when Josh taunted me for being a "nerd." Better my brother targeted me than him—a fellow nerd. I'd ignored Drew's participation. Before high school, we barely noticed him, but then Nora and I labeled him "the sad suck-up."

"Thanks, really. There are professionals for that kind of thing. Been there, done that. Didn't take."

"Elle, hey, all I meant was you shouldn't have to cope with this yourself."

There were four kinds of roasts. Breakfast Blend seemed the most innocuous, a nondescript sort of choice. I pushed the paper cup against the machine. "My mother hates hazelnut," I said. "All flavored ones. I have friends. I'm not alone."

"Of course you do. It's just that you've always seemed so independent."

"Your view of me was distorted, as this studious older sister. I had a boyfriend for four years. He looked after me, sort of."

Why divulge this information: defensiveness—*I'm a normal person!*—or some other motivation?

"Does he know about what's going on?" He flushed.

"No, we don't stay in touch. He's at UCLA now."

"What about social media?"

"Have I posted about Josh? No." I thought of Anna Nuñez, with whom Sam wasn't Facebook friends and whose comments he'd never read. "Haven't tweeted about it, either. And Sam isn't spying on me, anyway."

"That's not . . ."

"Sam isn't interested in me anymore. He has a new girlfriend," I added quickly. I was the spy. A couple of months ago, I'd seen a photo of him with some long-haired Whippet of a woman on Instagram, his arms around her curved waist.

"Sorry. Didn't mean to pry."

"That's okay." I softened. "Sam and me—that's the normal stuff. People break up all the time. This, what's going on now, is the surreal shit."

"Want me to come in to see Josh with you?" Drew's voice wavered, and his uncertainty moved me. "If your parents let me."

"That's really sweet of you. I probably have to deal with him myself."

"You're too hard on yourself."

"I used to think so," I said, at the cash register now. "But maybe it's the opposite. Maybe I'm too easy."

Other than the nurse at the front desk, no one was in sight on Josh's floor. The silence felt prescient, like the stillness before the killer crept out of hiding. I knocked lightly on the door to Josh's room. When my mother opened it, I glimpsed my father in a chair next to the bed, kneading the space between his brows with two fingers. All I could see of my brother was his waxy toes peering out from the gauze bandages. The sight made my vision blur.

"Thank you," my mom said, quietly, as she waved me away from the room.

"Is Josh still sleeping?"

My mother stepped into the hall. "He's in and out."

"We can go to the waiting room until he's up for visitors."

"Turns out, it's not a good day, Elle. I know you drove all this way, but it's just too soon."

"I haven't been allowed to see him at all!" Despite my fear of witnessing the scars and disfigurement up close, I yearned to express contrition and proclaim that I loved him. "You guys are with him all the time."

"That's different," she said. "We're his parents."

My mother pushed back her shoulders, the two cups balanced in her hands, the scales of justice. I always believed she'd missed her calling as a prosecutor. My parents had met in law school, but my mom never practiced. Soon after they'd married in her third year, she'd gotten pregnant with me. While she'd received her degree, she never bothered to take the bar exam. That could wait, she'd reasoned, a promise to herself—like a first-class cruise that she'd never take. Once Josh was in preschool, she'd obtained her realtor's license. "So much easier for a mother with two small children," she'd explained to us as she cooked dinner or straightened out the bedsheets.

I countered with, "I'm his sister."

"I'm well aware of that."

"How lucid is he?" A suspicion arose that my brother wasn't even behind this decision.

"The morphine makes it hard to tell what he remembers."

"Can't I just sneak in, then?"

"No, Ellie," she said sternly. "Not today."

My usually strong will crumbled. I was no match for my mother, never had been. I was her "smart, sensible girl" before the incident at Anna Nuñez's; then I became someone else: a suspect at worse, a disappointment at best.

"Can I see Dad before I go?" I asked.

"I'll get him."

"Let me help." Drew pushed open the door for her.

I stared at the barrier between me and my family, the thick frosted glass.

"She's tough on you," Drew said quietly.

"You have no idea."

My father slipped out, gaunt, in wrinkled clothes, his belt buckle tightened to hold up his loose pants. He had the beginning of a beard, and his hair slid over his eyes. I'd never seen him so ungroomed.

Elle-Belle, I wanted him to say, folding me into his arms. *Come in with us.*

"Hi, Ellie, Drew," he said, his voice scratchy.

"Mr. Stone." Drew tipped his head.

My father's kiss on my cheek was light and dry. He didn't whisk me away, as I'd thought he might. Privacy was a luxury he seemed too distressed to require. "It's been a bad morning. Josh isn't out of the woods. I thought when he woke up, it would be . . . better." He stopped, winded. "I just wish I could change places with him."

I should have agreed: *Me too.*

"Does he even know what's going on?" I asked.

"For a while, then he seems to forget."

"Has he talked about what happened?"

"He gets agitated when he realizes where he is and why. We try to keep him calm, reassure him that he'll be all right."

My mother peeked her head out and waved us over. "I told Josh you were here. He asked to see Drew."

"Why?" Drew's mouth stretched into a fake smile.

"He has a question for you. But please, be brief."

"Not me?" I asked, a tourniquet squeezing my body tight.

Josh would never forgive me for deserting him. Whatever tension had been between us the last few years, he was my only sibling. I'd taken for granted that we'd reconcile once his addiction was behind him, once we'd both matured, a realization that had been buried inside me, like a future self.

Drew turned to me as if to ask my permission, then seemed to think better of it.

"Ellie, we have to respect Josh's timeline." My dad addressed Drew. "I can understand being nervous. Do you want me to come in with you?"

"No, thank you, Mr. Stone. I'll be all right," he answered in a respectful voice. "He's my friend."

Alone with my parents, I scraped at my cuticles with my thumb, controlling my distress over being forsaken rather than engaging in conversation.

"Don't do that, Ellie. You'll make them bleed," my mother said. This was a refrain from my childhood.

I shrugged. "It could be worse."

"You're right." Her hands were quivering ever so slightly, and her elbows seemed clamped to her sides. "It certainly could."

"Peri," my father said in his "we've talked about this" tone. "Let her be."

When Drew emerged, a few moments later, his face looked blotchy, as if he'd been crying. But his eyes were dry. We exchanged a quick, sad smile. There was something between us now, formed by heartbreak and our proximity to devastation.

"What happened?" I whispered as we walked away.

"Give me . . . a minute," he said, a skip in his voice.

As the elevator was crowded, we didn't speak. Outside, the humidity clawed at my skin. The cars and people—all that movement—blurred, and I stopped walking. Nora would have directed me to fill my chest cavity with air, hold my breath, then let it out slowly. I followed her instructions, training my eyes on a minivan until it reverted to a clear image.

He grabbed my forearm. "I can drive."

"That's okay."

"Please let me," he said, and I acquiesced.

"How did Josh seem?" I asked once we were on our way.

Drew made a whistling sound.

"That bad?

"Yeah, sorry."

"Did he realize he was in the hospital?" When Drew nodded, I asked, "Did he understand why?"

"We didn't talk about that."

"My mom said he had something to ask you."

"He wanted to keep it private."

"Did he actually make any sense? My parents say he's confused and out of it most of the time."

Drew swiveled in my direction, his brows stitched together. "He was coherent for the few minutes I was with him. He asked me to take care of you. He said you had it hard, even though you made things look easy."

"Really? That doesn't sound like Josh." But what did I know of my brother anymore? What did we really know of each other?

"I guess being this injured changes someone inside, too."

"Why would you need to take care of me?"

"In case he doesn't make it." Drew's voice sank.

My body felt sodden, heavy and weak. "That was never his job."

"I told him of course I would."

Out the window, the clouds dipped low. I took a sip of my water, retrieved from my bag. The streaks from Josh's sports drink, made the night of the fire, were like tears. Who was this transformed sibling, with the heart of a valiant knight?

I must have dozed because when my eyes cleared, we were in the city.

"Hey," Drew said. "You were out for a bit. I can park on your street, then take the subway."

"That's really nice of you." I meant all of it: the drive home, sharing Josh's secrets, his magnanimous response. I poked around my bag for my peppermint gum. I popped a stick in my mouth and offered Drew one.

Outside my apartment building, I smelled his minty breath when he turned to say goodbye. Instead of leaving, he did this thing with his hand, scooping me up by the elbows and lifting me onto my toes. "You were always the smartest one in the room."

"Not true, Columbia. And what does that even matter?"

He had a misty-eyed glaze. "I was quoting Josh from when we were growing up. He nicknamed you Hermione."

"That," I said, smiling, "was a long time ago. You always made fun of me. I thought you hated me."

"That was never the case. The opposite, in fact." His voice so soft, like cashmere. "I had a crush on you years ago, when I was a kid."

I stared at Drew, this newly buff version of the boy who'd worn jeans a size too big, as if he could hide inside the flapping fabric when he walked. His awkward gestures, like a poor copy-cat version of Josh, his smirks and condescending tone of voice came back to me, but no snippets of conversation between the two of us. In fact, I couldn't recall a single exchange.

Was everything I'd ever believed about him wrong?

"Want to come in for a while?" I asked.

"Are you sure?"

I nodded, surprised by this longing to be with him.

Inside the apartment, my body leaned into his. *Stress-fucking.* A familiar college phrase used to describe the upswing in hookups around midterms and finals. But this urge felt deeper—and, also, wildly inappropriate.

"Are you sure?" he whistled in my ear.

I couldn't answer that question correctly, so I let my body take over. We scrambled and lunged a bit, then tugged at each other's clothes tentatively, without success. I paused for a moment, tensed, and he withdrew without resistance.

Where is Nora?

The place was dark and quiet, only the hum of the air conditioner—which meant my roommate would return soon. No yoga classes this afternoon unless as a last-minute substitute, nothing but laundry and grocery shopping on her agenda.

"Okay," I whispered. "Bedroom."

We shimmied in that direction, Drew laughing, me shushing him.

"There's no one here!" he said.

"She'll be back any minute. She thinks of you as the asshole who made fun of us for taking calculus in high school. And *this* is . . . so weird."

"It's not. It's really not! I was just a kid then."

Drew twirled me into my room, dipped me back, stretched one leg behind him, a complicated move. I heard him snap the door shut with his foot.

Giddy, I asked, "Are you sure you're not getting a master's in dance?"

"You discovered my secret."

He *was* a master of movement, this former awkward child. Drew cupped the cheeks of my ass, rolled me on top of him, and slid inside. I arched up, my legs wrapped around him, as tight as they would go. I was alive with desire even as the question flashed through my mind: *What the hell are you doing?*

Afterward, I lay flat, not touching Drew, who scrunched the pillow beneath his head and stared at the ceiling. He smiled. "I can't believe it. I'm here. With you."

The light blinked above us, under the scalloped glass fixture. "Totally bizarre, right?"

He laughed, an open-hearted, innocent sound. "It's amazing!"

"Don't you feel a little shitty now?"

He curled on his side, toward me, but didn't inch any closer. "Why? It wasn't . . . nice for you?"

"No, it was! I meant, Josh. He'd be grossed out. What we just did was . . . kind of incestuous."

Drew blinked quickly, as if startled. "It's nothing like that. And what good does it do if we're too depressed to be there for him?"

"I don't think he meant sex when he said to take care of me."

"Don't worry. We can stay under the radar."

I shut my eyes and imagined that when I reopened them, the other Drew would appear: my brother's sidekick-turned-finance-guy who'd never appealed to me. But when I observed him again, he was, indeed, not that person. "You're so different now."

"We all grow up, Elle."

Not Josh. He just unraveled.

"So, this"—I pointed between him and me—"will remain between us?"

"If you want it to."

"Under the radar is good for now, while things are so complicated for my family. I want to lie low until Josh starts to recover."

"Of course. Listen, my blurting out about my crush on you when I was, like, twelve . . . that doesn't mean I'm assuming anything."

"I'm in this super-weird state now."

He sat up and reached to the floor, slid his shirt on, half-buttoned, his chest hair an adornment. "If we decide to just be friends, that's okay."

"That's not what . . ." I propped myself against my wall, pulling the covers around my breasts like an actress with a no-nudity clause, and his lips curled into an easy smile. "I don't know what I want. Drew, I think about the fire all the time."

"You keep replaying it?"

"It takes up so much space in my brain. I can't shake the feeling that I left a lit cigarette in the house."

"Your mind is playing tricks on you."

"What if it's not?" I asked so softly, barely aloud.

"Is this because of what Anna Nuñez wrote online recently?"

He'd been checking, too.

I'd tried to resist social media but hadn't entirely. Audrey had set up a Facebook page for Josh, a virtual community that offered support for his recovery. Periodically, I checked the comments. A few of them referred to the rest of my family, sending best wishes. Anna hadn't mentioned me again, on her personal page, after her initial response: *Isn't this the Firestarter's house? Another "accident"?*

But she did post a close-up of her face, focusing on her scar—which was thick and pink and angry—without makeup covering it. Her status: *This is AFTER laser treatments.* When I saw that picture, my shoulders contracted, my body slouching in on itself in self-incrimination: *Look what you did to her! Of course she hates you. Of course she believes you burnt down your own house.*

Friends chimed in on both threads:

Has anyone heard from THE SISTER? She hasn't posted since.

Wonder what the police have come up with.

Maybe this time she'll pay for what she did!

No one referred to me by name, as if I existed as a town legend, a ghost of a girl.

"The thing with Anna was random," Drew said. "You were a teenager."

My tank top and underwear were shoved under the covers. I retrieved them with my foot and busied myself with dressing. We sat in silence for a couple of minutes. I could hear Drew's even exhales, like a metronome.

"What's going on with the police investigation?" he asked after a bit. "I read something about it in the *Star Ledger.*"

"I don't subscribe to that paper." A local New Jersey one, not widely read outside the state. I tried to pacify myself with the lack of national readers, then wondered how many followers the *Ledger* had on Twitter. "What did the article say?"

"Not much. That it's ongoing."

Good! "I don't want to upset my parents by asking. The sergeant who questioned me brought up the possibility that Josh owed money for drugs. They don't seem to have any real leads."

"They'll probably deem it an accident."

At the edge of my thoughts, a question pecked away. I'd been ignoring it for a while. "When you said that thing about Audrey not being an arsonist, was there something you weren't telling me?"

"Like what?"

"Like she'd been at our house that night—while I was gone?"

"I don't have any idea where she was."

"Then what? You're holding something back."

"It's too ridiculous to mention." Drew scratched his cheek, looked aslant. "Okay. Josh complained, last year, that Audrey had started smoking. He blamed art school, and I laughed 'cause that's such a cliché."

"Do you think she's capable of . . ."

He stretched his arms up in the air, then jumped out of bed. "Stop, Sherlock! I'm starving!"

"I have no food."

"Let's go out for dinner."

We bolted out of my room as if a prize lay on the other side of the door.

What met us wasn't a prize. It was the sound of the key in the lock. In the living room, Nora stood, holding a tote bag of groceries in each hand.

"Hi," I said, too cheerfully. "Drew drove my car back from the hospital. I was too upset."

"I'm sorry. Must have been really tough seeing Josh."

I nodded, offered nothing.

"Hi, Drew," Nora said. "So, did you guys just get here?"

"Not just." He smiled, his eyes crinkling at the corners.

"We've, umm . . ." I said.

Nora smiled back with a cool, disappointed gaze.

chapter eight

At the Cuban restaurant, Drew's face was alight with joy, his shiny-teethed smile, glittering glances my way. Every gesture was quick, up-tempo.

"Can you imagine the good luck?" Drew asked, drumming the table. "Hundreds of people died, and my friend is posting pictures of blue-footed boobies and sea lions on Instagram."

"What were we talking about?" I asked, having floated away, Nora's expression flashing in my mind.

"The guy from my seminar who went to the Galapagos Islands with his family. He missed the earthquake in Quito by less than a day."

"Right." My fork was lodged in a splice of papaya, although I hadn't eaten much of my tropical salad.

What are you doing, Ellie? Nora's voice filled my head. *This is the kid who opened your bedroom door just to gawk and call us geeks, while we did calc problems. That time you and Josh got into a fight over his finishing your stash of chocolate-covered pretzels, Drew gave you the finger. He laughed when you called Josh disgusting and threw his dirty cleats off the dining room table.*

Drew raised his beer. "My school is filled with people like that, Gatsby people."

"Gatsby ended up dead in his pool."

"I meant the other ones, Tom and Daisy, the ones who smashed up people's lives and retreated into their money."

"But," I said, back in my body. *He ended up at an Ivy anyway, Nora, despite all the video games.* "That analogy doesn't really apply. Your friend had planned to leave beforehand. He didn't cause the damage."

"You're right, of course," Drew said, jovially. "And who am I kidding? I may not hail from East Egg, but I'm the same. I'm just as lucky." He reached for my hand. "It's not like I've forgotten about Josh. I'm just happy to be here with you."

None of Nora's familiar scents awaited me at home, not incense, or spices, or flowers from the bodega. She was cross-legged on our living room couch, throw pillows stacked behind her, computer on her lap. She was wearing a baseball cap with the logo for the non-profit performing arts organization that had hired her recently. The associate production manager job thrilled her, the money less so. She'd rejiggered her schedule to continue teaching yoga on nights and weekends.

"Busy with work stuff?" I asked.

"Umm."

"K. I won't bother you."

She craned her neck, her back straightening to perfection. "How'd it go with Josh?"

"Strange."

"How'd he seem?"

"He wouldn't see me. He spoke to Drew."

"God, Elle. That sucks. That must have been awful for you." When I didn't respond, she paused. "I guess you and Drew are . . . what? Friends now?"

"Something like that."

Her eyebrow raised, Nora said, "What does that mean?"

I shrugged, glanced out the window behind the couch at the gray sky, the first drizzle of rain.

"I thought you weren't a fan. You always said he was pathetic, the way he worshipped Josh, like he wanted to *be* him. Plus, he was mean to you."

"Million years ago. He's changed. You can see for yourself."

"Sure. He's lost weight and dresses better."

"C'mon, he's grown up. He's self-assured, smart, driven. He's really different."

Nora clicked her tongue. "You guys hooking up?"

"Just once."

"Jesus, Elle."

I twisted my bangs around my finger, a new habit acquired since not trimming my hair for months. "Why so judgy?"

"It's creepy, like you guys are hanging onto Josh by being together."

"That's not true. Drew confessed he used to have a crush on me."

"He made fun of you for being so studious. Anyway, even if he did, don't you see him more like a sibling?"

"No. You make it sound like incest. We're not related." How awkward to stand before her, like a suspect on trial, waiting for the head juror to read the verdict. "And we're not in a relationship. It was just sex."

"Does *he* know that?"

"Nor? Interrogation over."

Her eyes slid over me and back to the computer screen. "You're hurting. You're not a one-time kind of person. You're not casual."

"Maybe I am now. Everything's changed."

"Elle, you never even noticed him before."

"I noticed him."

How Drew popped up at our dinner table Fridays for pizza and salad and my mom ordered an extra pie, topped with pepperoni, just for him. How Drew and my brother would laugh and laugh, sometimes so hard they would choke on their own saliva. How Drew would say, "So, Ms. Stone, did you hear the one about . . ." and recite a terrible joke to make my mother smile. How once Audrey was in Josh's life, Drew's presence diminished and when he accompanied the couple, he hung back, one hand pressed against his heart as if standing for the Pledge of Allegiance, his mouth set in a hard line. How, even now, I questioned if Drew's attraction to me was all mixed up with his love for my family.

"Sure, you have now," Nora said, "since he looks good."

"I'm not that shallow." I perched myself on the other end of the couch. "He's there for me. He understands. My parents aren't; they can't be and I get that."

"I'm here."

"I love you, Nor. But it's not the same."

She bit her bottom lip. "What about Audrey? She must be hurting. You could talk to her instead of getting yourself into something that might complicate things later, when Josh is better."

"Audrey's a suspect," I blurted out. "Drew told me she smokes, too."

"So?"

"She could have come over to the house after I left."

She squinted as if to see me better. "The police suspect she was in your house?"

"Maybe. I wasn't in the room for their interrogation, obviously."

"How long were you gone before you turned around, under an hour?"

"How is that question being there for me?" I snapped at her.

"Just trying to follow." Nora clamped her laptop lid down. "Drew implicated Audrey?"

I combed my fingers through my hair, frizzy from the humid air. "This is coming out all wrong. He didn't do that. All I'm saying is, I'm not the only smoker who was mad at Josh that night."

"Do you think Audrey set the fire, or are you grasping for answers?"

"Stop drilling me!" I demanded, clammy from fear and anger.

Her voice quivered. "That's not what I was trying to do. You've been through something terrible. You need help, Elle, not from me. Professional . . ."

"Don't," I said, and jumped up, walked away.

I couldn't broach erasing my text—*Sick to death of Josh. Let him OD*—with her. Not when she was suspicious of the time frame that night, of Audrey's possible participation, of my mental health.

I lay on my bed, in the dark. But the lights from the bridge illuminated the few pieces of furniture, trinkets on my dresser across from me: a Capricorn candleholder, goat carved into the ceramic; a tiny snow globe of Big Ben from Sam's semester abroad; a glass vase filled with dried lavender.

"He needs our help, Dan."

That was my mother's voice, loud enough for me to hear through my half-closed door. A year ago, August, at the rented lake house in Vermont. I'd sworn off vacations with my family, but, having just ended things with Sam, I'd felt stripped raw, aching for a comfort that was no longer available, that hadn't been for ages.

"Dr. Yeung insists he needs our unconditional support."

There was always a new therapist or a psychiatrist, or both, with fresh advice; there had been since Josh's struggles began. I hadn't kept the dates straight after my father mentioned the first incident to me.

"There's a problem," he'd begun the conversation, "with Josh." I'd been reading about biodiversity and functioning ecosystems on my dorm room bed, junior year. My brother had been a senior in high school, accepted early admission to his first choice, a Division 1 university where he'd play midfielder for their soccer team.

The drug-taking was manageable until it wasn't, a pattern that ebbed and flowed but never abated.

"Support is different than condoning, Peri," my dad said.

The air was blanketed in a darkness that was thicker and more substantial than night in New York City, filled with scents of pine and soil and lake brine. As I'd peeked into the hall, the floorboards creaked. My mother, with her posture perfect and her pallid complexion, stood outside my brother's room, like a sentinel oddly attired in a silky bathrobe and ballet-like slippers. My father held aloft a plastic bag of pill bottles, while Josh, his face contorted into a villain's grimace, furiously swung to grab it.

"You invaded my privacy!" Josh screamed.

"You're on the property I'm paying for. Those drugs are my responsibility," my father said. He raised his arm higher, a gesture that wouldn't deter Josh if he was up for a physical confrontation. "And they are illegally obtained."

My mother turned toward me so abruptly it seemed she'd solved the problem. "Get back in there. This doesn't concern you."

As if I were a trespasser in our family.

No one contradicted her.

"Josh," I called out. "What are you doing? This isn't you."

He looked at me, his eyes clear and wide, and for a moment, he was my beloved brother again. "It is now, Elle," he'd said, gruffly.

⌐—·:·—⌐

In Washington Heights, I fell asleep too early and was plagued by a nightmare on repeat. Josh, in his footsie pajamas, with his blanket like a cape around his little-boy shoulders. "Elle, I'm burning." I patted the space next to me and beckoned my brother to lie down. He shook his head. "You'll catch it." The trees around the house were a blackish-orange blaze with the silhouettes of hopping kangaroos in the distance.

I awoke, over and over, until finally, it was morning. Outside my window, in the stark white of day, the faithful structure ferried cars to their destinations. My dad's text came moments later. It read: *Josh needs surgery on his hand tomorrow or he'll lose fingers.*

I responded quickly: *I could visit after work.*

I waited to be rebuffed: *That's ok, no need for you to make the trip. Will pass along your good wishes.* Instead: *That would be great.*

Pressure in my chest, my throat tight, and eyes full.

What time is the surgery?

First thing. 7AM. Come when you can.

Will be there.

I'd memorized the train schedule, which was inefficient at best, woefully delayed or canceled frequently. Twitter accounts were dedicated to the folly of NJ Transit, the massive disaster that was our poor infrastructure and antiquated equipment. But driving during peak commuting hours would be a worse slog. Mid-afternoon was best. In the shower, I considered my options, how to approach Rashad. Asking permission to leave early was risky after he'd issued his warning. But as long as I promised to meet my upcoming deadlines, to not file shoddy pieces, visiting my brother during work hours shouldn't be a problem. Rashad was a reasonable person. I'd try to get research done for the article due on Tuesday in advance.

The water pressure was low again, and mildew had grown in the cracks despite Nora's vigilant scrubbing. I hated that heat waves, flooding, droughts, and snowless winters plagued the earth, that Josh's back skin would be grafted onto his fingers, and still, I longed for modern tile work, good plumbing, and chrome faucets.

"Hey," Nora said when I showed up in the kitchen, my hair wrapped in a towel turban. "Good morning."

"Same." She was in her yoga leggings and crop top. "Class?"

"Yeah, Harlem at ten. You?"

"Catching up on work. Then food shopping."

"Sounds good," she said, cheerfully. Which translated into: *No Drew. No fucking up.*

Or so it seemed to me.

Normally, I'd share the news about Josh's surgery tomorrow, about my dad's solicitous message, about how I detested penning this piece on the Doomsday Clock. But now, I thought: *Keep it light.*

Sorrow swatted me. It felt like another huge loss, this schism between Nora and me.

Passing the nurses' station, I smiled, wondering if any of them recognized me. One, with a shiny forehead and mocha-colored corkscrew curls, smiled back. "Good to see you." It was clear from her expression that she had no idea who I was, that her greeting was the same for all of us, the traumatized visitors.

My parents and Audrey were huddled outside Josh's door. Which caused my pulse to skitter.

"Hi, Ellie," my mother said. In her brief embrace, I noted how her once muscular arms felt bony. She was even thinner than the last time I'd seen her, swallowed up by a linen shirtdress she hadn't bothered to iron. Her complexion was dove gray, her roots icecap white.

"I'm glad you could get away early."

My father came forward to kiss my forehead. "Josh is napping."

"Oh, good," I said. "How was the surgery?"

Audrey sucked on her lower lip and kept her distance. In her frayed denim pants, forest-green sweatshirt with "Pine Trees School" printed in white, and Toms canvas shoes, she looked like a model in a bug spray ad. Not her usual attire.

"Coming from work?" I asked her.

"Me?" she responded, surprised.

Obviously. My father had taken a leave of absence at the end of the semester, one colleague finishing up his Civil Procedure course and another, his seminar. My mother had given her client list over to an associate at her agency.

I pointed to the logo on Audrey's shirt.

"Yeah, I'm an assistant art teacher at a private school. Mornings, three days a week."

"Right. Along with the MFA?"

"I'm part-time," she said, tugging on her sporty ponytail, wispy tendrils loose around her neck. "Part-time everything now. The headmaster has been great about flexibility since . . ."

Where were you that night?

"Josh asked for Audrey," my mother said, shifting in her direction. "It's very kind of her to come all this way."

"I *want* to, Ms. Stone."

My mother circled an arm around Audrey.

"I thought Josh wasn't letting anyone in but you guys," I said.

"He wasn't at first." My mother lowered her voice as if my brother might be eavesdropping. "He couldn't tolerate the idea of anyone seeing him, not with the way . . . things are."

"But he's coming around," Audrey said. "Slowly. It's a process."

"What kind of process?" I asked, irritated.

"Acceptance, I meant."

"And this 'acceptance,' you think Josh will . . . *embrace* it." *Embrace* was the most Gwyneth-Goop-y word I could conjure up.

"Yes, eventually. He's stronger than he realizes."

"So, he's seen you, then?"

"Once. Only the once."

I glanced at my father, but he was studying the linoleum floor. Audrey. Drew. My parents. I was the only one with whom my brother refused to visit. "You guys were fighting that day, all day."

"Ellie!" my mother said in a sonorous voice.

Audrey's eyes spilled. "How do you know?"

"I was in the house. Were you?"

Audrey wiped her tears. "If you were there, you'd have seen I wasn't."

"Obviously, I left for a while."

"That's enough," my father commanded. "Ellie."

"I'm going to check on Josh," my mother said.

"How about me? Can I see him now?" I asked.

My mother glowered. "He's in and out. Let me check."

Left to ourselves, we three didn't speak. My dad was picking at his torn cuticles, the thickened, scrapped patch on his index finger.

The door cranked open. "Just for a few minutes," Mom instructed me. "He's having a rough time, post-surgery."

Cortisol coursed through me, my anxiety like a panting dog. I hadn't expected this allowance, hadn't prepared. Me, the person who always prepared.

Josh was propped up by two pillows. He was wearing that mask, which was shiny, like glass, highlighting his eyes, wide and dark. The lashes had started to grow back in sparse bristles. The scars that pulled down the side of his face created a tragic expression he might never discard. His scalp was wrapped in gauze.

Regarding him awake was even more frightening, the transformation.

I grasped one hand with the other, to keep both from trembling. "Hi, Joshie. How are you feeling?"

He stared, as if trying to place me. When he spoke, his voice was strange, as if disconnected from his body. "Weird."

I sat in the chair next to the bed. "Thanks for letting me see you."

"I had to. There's something," he said, his voice filled with urgency.

"What, Joshie? Take your time."

"It's all fuzzy. The doctor said I might never remember." He laughed a goofy, high-pitched hiccup of a laugh, like someone who'd inhaled helium. "Then again, I might."

"There's nothing you need to do except recover."

"If I don't get better, obliviate, for Mom and Dad's sake."

We'd seen the seventh Harry Potter movie together when it first came out, and that scene where Hermoine erases her existence for her parents' sake always saddened Josh more than me. "I wish I could. But I'm not a wizard."

He whispered, "Talk to Audrey about memory spells."

"I don't understand." I shuffled the chair closer to him. "Was she there that night?"

"Everything hurts. They keep saying this . . ." He cocked his head in the direction of the IV.

"The morphine?"

He stared at me, just for a second, his gaze clear. "They thought Ativan was so bad. The joke's on them, right, Elle?"

I hung my head down. "Joshie, I'm so sorry," I said too quietly for him to hear, not wanting to burden him with my confession, to make his tragedy about me. He was in no position to forgive me, if he ever could. I reached out my hand to touch him but dropped it on the bed. Even a touch could cause him more pain. *I should never have left you.*

"I'm so tired." He closed his eyes.

"Rest, honey."

"Ask Audrey what happened."

chapter nine

L isten all you want.

Most likely Nora was asleep, but I didn't care either way. Drew was on top of me, holding my hands above my head, pushing me down. But not without my permission. "Is this okay? Is this?"

"Yes," I answered, watching his mouth open, his eyes half close, not minding the weight on my wrists.

"Are you into bondage?" I asked him, half joking.

"No." He blinked quickly, as if startled. "I didn't realize . . . I'll stop if it bothers you."

"Don't."

Then his mouth was everywhere, and I was arching up to meet it and my mind emptied. I was just a body reaching and clutching and buzzing with pleasure.

We lay there in my bed naked for a while afterward, not talking. With my window blinds half-mast, the lights from the bridge acted like low-wattage lamps. Drew peered at me. "What is it?" I asked.

"I can't stop thinking about what Josh said to you. I'm sure Audrey was in town that night. He said she went to some party with a friend."

"We can't talk about this again, or I won't sleep." I slipped on my T-shirt. "I have to pee. Be right back."

The bathroom door was shut, Nora possibly inside. She often used her phone to navigate the dark rather than be pierced with the overhead glare. The shock of it, in the night, roused her. "Was up for an hour!" she'd say. "Just because of my tiny bladder."

But it was empty and damp from the continually dripping shower. The scent from the air freshener on the toilet lid was like a cheap floral perfume turned bad. On the cracked seat, I wondered if Drew would leave. And if that's what I wanted.

He was there, lying on his side, snoring softly. I eased the blinds down, then slid into bed, the heat from his body like a water bottle on my back. I felt a mixture of gratitude and apprehension. *So glad you're here, can you please go?*

"Josh," he cried out.

"What's wrong?" My phone read: 3:07.

He whispered my brother's name, then his eyes opened.

"Bad dream?"

"Yes." He blinked more quickly. His breath was like warm pine and pepper from the gin we'd drunk. "We were in the woods, and he was screaming. But every time I got close to him, he ran away."

"I have nightmares like that, too."

He reached for me, and we held onto each other, dozing, until my alarm sounded.

"Ellie." He patted my arm. "Hey, gotta get up."

"Uh?" I jerked awake, seated, shirtless. I lunged for my top and rustled it on. "What time is it?"

"Seven fifty-five."

"Oh, shit!"

"I left the shower running for you. It's warm."

I noted this Saks Fifth Avenue model before me, shaved and showered in his pressed suit, ironed shirt, Italian leather shoes. He'd arrived at my place with a bottle of Hendrick's and a garment bag that he'd hung in my closet. My first instinct had been to protest.

Then I recognized that he wasn't being presumptuous. I'd called him. When he suggested coming uptown, I'd agreed. It was what I'd wanted. If I also wanted him to disappear on demand, at my convenience, that wasn't his fault. He had a schedule, obligations, an important internship. Drew was behaving like a rational adult, while I was an ambivalent mess. And one who was going to be late for work.

How many second chances would Rashad allot me?

Nora's hours were ten to six, so I had leeway. But this arrangement—three people, one bathroom—wasn't sustainable.

Drew kissed me on the forehead the way you would a child. "I have to run," he said. "Talk soon."

"Definitely," I said, and meant it.

Unequivocally. In that moment.

My dad's call came while I was watching the barista steam milk for a grande cappuccino over my lunch break a couple of days later. I pressed decline on my phone; it was too loud in the shop to carry on a conversation. The espresso machine hissed and clanged; someone in the chattering, crowded shop honked like a snow goose.

I took a second to text my dad: *At work. Talk later?*

I heard the follow-up ping but couldn't check now. There was a line of NYU students twenty minutes long, some listening to podcasts and Spotify, others texting, many engaging in frantic chatter. One woman, with nails polished in alternating green and black, leaned her head against her friend who had RBG's face ironed on her sweatshirt. "This is the worst coffee in the city," she said.

"Stop kvetching," RBG said. "Blue Bottle was a zoo. Just hold your nose when you swallow, like you do with Kyle."

"I won't dignify that. Want to split a lemon loaf?"

They kept coming, this rush of keyed-up undergrads. I envied their sense of frenzied purpose. After joining the others in the pickup line, I read: *Call now.*

I felt a surge of fear.

My father's voice was like the low growl of an animal. "Josh is gone."

"Gone where?"

A memory came into my head: my brother at eighteen months—in his diaper, T-shirt, and pastel blue socks—bolting from our yard and ending up at our neighbor's house at the top of the block before my mother realized he was missing. It was a torrid summer day, the air a thick, damp blanket, and my mother had dozed off.

"They couldn't save him."

The words made no sense.

Save him from what? But my knees caved so that I was squatting on the floor, my head cradled in my hands. I whispered into the phone, "I'll call you back."

Above me, a young woman was asking me a question. All I could see were her black boots. It was dangerous to glance up at the spinning room; better to hug my legs closer to me. She handed me a cup of ice water and, after I'd taken a few sips, gently lifted me to my feet.

"Gross! Smells like puke," some guy shouted. "This place is a sewer!"

The woman guided me toward the back, to the bathrooms. "Let's get you out of here," she said. She held my head down, like a perp being directed into a police car. "Focus on the floor. Don't want you to barf again."

"Sorry," I said.

"They'll deal with it. You still nauseous?"

"Just dizzy."

One door had the red "occupied" sign next to the handle. She pushed open the other one. "Wash up. Can I call anyone for you?"

"No, thank you," I said.

Alone, I turned the lock. I couldn't think what to do next. If I sat on the toilet seat, I wouldn't get up for a long time. I tore off my peacoat and ran it under the water, pressing down on the soap to try to rinse out the stench. The face in the mirror was mine, full brows and big features—eyes and lips and round-tipped nose—but with an odd, grayish tint.

I texted Nora: *need help.*

She could have been in a meeting or unable to respond for any number of reasons during the workday. After a few seconds, I texted Drew: *can you meet me now?*

done early?

sick.

The lie was all I could muster.

b right there. I'll grab a cab. What's the address?

I'd written to my father—*coming home*—when someone knocked on the door. "You almost done?"

I didn't press send but gathered my wet coat in my arms and stumbled out. All I had to do was grab my backpack and make it to the street.

The clouds were murky. Two girls were laughing on the shop's bench, under the mermaid's star crown on the logo. A text wouldn't suffice. Adrenaline flooded me.

"Where did you go?" my dad asked as soon as he picked up.

"How did this happen?" I asked, shivering.

"Sepsis."

"When?"

"It started less than forty-eight hours ago with 105 temperature, his heart rate dropped . . ."

He sounded so far away, on another continent, in another century. "The doctors thought they could get it under control. But they couldn't save him."

"I'll be right there." I looked out at the buzzing traffic and tried to recall how to travel such a distance.

"Come tomorrow, first thing."

"Why not now?" I cried.

"Too much to arrange. I don't know where we'll be."

After he hung up, I held out the phone, like a toddler asking for assistance with a mechanical toy. The sky crackled and a few drops fell. I doubled over at the waist and gagged, bile rising.

Someone grabbed my elbow. "Poor thing," Drew said, a crease between his eyes like an elastic band. "You're shaking. Let's get you home."

I thought of Nora, how she'd find me with Drew, of her judgment.

"Can we go to your place? Is anyone there?"

"Ty is at the library right now. He'll probably be out late."

"That's okay."

In the taxi ride uptown, I thought about contacting Rashad. But I couldn't make sense of it, what I'd say and why work mattered.

Drew's apartment was overheated and stuffy, the scents of black beans and beer heavy in the air. Drew led me into his bedroom, then peeled off my coat. "Stomach virus?" He scooped up the balled peacoat that still stank of vomit and stuffed it in his laundry bag. "I'll have it dry-cleaned. Food poisoning, maybe?"

If I didn't say the words, the past would continue unabated. I sat on the edge of the bed.

"It's not food poisoning. Josh is dead."

Drew groaned. Then his face slackened, his eyes watered. "I don't understand. He was getting better."

I repeated my father's report of the events.

He sunk down next to me, reached for my hand, and covered it with his own. He sobbed quietly, saying, "Poor Josh," over and over. When he finally set his gaze on me, he was dry eyed, but his cheeks were flushed. "Ellie, you . . . I'm so sorry. And your parents! They must be crushed." It was as if revelations were coming in waves that he had to navigate, to stay afloat. "Were they with him . . . when it happened?"

The thought yanked me down onto his bed and I stared at a spot on the ceiling, a small stain, to ward off dizziness.

He rubbed my back, under my shirt, with his warm hand.

"I don't know," I said, "who found him."

"I shouldn't have asked." He found the spot at the knob of my neck that always ached from long hours at the computer and massaged it for a few seconds. "Let me get you something, a drink? I don't have anything but beer and water."

"Water."

When he left for the kitchen, I lay still and stared first at the stain and then at his wall. There was a print on it of Hannah Arendt and her shadow. The part of my brain that was still me wondered why it was hanging there. I waited for Arendt to flick her cigarette into the glass ashtray. Her ring and pinky fingers were curled so delicately, like a seashell, a sharp contrast to her clever face. She could stare death in the face.

Audrey.

She didn't know. While she was in my contacts app, Audrey's schedule was a mystery. I pressed on the mobile number, unsure what to say to her voicemail.

She answered with a hesitant, "Hi?"

"It's Ellie," I said, my breath catching.

"Yeah, I saw." She paused. "What's up?"

"Where are you?"

"Home. Are you nearby?"

"No, Manhattan. I have some bad news."

"Oh, no! Is Josh in a coma again?"

"It's worse than that. He . . . It's hard . . ."

An audible gasp when I finally formed the words. "No, you're wrong! I'm sure of it. I was just with him."

For a second, it seemed possible I'd been misinformed.

"Is this an FB prank?" she asked. "Anna Nuñez?"

"My father told me."

There was nothing at first. Then a wail so piercing, I said, "Stay where you are. I'm coming."

"This can't be happening," she howled. "I promised him it wouldn't, that I'd be there for him. This is all my fault. This can't be true!"

"Just hold on, Audrey. Okay?"

My clothes were folded on Drew's chair. The shirt with the stench and the sweat had to go. In my bra and jeans, I dashed down the hall, nearly crashing into Drew, who held a mug of reheated wonton soup and a glass of water on a dinner plate.

"I'm going to Brooklyn," I said. "Can I borrow a shirt?"

"What! That's crazy, Elle. Eat this."

Some impulse was drawing me to her. Would she divulge a secret that would solve the mystery of that night? Would I discover a hair-

line fracture in her assurance that she hadn't been in town? Or would
we connect like twins, born out of sorrow?

"Audrey's a mess," I said.

Drew stared at me. The plate clattered in his hand, and he steadied
it with the other one. "Let me come with you."

I shook my head. "She wouldn't want that."

"I know. I'll wait outside."

"You'd do that?"

"He's my best friend. I told him I'd take care of you. Drink the
water at least. Let me get you clothes and clean off your jacket."

The subway frightened me. Underground, juddering forward, my grief
might be rattled loose. Drew held my hand and navigated the train
changes. On the first one, there were no seats, but I grabbed a pole at
the end of the row near the door. Drew's fingers nearly crushed mine;
we were like two sailors clinging to a capsized boat. Yet instead of a
roiling ocean, there were patches of floor underneath us, much of it
filthy from sticky liquid, newspaper scraps fluttering, soda cans rolling.

It dawned on me that Audrey hadn't responded to my request to
stay put, that she could be gone by now.

The G train was quick. We emerged into an unfamiliar part of
the city, one that was dense with a young, noisy crowd. My mind
flashed to when Sam and I had taken a short vacation to Amsterdam,
the one stamp in my passport. When we landed back at Newark Airport, I'd said, "This is the ugliest place on earth." He'd laughed, "I read
Kuwait's airport is even worse."

I'll never be that happy again.

My body felt jiggly and weak, but Drew was clutching my hand.
He hadn't let go.

I texted: *I'm on Myrtle Avenue. You still home?*

I stared at the screen.

Yes.

I'll be right there.

k.

Audrey's apartment was fifteen minutes away, according to GPS, a walk we'd have to repeat on my return trip. Maybe she had a couch to crash on.

"We'll take an Uber back," Drew said. "I'll be outside waiting."

I scanned the street, a sandwich place, a deli, Huang Noodles. "Why don't you hang out in a restaurant?"

He shook his head. "Can't be with people now. I'll be all right."

"Okay," I said, wanting to show gratitude, some gesture. I kissed his cheek, which felt hot and damp.

Audrey buzzed me in, and I climbed the three flights of stairs. She was standing in the doorway, in an oversized shirt and leggings, her skin marred by pink splotches, as if feverous, her pupils dilated. I followed her past the open area, down a hall, and into her cell-sized bedroom. There was a platform bed and a desk facing a window.

"My roommates will be back soon, so better if we stay in here," she said. "Shouldn't you be in New Jersey?"

"Tomorrow."

"You were supposed to be there." Her voice trilled as if she couldn't find the right pitch. "It's just a weird coincidence that this happened while you were gone."

"Can I sit down?"

She pulled open a storage drawer under her mattress and shoved the shirts piled on the bed into them. "Go ahead. You smell like . . ."

"I threw up before. Sorry."

"Want a drink? I have . . . Perrier, maybe juice."

"Perrier is good."

Her walls were empty, other than a pin board with photos of her and Josh on it. I was hyperventilating. The air was so thin, I glanced up at her ceiling as if an oxygen bag would fall from it.

By the time Audrey returned and handed me the glass, I was exhaling more slowly. "Thanks."

She slunk onto her desk chair, releasing her head into her hands— the heaviest part of her. Just for a moment. Then she looked past me with a confused expression, as if she'd lost her way on a dark road. "He was doing better."

As I repeated my father's explanation, I watched hope leach out of Audrey—that last grasp before reality set in—her face growing gaunt as it might with age.

"*I* should have been there with him," she said in a chilly tone.

"Don't do that to yourself. I was supposed to stay with him in the house."

Staring at something beyond me, she said, "He's twenty-four years old. An adult." Tears bloomed. "People live by themselves at that age. No one should have had to monitor him, his stupid choices."

This sounded like an old argument between her and Josh. I wasn't going to referee, especially now, when it was too late.

"I only visited him once when he was awake," I said. "He was pretty out of it from the morphine. But he told me to talk to you."

She bent over, as if she didn't have the strength to sit anymore. Her hair spilled, Highland red. "Fuck. He was mostly asleep when I was in the room with him. When he talked to me, he didn't always make sense. He didn't remember stuff. I just kept saying I'd be there for him, over and over. As if that would help."

"Auds, you need to lie down?"

"What do you want to talk to me about?"

"He said to ask you what happened."

She bleeped, "It's not what you think."

"I don't think anything. I just want to know what Josh meant. Did you meet someone else? I'm not judging."

"Not like that!"

"You mean, just a fling?" How creepy to be questioning Audrey about her sex life with my dead brother.

Josh is dead.

I waited for a cry to escape my throat, as it had hers. But I was like a penny dropped into a well, sunken into some watery bottom.

"No," she said, more firmly now. "There was a party in town the night before the fire. It was for our high school class. My friend Maddie wanted me to go with her. Josh thought the party was a bad idea; he wouldn't come with us."

"'Cause he was embarrassed? 'Cause his life was a mess?"

"He said the guy having the party was an asshole. He was on the soccer team . . ." She wandered off.

"What's the guy's name?"

"Rory Martin. He wasn't someone Josh hung around with outside of team events."

No recollection of him. I shook my head.

Audrey rubbed her eye, leaving a few dots of mascara under it. She appeared so fragile. "I planned to go to the party for a while, then have Maddie drop me at your house afterward."

"Did she?"

"I never made it to your place. Josh warned me about the kind of people who would be at the party. He was always saying I wasn't careful enough, that I was naive."

Officer Volpe whistled in my ear: *Do you know if your brother owed someone a substantial amount of money for these substances?*

"What did he mean by the 'kind' of people?"

"He was being protective of me. Back in college, there were some dickheads who'd show up at parties; they drank too much and came onto me. I used to complain about it, which really frustrated Josh." The dots of mascara looked like beauty marks under her glistening eyes. "But yeah, I was upset. At this point, I'm the one handling my life, right?"

"Yes."

"It's not like Josh doesn't have ideas, plans for the future. He just can't get it together to do it yet."

Because he was an addict. I couldn't bring myself to correct her use of present tense. "Like what?"

"He has good instincts about people, so anything that requires that."

This was too much to bear. "Back up. Why didn't Maddie drop you off at our house?"

She looked away, her hair a mess around one shoulder. "I woke up in Rory's den, lying on the floor. It was almost dawn. I had to walk a couple of miles home. Josh had called and texted me . . . *eleven* times." She said the number as if mystified, by his insistence or her lack of response.

"Why would your friend leave you there?"

"Maddie said I insisted she go, that I was having fun. I'd get a lift. She texted me later and asked if I'd gotten back to my mom's."

"You don't remember saying it was all right for her to go?"

"Things got fuzzy." She wiped her nose so roughly, her nostrils turned red. "My underwear was off and there were bruises. It burned when I peed. I blanked out on the rest . . . having sex."

I felt a sharp twisting pain in my torso. I leaned toward Audrey, my hand reaching out. "Then you didn't consent."

"Maddie says I was laughing and cracking jokes and flirting with guys. But I wouldn't have sex with some random guy. I mean . . . I was with Josh."

She sounded not quite convincing. "Do you think it was assault?"

"Yeah." Her voice was rubbed raw.

"Did you tell Maddie or your mom?"

"No. Especially not my mom. I told her I forgot I had a group project and took the train back to Brooklyn. I didn't see Josh, at all." She spoke in a lower volume, as if someone's ear were pressed into our conversation. "You can't share this with anyone. This is private."

"Of course not."

"I had a beer and one cup of that punch. That's not enough to black out."

It struck me that she was speaking from experience. "Were other people having the same reaction to the punch, passing out, or sick?"

"Not sure."

I'd read an article in college that claimed one out of thirteen girls reported having been molested while blacked out from roofies. "Someone could have drugged your drink."

The same someone who might have burnt down our house.

"Why would anyone do that? These were just kids we knew from high school."

"Cause some guys are sick fucks, that's why. Do you have any memory of who it was?"

"The sex guy? No. I thought this wouldn't affect me so much . . . emotionally, since I was knocked out the whole time."

"And what about Josh?" I didn't want to lead her to a conclusion she wouldn't have made on her own: that there might be a connection between the rape and the fire. That Josh had owed a guy at Rory's money, maybe a lot of it. "Did he know?"

She nodded slowly.

"When?"

"Later that afternoon, once I got back to Brooklyn. He kept asking me why I wasn't spending the day with him as we'd planned. He thought it was because you were there, 'babysitting him,' and that I was finally fed up."

"That's what you were arguing about?"

"Yeah, at first. When I explained about . . . he freaked out. I needed to calm him down. Then he asked if I was going to the police. I said no way. I didn't want to report it. I just wanted to forget." She had a pleading shine in her eyes, as if there might still be time to fix things. Then the reality washed over her again. "Now, I'll never forget. Any of it."

"Auds? Me either."

chapter ten

The long hours after the burial were winding down. The second hand of the skeleton clock on the wall made a clicking noise as it struck 1:00 p.m.

"What can I do to help?" I asked my mother as I followed her into the small kitchen.

"I guess we should have coffee."

"Where are the good mugs?"

Then I remembered: the ceramic teal dinnerware was gone, along with all of our possessions. This rental was a small cape that resembled an elongated trailer home, only constructed of wood. The door and shutters had been painted a bluebird blue, a cheerful color that only reinforced how sad the place was otherwise. The front steps were cracked, and the paint on the wrought-iron railing was peeling. My parents had hoped to close on a new home before Josh was released from the hospital.

"There are a couple in that cabinet," my mother said, pointing. "First let's pack this stuff away."

I tucked the Tupperware containers of brisket, potato and egg salad, roasted chicken, baby carrots, and cold broccoli into the refrigerator. I moved aside the platter of cheeses, covered by aluminum foil.

"Throw out that vegetable dip. It's awful," my mother said. She stored the plain bagels—the Black Russians, pumpernickel, and whole wheat had been eaten—in the bread box. "Thank God, everyone else is gone."

I pictured Drew in the other room, standing next to Nora and Audrey on the old taupe couch in their black dresses, Audrey in matching tights. We'd come together, the four of us.

"What about shiva?"

She scowled. "I couldn't tolerate that."

I understood. The weeklong ritual would exact too great a toll on her. She'd want to squeeze the necks of relatives with living sons. All those murmurs and clucks and tears of condolence: "May his memory be a blessing."

I hadn't thought of *Wuthering Heights* since high school. It was a tale for other girls, not my kind of romance, with its suffocation and darkness. Now, looking at my mother—her long, regal face, her high, close-set eyes smudged with grayish-brown circles—I realized she'd rather be haunted by my brother than left with the "blessing" of an empty peace. Even madness was better than abject loneliness.

My poor father.

"I should never have left the hospital," she said. "How could I not have been there?"

"It was nighttime. You needed to sleep."

She shook her head. "The doctors should have made it clear. They should have warned us how quickly things could turn. I'd never have left his side."

"Mom, I'm worried about you."

She was forty-eight years old but looked a decade older now. "Dad spoke to a psychiatrist, got me an 'emergency' appointment yesterday. So that I could get through . . . this. Whatever that means. The rest of my life?"

"How was he? She?"

"Cheryl Weissman. Very cheerful, young, with an overbite." She pushed her top teeth over her bottom lip. "Maybe once she pays off her medical school loans, she can afford orthodontics."

"What did she give you?"

"Some antidepressant which, apparently, can take a few weeks to work. What use that is, don't ask me. And another drug to help until the first one kicks in."

"That sounds okay."

"You want them?" My mother's eyes brimmed. "They make me jumpy. But nicotine raises dopamine levels, so maybe you don't need them."

"Mom." I stared at my cheap black pumps, purchased during my shopping trip the day before. "I stopped smoking."

Not true. In fact, I wasn't monitoring myself anymore. Some days, I'd smoke five cigarettes; others, ten. I waited for her to say, "Too late."

"That's good," she nodded. "Anyway, I don't want to block the way I feel, the rage over losing my son."

There it was: caught in my throat. My chest. In the back of my eyes. All of these places in my body congested with grief, guilt. But I had to keep going, the whoosh of wind in my ears, the world a dazzle of light, to Houdini my way out of the chains of emotion.

"Let me make the coffee," I said.

"Thanks. I have to change and throw out this skirt. I can't bear to wear it again." She smoothed out the silky material that fell to her ankles. "Unless you want it?"

"That's okay." She was a size 4 to my 6 and, at five foot seven, three inches taller. Even if I lost weight, I'd have to hobble around in heels. "I'm too short."

"You could have it altered instead of it going to waste." She clapped her hand over her mouth. "Listen to me. My boy is dead, and I'm talking about not letting a skirt go to waste."

"Mom."

She clasped me to her and whispered in my ear, "How will we ever recover?"

Once she released me, she hurried away. I scooped out the coffee, which I could prepare for Nora, Drew, Audrey, and my dad. The only other person still at the house was my aunt Celeste—who planned to stay as long as needed. She'd slipped upstairs to lie down, call my uncle. My only relationship with Celeste revolved around my mother. On the rare occasion when she contacted me, it was for one purpose. "I can't reach Mom," she'd say.

I poured the half-and-half creamer into a mug.

"Let me bring them in," Nora said, standing beside me. "We'll catch the train if you want to stay here."

Nora's hair was chopped from the nape of her neck to her earlobes, no more spikes. Her nose ring was gone. She was less yogi now, more "managerial," hoping to move up at the nonprofit.

"That's okay, I'll give you a lift. We'll go soon."

"Maybe stay. You can't hide forever behind that veneer of strength, Jessica Jones."

We'd watched the first two seasons of the TV series and Nora had remarked that I resembled her—the actress, not the comic-book character.

"I think I'll go to Drew's for . . . a while."

"Is that a good idea?"

"If it makes me feel okay, why not?" I stared at her. There was a small beauty mark on her neck, exposed for the first time. "You've been judgy about him since I told you I slept with him."

"Ellie, you're hurting. Just forget it."

"Tell me what your issue is with him."

She squinted at me. "I don't have one."

I thought of his hands cupping my butt as I moved on top of him, his groans as he flipped me over. How the sex was the only temporary relief to the sludge of my existence. "I like him."

"Just slow down. Give yourself time to mourn."

"What if this is how I mourn? Drew is the only part of Josh left that isn't ruined. My parents' lives are destroyed, and I'm the reason."

"You're *not*, Elle." She raised the mug to her mouth but didn't drink. "At least take off from work."

"I used my sick and vacation days when Josh was in the hospital. Family leave doesn't cover siblings."

"I'm sure they'll give you more."

"No." Why couldn't she grasp that what she was proposing was antithetical to who I was? I plowed ahead. Having lost Josh, should I abdicate my identity as well?

"You need to process what's happened," she said softly.

"Sorry if my way of doing things, of 'processing,' doesn't meet your standards."

The air bloated with tension.

"That's really unfair, Elle. But you're grieving. I get it."

I glared at her mouth, which was pursed. It was wide, with lips that curled slightly up while mine dipped down. We used to compare their shapes; also, the size of our eyes (mine larger) and the length of our noses (hers shorter). I'd envied the delicacy of her features. Now, they struck me as pretty but forgettable. She could be anyone.

"Sorry. We're not the same anymore. That's all I meant," I said.

"I love you. I'm here for you." She touched my shoulder, lightly.

"I can't . . . talk about this anymore."

The closest bathroom was down the hall. As I raced toward it, I caught a glimpse of my father seated on one of the armchairs, his head dipped back, as if in sleep. I should have ushered us out of the house. But instead, I locked the door of what my mother called the "powder room." The urge to cry was so strong, my face hurt. But no tears came.

There was a knock.

"Use the other one!" I shouted, certain it was Nora.

"I wanted to see if you were doing okay," Audrey said.

"Hold on."

Opening the door, I nodded at her. She was so pale that her freckles, which formed a trail over her nose and cheeks, were muted.

"Your dad is taking Nora to the train," she said.

"Where? South Orange?"

"He didn't say."

"She asked him? On the day of his son's funeral?"

"He offered. I got the feeling he was eager to get out of here, go for a drive."

"So, ready to get back to the city?"

"I'm going to stay overnight at my mom's. She's on her way to pick me up."

There was the dull thump of my heart. "Stay in touch?"

"Sure," she said, sounding tentative.

We were in new territory.

My mother was on the couch, her eyes closed. Her arms were joined and cupping her belly, the way women did when pregnant. "Ellie," she said. "Dad wants you to wait before leaving. He has something he needs to go over with you."

"What is it?"

My mom shook her head and rose slowly. "I need to lie down. Please thank your friends for coming."

As if to a party, a family gathering.

By the time my father arrived, there was only Drew and me left. We were holding hands on that ratty sofa, and the second my dad saw, I removed mine from his.

"Hi," I said, springing up, "thanks for taking Nora."

"She wanted to call an Uber, not rush you to leave. That seemed unfair. She came all this way."

"Mom said you needed to talk to me."

"That's right. Should we go into the kitchen?"

"No. I can leave," Drew said.

I shook my head, wanting the protection that being with him imparted. "It's okay."

Disapproval registered in my dad's eyes, but he fixed his attention on me as if we were alone. "Listen, Elle, there's a good chance the police will want to interview you again."

"What? Why?" My voice boomed in my ears.

"Now that there's a death involved, the investigation will change from arson to murder."

Fear spread down to my torso as if I were standing too close to that fire, the fire that would never stop burning now. "I thought they were ruling it accidental."

"They likely still will. But there's some new information. Mom keeps in touch with the sergeant in charge. I wish she wouldn't, for her own peace of mind."

"What new evidence?"

"A percipient witness. A neighbor who says she saw something."

I drilled him. "If this person perceived the event, why come forward now? Which neighbor?"

"The police wouldn't disclose who he or she is for privacy reasons. There might not be enough evidence to build a case anyway."

"Did *they* see someone torch our house?"

"They didn't tell us," my father said.

"Can you come with me when they question me, as my lawyer?"

"You know I can't. I can ask Stanley Porter if it comes to that."

"Dad, you didn't recommend anyone the first time they interviewed me. This is freaking me out."

"It will be all right." His voice was flat. "It's just procedure."

"Don't worry, Mr. Stone, I'll help look out for her." Drew squeezed me to his side.

"Josh asked him to," I said quickly, pulling away at the sight of my father's expression. His face tightened, his forehead crinkling in consternation.

"Yes, he did, sir, the last time we spoke," Drew said. "I'll meet you at the car, Elle."

Once we were by ourselves, my dad said, "Josh was incoherent or confused when he was awake, which was, maybe, half the time. I think Drew is saying this to impress you."

"He wouldn't do that. Anyway, it wouldn't . . . make a difference."

My dad rubbed his chin, back and forth as if sanding wood. "What's going on with the two of you?"

"He's a friend."

"*Josh's* friend. It feels wrong for you to be dating him now."

"I'm not *dating* him."

"Whatever you call it. Hooking up."

"Jesus, Dad. I wouldn't do that," I lied. "I loved Josh, too."

"Drew is a good kid. But he comes from a troubled family." He squinted, as if disregarding me would aid his recollections. "That father of his was involved in some fishy business before he ran out on his family."

"What fishy business?"

"Illegal. I don't have all the details. From what Mom told me, it was really rough on Margaux but worse for Drew. Jerry Colins essentially abandoned his son when he remarried. Now, with Josh gone, it's got to be really rough on him."

What about me?

"Drew will be fine. I just want you and Mom to be okay."

My father's posture shifted abruptly, loosened. He hugged me and kissed the top of my head. "You too, honey. Take care of yourself."

Across the street, a woman in a straw hat was potting plants in her window box. Her stucco house was small and in need of a power wash. She gazed up and waved at me. My parents had never introduced themselves to the neighbors, never shared any piece of themselves. I nodded, not having the energy to wave.

Drew had started the engine, the air conditioner running. "You don't need to say it," he said. "I fucked up."

"It's not you."

He was watching the road, both hands on the wheel, steady. "I only wanted to reassure your father that you weren't alone."

"He thinks we're a couple."

"Is that so terrible?" Drew asked, frowning. "Does he dislike me?"

"Of course not. He thinks the timing is bad."

"We can smooth things over with your folks—later."

My gut cramped and I tried to adjust the seat belt, which was too tight.

"You have to admit, it's like a burden's been lifted," Drew said, "not having to pretend anymore."

"I wasn't pretending."

"Just . . . we can be out in the open now. I can come clean."

"What do you mean?" I stared at him, afraid of another revelation.

He smiled, his teeth so white, as if he'd polished them this morning. "I'm falling in love with you."

"Oh, Drew, I . . ."

"It's okay. You don't have to say it back, yet."

Yet.

"I could be going to jail."

"Of course you won't." His voice was sharp, and I thought of what my dad had said about his father.

"I'm scared about the police."

"What could they have seen? It's not as if they found evidence in the house, something that caused the fire. Right?"

"When they first interviewed me, they mentioned drug dealers. I laughed at that." I thought of Audrey and glanced at the floor, so my face wouldn't reveal my furtiveness. "Do you believe Josh would get mixed up with people like that?"

Drew shook his head. "I don't know, Ellie."

"I almost wished Josh had been involved with criminals who would do something so insane just to get me off the hook. But I guess he wasn't, or the police wouldn't want to see me again."

"Did your dad say they found anything new?"

"No. Only what you heard. He offered his friend as my lawyer."

"Slow down. Let's see what happens."

"I thought my dad would protect me somehow," I said, feeling raw and young and selfish. "He seemed so unconcerned."

"He's in shock over Josh."

"Me too. I need him. I can't go through this alone."

"I'm right here."

"Thank you." I sagged down in my seat and faced the road.

I focused on the gray highway and the flat New Jersey sky. Everything felt loose, flying away from me.

chapter eleven

My body was running on the dregs of adrenaline, the fumes of sleep. In the deep furrow of night, I'd check for updates on the FB memorial page for Josh that Audrey had created. Members of his college team had posted photos of him on the field in a blur of action. In the older pictures, he appeared in his high school soccer hoodie, beer in one hand, his other arm around Audrey's shoulder or making a peace sign with one of his jock buddies. He was at a party, surrounded by fellow athletes. He was wrestling a kid with a tattoo of a tiger on his neck. He was holding a St. Bernard puppy in his arms and his eyes were aglow.

His friends shared their memories, tributes, and well-meaning platitudes: *Can't believe I'll never see you at Chloe's Kitchen again. You're the only guy I ever met who liked pineapple on his pizza. I'll never forget how you won the game against South Orange for us. Love you, man. Miss you forever. Life is fleeting! No one's future is certain! Josh, you prove that only the good die young.*

Reading these, my face felt like a crushed fruit, wet with juice.

I stayed with Drew that first week, finally dozing in the pitch before dawn. When I woke up, I'd forget where I was. Then the sight of Drew's feathery lashes, the few coils of hair on his forehead, the muscles in his forearm, reminded me of our sex hours earlier. The pleasure was an antidote, even with the pressure of him pinning me down, whispering, "I'll be gentle." Drew had repeated, "I love you," after groaning on top of me. I'd dismissed it as "sex talk," reassuring myself. I hadn't echoed those words, but the "yet" haunted me with expectation. His declaration was a hook around my middle, a hand over my mouth, a provocation to flee. But I didn't flee. Drew anchored me to life.

Rashad offered me a remote-work arrangement for two weeks, which I accepted. The article I was writing was on the Australian bushfire season that affected up to 80 percent of the continent, covered over 100,000 miles, and destroyed nearly 3,000 homes. Staring at the research, I felt unmoored, queasy, as if the assignment were retaliation—which, of course, it wasn't. By the first afternoon, I missed the office, the sense of comradery and grounding, the normalcy it provided. On day three, I went back.

When are you coming home? Nora texted me that morning.

Soon. I'm at Terrafeed.

Already?

Was she insulted that I'd returned to my job before our apartment?

Yes. Will call you tonight.

Later, she messaged me again: *Please, don't pay attention to social media today. Love you.*

I ignored her request. It was easy to find. Our local paper had run another piece on us, a special feature about Josh's "tragic death." This time, the writer cited my Firestarter moniker and a brief background on how I'd gotten it but clarified that the police had not yet determined if *this* case was arson. I froze in my swivel chair. How could an editor have included this defamatory reference when the garage incident held no significance to the story? It was tabloid-quality speculation. Two spelling mistakes and a sentence without a period at the end: that's how. No one was checking. I googled the writer's name. There were pictures of her with Anna Nuñez, the two of them bent over in open-mouthed laughter, glasses with paper umbrellas in hand. From her online history, I learned they'd met at Rutgers.

The thought crept into my mind: *What if Anna lit the fire as payback for what I'd done to her?* Yes, it was more than a decade later. But something—another rude comment about her scar, like the one the students made at college, a rejection or insult—might have compelled her to retaliate against me and my family.

I gagged, which catapulted me to the bathroom. After I forced myself to throw up, my throat stung and my body shook, but the tension above my eyes lessened.

Jae said, "You poor thing. You look wrecked."

"I'm going to take a quick walk and a smoke to wake up."

"Restoril works for Lily." Her partner.

"Good to know."

"Or just get a script for Ambien like everyone else," she said.

"My freshman roommate took that. She would eat these gravy-flavored chips and talk about how her boyfriend wanted her to have a threesome—in her sleep."

What if, doped up on Ambien, I spilled secrets to Drew? *I'm not sure I love you. I still wonder if I left a cigarette burning that night.*

"Did your roommate remember what she said?"

"Never."

Outside the office, the dull light didn't sting my eyes. There were so many bodies in motion, but the noise level was lower. Since Josh died, I'd tried valerian, melatonin, and Benadryl. The first two were useless. Only the antihistamine knocked me out for a few hours, during which I dreamed that, while driving on the GW Bridge, I frantically phoned Nora. "I didn't put it out. Should I go back?"

She said, "I can't cover for you anymore. The sergeant is here with me."

At Walgreens I grabbed: homeopathic tablets, a bottle of berry ZzzQuil, a copy of *Mindfulness* magazine, and a tube of concealer. The women at the checkout both looked bored, one picking at a nail, the other stifling a yawn. They probably would have rung up my purchases without a glance my way, but I chose self-service, embarrassed.

I was trying to recover. I'd even looked for therapists.

The ones who advertised used terms like "transformative tools," "creating safe havens," "inner self," "collaborative transaction," and "supportive space." There were a few who specialized in bereavement counseling. What did their poorly worded pep talks matter? I couldn't afford to be such a snob. Yet they warned that it was important to find a good fit, which, like therapy itself, was a process.

I didn't need a process; I needed a medication to help me settle down. I'd researched psychiatrists. Very few were covered by insurance, not here in the city, anyway. I left email messages for three on my plan. That was days ago, and none had responded.

In the entranceway to the pharmacy, I sank down to a squatting position, waiting for a wave of dizziness to pass. Dehydration. A couple of teenagers walked by me without a glimpse.

"You okay?" a woman in a pink pussy hat asked. She had no visible hairline and no eyebrows. The hand she offered me was bony and chapped red.

"Yes." I shot up by myself. "Thank you."

A cancer patient coming to my rescue was too pathetic. I had to rally.

I'd gather the courage to call my dad about the Madison Avenue psychiatrist. The one with the inviting smile, the slick site with the gray-and-white, moody illustrations of rain and wind and a price tag of $550 for the initial hour consultation. There was a video of her speaking to potential patients in a soothing voice. The skin around her mouth was distracting, puffy, with little slits from some sort of injections. I'd do it as soon as I arrived back at my apartment.

At the office, I texted Drew, explaining I needed to go home, that things were better with Nora. Could we see each other that weekend? Could I get my stuff then?

Sure. Whatever is best for you.

He sent a kissy-face emoji.

I hesitated, then returned with a solid red heart.

That evening, I got home before Nora, who was teaching a yoga class. It was wonderful to be back with my view of the bridge, the smell of Nora's cinnamon and clove incense, her stash of dried fruit, oat milk, and vegan brownie bars.

After eating a quick salad, I phoned my dad.

He answered with, "Oh, Ellie, your mother isn't well. I'm so worried about her."

"What's going on?"

"She's not eating. She's sleeping too much and, when she's not, she cries for hours."

I leaned forward on my bed. "Isn't the medication working?"

"She couldn't tolerate it. The doctor switched her to another one."

"But something will work, right? She's still in shock."

"Dr. Weissman suggested hospitalization if she doesn't improve soon."

I tucked my legs in cannonball position. "That's so extreme."

"Ellie, what can I say? I can't lose her, too."

"Dad, I'm sorry," I said. "I'm so sorry."

"I know you are."

If I lined up my apologies, they'd circle the globe like the equator. But regret wasn't restitution. "I'll come this weekend."

A good daughter would jump in her car, would drive above the speed limit to reach her parents, would try to relieve her father of his mounting panic and her mother of despair. She'd move in with them, shop, run errands, cook, give up whatever threads of independence she was hanging onto—if that's what it took.

"Unless you need me sooner?"

"Thank you for offering, honey. Not right now. The only person Mom seems to tolerate well is her sister."

"What about you? What do you want?"

My father's laugh was devoid of joy. "To wake up, for Josh to be alive, and for all of this to have been a nightmare."

"Yeah," I said. "Me too."

I couldn't bring myself to burden my father when the police contacted me. I decided to forgo a lawyer and have Drew accompany me instead. He wouldn't be allowed in that dull interrogation room, of course. But knowing he was waiting in my car was like a good luck charm, a rabbit's foot in my pocket or a hamsa on a chain around my neck.

Volpe wasn't there, which made me feel hopeful. Sergeant Abbott introduced Detective Parrish, a young, muscular woman with toffee-brown hair pulled into a tight braid down her back. She stood next to the table where the sergeant was seated with his notepad.

"Hi," I said, with a smile, and she nodded without a flicker of one in return. The hopefulness vanished. Detective was an upgrade, and this one seemed as dispassionate as an android.

"First of all," Abbott said, his hands clasped together, his thumbs knocking against one another, "our condolences for your loss."

"Thank you," I said, noting that Parrish's eyes were fixed on me.

She said, "The reason you're here today is we've gotten some new information." She had a husky voice, like a cabaret singer who'd inhabited too many smoky rooms.

"About me?"

"A few things have come to light that we want to go over. Just to be clear: this isn't an interrogation, so you are free to leave at any time. We're still trying to piece together the sequence of events that night."

"Okay, sure," I said, twisting one leg around the other, like in eagle pose. "I mean, I want that, too."

"Good. Do you know anyone who drives a silver sedan?"

This took me by surprise. Was this linked to the drug dealer theory, and if so, why ask me? "Not sure. My car's blue. It's right out there in the parking lot. Do you want me to get you the registration?"

"No need. We can look that up," Abbott said.

Parrish pulled out the chair next to the sergeant and sat in it with a soldier's rigid spine. She flipped open her own notepad. "A neighbor said they saw a silver vehicle outside your house when they first noticed the fire."

It had to be Mrs. Goldsmith. I pictured the older woman that night, that lilac robe and bracelet around her ankle with those bulging veins. Her view of our house was a clear one. Then I thought about Mrs. Peterson, how she'd raced to my rescue when no one else on the street had appeared. I wondered what she'd observed. But why wouldn't either of them have mentioned this before? What took so long?

"Outside, where?" I asked.

"Pulling out of your driveway."

"That doesn't make sense. There wasn't anyone there but me, and I'd left before the fire started."

"If you weren't there, you couldn't observe if anyone else showed up," Parrish said, checking her notes, "during those forty-five minutes to an hour window."

"Okay," I conceded.

"We're wondering if someone was planning to come over, that you know of."

Audrey? I tried to conjure up an image of her arriving at our place when I'd been home over college breaks. What size or shade was her car? Nothing clicked.

"No. It was late."

The sergeant said, "I have here from our last conversation that you stated your brother had been arguing with his girlfriend on the phone and that you weren't sure if she was in the area."

"Probably not. She lives in Brooklyn."

"Yes, that's in here, too. But as you said in your previous interview, her mother lives in town, and you implied she could have been staying with her."

"Look, I don't know where Audrey was that night. And anyway, she'd never deliberately do anything like you're suggesting. You'd have to be sick to do something like that."

Parrish's neutral expression didn't change. "Just to be clear: you're referring to an Audrey Findley?"

"Yes. I don't want to talk about her, if that's okay."

"That's your prerogative."

"I don't know of anyone with a silver car. My mom's car is gray," I conceded, thinking how easily I divulged this information. "She was away, though. They took my dad's that weekend. It's black."

"That's all right," Parrish said. "We know your mother's vehicle was there in the garage. She's not a suspect."

"Am I?"

"No," she said, studying me for a moment.

"Do you think it was a drug dealer's?"

A momentary frown. "Why do you ask that?"

"Oh, well, Officer Volpe brought that up last time I was here."

She exhaled silently, her chest falling. "There aren't any suspects as of now."

I nodded, not believing her. The window blinds were rolled halfway up, and I noticed my Hyundai in the afternoon light. It crossed my mind to offer up my suspicions about Anna Nuñez. Josh defending me: *Sounds like a spoiled bitch. That girl lied to her.* But such violent revenge, even if Anna hated me . . . well, that was another level of fury that would be hard to verify.

"How could anyone see a car's color in the dark?"

"The blaze lit up the area."

"They would have to be paying close attention," I said. "So, why wouldn't they have come forward before now?"

The two of them exchanged a glance; it seemed obvious that Parrish was in charge, but she waited a beat to answer. "People tend to talk more after events change."

I held my breath so as to not cry. "You mean because Josh died?"

"That's correct."

"Maybe someone was just turning around in our driveway? Like they went down the wrong street."

"Could be."

She didn't sound convinced. I glanced at Sergeant Abbott, but he was staring down at his notes.

"There's one more thing," she said. "It concerns a Mrs. Bea Nuñez."

For a second, I felt confused. "Did something happen to her, too?"

"Mrs. Nuñez came in to give us some information."

I could smell my own sweat under my shirt and jacket, that skunky stink of fear. I should have taken my father's advice and brought Stanley Porter along. "About me?"

Parrish said, "She brought up a case that had been settled out of court, one that involved you and her daughter when you were both juveniles."

"Fifteen and a half," I said. "An accident."

"She showed us a picture. The young lady's face is scarred from a burn she received."

Was this a test of how I'd behave under pressure?

"Why are you telling me this?"

Abbott's thumbs were at it again, but Parrish didn't flinch.

She said, "Please let us know if anything else about that night comes to mind."

"What if I find out who has a silver car?"

"That's our job."

"I'm a journalist, so I tend to want to get to the bottom of things."

"Leave the police work to us," she said with a sliver of a smile. "You are free to go."

In his bed that night, Drew's breath was hot in my ear. "I know it's not your thing, but Ty has weed." His roommate: Tyler. "It might relax you."

"No, thanks. We can still fool around if you want," I said, too groggy to care either way.

"I'm always up for that." He leaned into my back, hard.

Drew had suggested we have more frequent sex and try new

positions. He claimed it was his remedy to heartbreak, and I wasn't offended.

"But you seem exhausted," he said.

"Yeah, next time."

"You know, it's not a big deal, taking something to sleep once in a while."

I rolled away from him, onto my back. My arms and shoulders ached, as if I'd been lifting weights. I explained my frustration with not being able to nab an affordable psychiatrist, the same sad tale.

"That's crazy. I'll pay."

"Drew, no. That's nice of you, but no."

All I could see were his eyes gleaming in the shadowy light from the moon. "Look, it's no big deal for me."

"I can go to my PA. She looks twelve, but she can probably prescribe something."

"Good. In the meantime, I can get you a few pills tomorrow."

My spine elongated. "Did you do that for Josh?"

"What? Of course not! Do you know how easy it is to get sleep meds, like everywhere, every campus in the country, every party, every friend?"

"I'm sorry. I never paid much attention to that stuff."

He nuzzled close, again, kissed my neck. "You're a purist, but that doesn't make me a drug dealer. I'd never give Josh anything."

"I'm not a purist. I smoke; that's worse."

The fact that cigarettes were carcinogens and terrible both for my health and for the environment had always nagged at me. But the feeling of superiority over Josh came from playing by the rules, from following the law and staying in control. Now, I wondered why the rules part had mattered so much when the codes were arbitrary. Everyone—even the best citizens, the ones like my father, who taught jurisprudence—could see the enormous gaps between law and justice.

He said, "I'm not talking about scoring you Oxy."

"Yeah. I'm afraid of taking anything addictive, with my family history."

"It's not like you come from a clan of heroin addicts."

"Never told you about my grandmother who snorted coke?"

"You did mention her, once." We shared a thin laugh. "Please, Elle, I'm in a position to help you. Let me."

"Don't spend a lot of money," I said. "If you can get me a few Ambien, that would be great."

"Um." His tongue was on my breast, his fingers moving up my thigh.

The price of the pills.

chapter twelve

L ate October felt like early spring. My weather app read 64 degrees. Humanity was that boiling frog, unaware it was being cooked to death. There was a new fire burning in Sonoma County, California, and just my luck, I was assigned to write about it. Then another article on climate grief.

All I wanted to do was research the silver car that had been parked, however briefly, in our driveway on that night less than two months ago. I tried. All vehicle and registration information were off-limits to the public.

I'd seen my physician assistant, who scribbled a prescription for Klonopin five minutes into my visit and instructed me to exercise more and consume less caffeine. In order to avoid getting hooked, I was determined to ration them to three times a week. An arbitrary decision, backed by emotion, not science. Without the jolts from caffeine, my muscles slackened, and my neurons fired too slowly. Still, I slept poorly and not enough. The skin around my eyes grew sore as if exposed to long swims in a chlorinated pool. My teeth felt as if they were screwed into my gums too tightly.

The night stretched out further and further, a dusty highway in a flat field. For the first time, I understood Josh's Ativan use.

Too late.

Sunday evening and, outside my window, rain dripped, like the last drops rung out of a washcloth. In bed, I read my notes from a psychologist I'd interviewed on the mental health of climate change activists. She equated their despair with being trapped in a gas chamber, not knowing when the valves would be turned on. I'd ended up sidetracked, researching images of Nazi spigots, with porcelain handles and swastikas etched into them. After the war, they were auctioned off to collectors, many of whom were Jews.

I dreamt that I was rummaging through the rumble of our old house, which was now a pile of burnt wood and singed plastic bottles. Filthy from soot, I was barefoot and wearing an old nightgown that reached to my bloodied knees. There was a silver Mercedes parked in our driveway, an old model with a long hood and giant-looking front wheels. I couldn't piece together what was happening. Then I found an old steel pipe with a chorus line of swastikas running down it and I knew. Doomsday was coming.

I awoke to a conflagration in the sky. It was only sunrise.

"Rashad asked for you," Jae said, as soon as I got to my desk a half an hour late. She cracked her gum.

"Okay," I said, nonchalantly. My heart knocked. "What did he want?"

She shrugged. "Didn't say. He was at your desk like ten minutes ago."

I stared at my desk as if it had betrayed me. "Okay, thanks." I looked at my laptop for a few seconds before entering my passcode. I texted Rashad and he responded immediately, *Come see me.*

Now?

Yes.

The lack of context wasn't uncommon, or not entirely. Rashad sometimes communicated in person about a story in progress, al-though the phone was his preferred choice. My legs took me to his office slowly. It was a place they didn't want to go.

"Hey," I said, as I entered.

He was arched toward his computer. He gestured for me to shut the door, then to sit down across from him.

"I'm sorry I was late," I said. "But I finished the research on the Sonoma piece."

"Ellie, that's not why I called you in. We know you've been going through a hard time, which is why we hoped the leave of absence would help. What happened to you, your brother's death, well, I'm just so sorry."

"Thanks."

But.

When he finally looked at me, his eyes seemed more deep set than usual under those thick brows. "This is such a touchy subject, I'm a bit out of my depth. It's part of our commitment to employees, to check in when they're struggling."

There was a shift in my chest, room to breathe. "Thanks, I mean, yeah, it's been hard. But, um, I'm getting some help so . . ."

"That's good," he said, without conviction.

Was I required to provide some kind of progress report on my mental health?

"It might take a while to . . ."

To what? To recover? That sounded callous and small, as if I'd torn a tendon. To grieve? That wasn't a word compatible with the office, unless referencing my research. "To get back on my feet."

"What I'm about to say is awkward and unfair after what you've been through." When he frowned, his mustache bled into his stub-bled beard. "Management is putting you on notice. You'll have to prove yourself a bit, that you're still up to the job. It's a three-month plan . . ."

The hum in my head was so loud, I couldn't discern my thoughts. "It's hard for me right now . . . I'm wondering if we could work something else out. Something better for both of us. How about I go part-time for a while, or a freelance situation? I realize that wouldn't include benefits."

Rashad interrupted my free-floating plea. "I'm afraid that can't fly, Ellie. Our budget's set. It only allows for full-time staff at the moment. We're trimming, not adding alternative work arrangements."

"I get it."

"We're all just trying to hold on. Things are going to get even busier for everyone for a while."

Darkness rose inside my head, like smoke. Oh, how I loved it here! My work was my identity, a call to duty. At least, once upon a time it had been. But dealing, at breakneck speed, with the planet's ravages— the droughts and dying sea animals, the wildfires and the record-breaking heat waves—was agonizing in my current state of mind.

"I guess I have to resign, then."

"Ellie, are you sure that's what you want?" he asked in a measured voice. I gleaned the relief underneath. Problem solved, without his having to play villain on behalf of the company.

"Do you need more notice?" I stood up, a woman made of gelatin. "Should I stay until the end of the week and finish this story?"

"That won't be necessary. It would be great if you could give Harper your notes."

"Okay." Obliterated in an instant.

"I'll make sure you get your last paycheck. You're extremely talented, Ellie. If I can help you in the future, please be in touch," he said, and reached out to shake my hand.

He didn't offer a recommendation.

"Thanks."

"What's up?" Jae asked as I shoveled my stuff into my backpack: pens, three books, the small papier-mâché doll that Sam had brought me back from a trip to Japan. He'd told me this Okiagari-koboshi doll, which sprang back up when knocked down, symbolized resilience and perseverance, reminding him of me.

Not anymore, Sam.

"Later, okay?" I said to Jae. "I have to talk to Harper."

"Sure." She sounded uncharacteristically chipper.

There wasn't going to be a later and she must have sensed it, probably thought I'd been laid off. And I wasn't about to discuss my situation with Harper in person; I'd forward her my files with the subject line: "Rashad wanted me to send these to you." I couldn't reach the street quickly enough.

It felt better to walk the fifteen blocks uptown to catch the local subway than backtrack downtown to the closer stop. I headed away from Eleventh, once nicknamed "Death Avenue" due to the frequent occurrence of accidents between freight trains and street traffic. The windows of the factories and warehouses once had stretched across the shadow side of Manhattan, staring blankly at passersby, the eye-holes of empty skulls. The stench of dead animal flesh from over two hundred slaughterhouses had hung in the air. Before restaurants serving pho and ramen and kimchi, a bridal boutique, a Starbucks. Before rising tides threatened to swallow this island.

Triage.

That word, in Sam's voice. He loved to use it when his workload piled up, around exams, from taking five courses a semester, a couple with labs. "Whose lives are you saving?" I'd ask, pissed that he'd chosen the Bunsen burner over me. But it was useful, the idea of choosing which emergencies to treat, how to make order out of anxiety.

I can make next month's rent.

The two-week salary would cover that, but not other expenses. A woman smiled wanly at me, as if to say: *I get it.* She was carrying a toddler, his sleeping face stamped into her neck. But hanging from her shoulder was a Stella McCartney tote bag, worth close to a grand.

Triage.

What did I do? Go back right now and beg.

A male jogger flung sweat from his hairband my way. A couple of models, impossibly tall and thin, were chatting in some Germanic language. I let them sidestep me.

Talk to Dad again about floating me for a while.

It'd be asking him to take money from necessary funds, most likely his home insurance reimbursement. Could he handle that with my mother's depression?

My car on the C train smelled like curry and perspiration. The teenage girl across from me was cracking open pistachios and littering the floor with their shells. The man in a baseball hat next to her pushed them aside with his feet. I admired his nonchalance.

What asanas would Nora recommend: child, fish, corpse? She was no longer home in the afternoons, so I'd have to wing it, try them all. Or none. Let the panic flow unimpeded.

At 168th, I stood on the platform, waiting for the A line, next to the pistachio girl. She'd stuck her paper bag of nuts into her canvas satchel and was wiping the crumbs out of her green-streaked hair. My desire to hit her was gone. She probably had some crap job serving lattes to rich people. Soon, I could be in her position. If I were lucky.

Maybe it was the poor ventilation that caused the wave of vertigo in the elevator. Maybe it was terror. I leaned back against the walls in a squat. "Are you all right?" the only other person inside this box asked me. He was a young guy with an afro fade and a violin case tucked under one arm.

"Yeah," I said. "A little dizzy, that's all. Just need to eat."

We reached the double wood doors to 181st Street at the same time. He turned to me and said, "You get yourself a slice, okay?"

"Will do." I wanted to follow him as we exited, his easy stride. When he waved to a short woman across the street, leaning on a cello, I saw him grin, his eyes bright.

My cheeks and lashes were wet. But I didn't bother with that. What mattered was wiggling my way out of this. Was there a prosperity pose I could strike? The discussion of what would happen, how I could remain Nora's roommate, rattled in my head.

I abducted her sauvignon blanc from the fridge and poured what was left of it into one of her stemless glasses. Since I mostly drank on dates and rarely alone, the bottles of wine were all hers. Today, I'd make an exception.

I was lying in the dark, perusing content writing sites online when she came home. A plate with a half-eaten peanut butter sandwich sat next to me. My friend moved it to my night table, rearranging the wine glass next to it, and sank onto my bed. "What's going on?" she asked.

"I'm unemployed. Job searching."

Nora's mouth formed a pink line. "There has to be someone you can appeal to at your company."

"I wasn't fired. Rashad called me in to talk about how I was put on notice and needed to work even harder. I can't."

"C'mon. They have to make allowances for cases like yours. Rashad loves your writing. You're a great journalist."

"I can't write about the end of the world day after day."

"Of course not. You went back to work after a pathetically short leave of absence. Maybe you can just ask for more time off."

"Nora, what country do we live in? I have to figure something else out. Something mindless."

She wiggled one of her dewdrop earrings. "Can I help?"

"Dunno. How's your stock portfolio?"

"Never better."

We shared a gallows laugh.

"If I can't, you're going to have to find a new roommate. Quickly."

She moaned. "No. I can help for a little while."

"No way, you're working two jobs. I'm not doing that to you."

"Where are you going to live?"

"New Jersey, my parents' rental, I guess."

We stared at each other in the dim light.

"Listen, I'm sorry I told you to do that . . . before. We have to strategize," she said. "What about tutoring SATs? I could ask my friend Jasmine."

"Thanks. Those agencies prefer people who went to, like, the top three schools. Didn't she go to Yale?"

"Princeton."

"Worse!"

"Don't denigrate yourself." She bowed her head. "I can contact Jasmine. Also, I have a couple of friends who freelance. Maybe they'll share their editors' info with me."

"Thanks, Nor. But right now, I'm not ready. I can't focus. I should become a sex worker. OnlyFans. I wouldn't even have to touch human flesh."

"Elle," my friend said, caressing my arm. "You'd suck at that. Not the sex part. The faking it. Call your dad."

"I can't. Sorry, I drank half a bottle without asking. I'll replace it tomorrow."

She waved away my suggestion.

⸻ ·•· ⸻

The next morning, after taking one of the Klonnies (as I called them) and getting a full six hours of sleep, I shuffled back to my room with my mug and protein bar. That afternoon, I was going to have to do some serious grocery shopping, as I wouldn't be able to splurge on even cheap takeout anymore. Nora had been on my case to "eat clean." Not for vanity's sake—I was slim with a small appetite by nature—but because my food choices were lazy. Now they'd be deliberate, based on cost. *Rice. Beans. Ramen noodles. Cans of tuna.*

A sensation from the subway returned, a momentary vertigo, as if I'd been wrenched upside down. I stared at a cobweb on my ceiling until the spinning subsided, then texted my dad. He awoke at dawn these days, and it was already past eight o'clock.

I lost my job.

Lost. As in: if I dusted under my couch or tossed the contents of my backpack on the floor, I might find it.

Oh, Ellie. How did that happen?

I torched the building!

Budget cuts.

It took a few minutes for my father to respond. *I'm so sorry. What are you going to do?*

Calling the student loan people.

Can you get a deferment?

He wasn't making this any easier for me.

Can we talk later today?

Yes. I need to get your mother settled. Give me until the afternoon. Will call from work.

⸻ ·•· ⸻

By noon, I still hadn't even showered. But I had spent over an hour on LinkedIn and Glassdoor. When my dad called me, I was reclining with an ice cube, in a dish towel, on my forehead.

"Is now a good time?" he asked.

"Yep," I said.

"Listen, Ellie, I don't mean to pry. But what kind of shape are you in? I mean, financially? Do you have any savings?"

I gulped down my disbelief. "Savings? Dad, I owe loans for college. I'm not a banker or a consultant. I work . . . worked . . . at a news site."

"What's the chance of you finding a new job in time to cover your bills?"

He sounded like my accountant—if I'd had one—not my dad.

"Well, the economy *is* booming. Especially for Gen Zers not in law, finance, or tech. Tons of opportunities for full-time jobs with benefits. Maybe Bezos or Zuckerberg will offer me—"

"Ellie, I can't now . . . Looks like the best thing is for you to move back home."

I rolled, my legs tucked under me, face down into the mattress. "I thought you said Mom is struggling. Do you guys really want me around?"

"You are our daughter."

"Nora's going to get me tutoring jobs," I exaggerated. "I can't do that remotely. Can you help me out just for a couple of months?"

"This is a terrible time for all of us."

"Of course. I know that."

"Listen, Ellie, I realize this isn't convenient. But obviously, Mom isn't going back to the agency, not for the foreseeable future. Money is tight. We have to find a new house by the new year, and even though the insurance will help pay, there will be extra costs."

"I get it."

"We have to come together as a family now." His voice caught. "The three of us."

"I don't know . . ." *if I can do that.*

"You need to have your own life, of course. But, while you are job searching, you could commute for a while. Save money. Pay off some of those loans. Just until you're solvent again."

A frantic sparrow was flitting around my brain, trying to break free. I imagined it flying out of my ear, out of my window, alighting on one rooftop, then another, all across the city. But never soaring over the bridge, never trapped in a tunnel, never crossing state lines.

"Dad, I have to go."

I tore through my friend list on Facebook. There had to be people whose couches I could crash on, doors I could enter late at night and exit early the next morning. I'd be willing to live out of a duffel bag, Marie Kondo my stuff. I'd widen my job search to other cities—almost all were cheaper—Nashville, Austin, Philly, Portland, Columbus.

Drew: *What are you up to?*

Me: *Job search.*

Why??

There were limits to how vulnerable I wanted to appear—to anyone. Quitting raised questions about my lack of resilience, my mental stamina.

Layoffs.

Oh, no!

Yep. Have to find something ASAP if I don't want to end up in NJ.

Brb. Going downstairs.

Did he have the leeway to break into his workday to leave the office? He was just an intern, but maybe that was why he was allowed flexibility. I had no idea how his company operated.

"Hey," he said into the phone. In the background was the whine and honk of traffic. "Unfuckingbelievable."

"Yeah."

"Elle, you can't move back there now."

"Not a lot of choices," I said, yanking on the ends of my hair. "I need an income to, you know, cover bills."

"Of course. But that doesn't mean . . . Listen." He paused. "I have to run it by Ty, but it won't matter. It's basically my place; I pay two-thirds of the rent. You can stay with me as long as you need to."

"That's really nice of you," I said, testing my reaction. Not ideal, awkward, but not as bad as living with my parents, which would be like being locked in a tomb. Suffocating. Pitch-black.

"Isn't it too soon?"

"I'm not asking you to move in with me." A hard-edged laugh. "Not as a girlfriend."

"Yeah, no. It's so nice of you. I didn't mean to be ungrateful."

"It wouldn't be like that. We'd be free to see other people. That didn't come out the way I meant, as if I'm entitled . . ."

"Believe me, that's the last thing on my mind. I'm in emergency mode."

"Exactly! I have a pretty big place. There's even an extra room. It's only big enough for the futon in there and a desk. But you could use it if that would make things less awkward."

"Are you kidding?" I asked. "How much would that cost?"

"Nothing. That's the *point*. It's yours, however long you need it."

"Oh, my God," I exclaimed. Giddy with relief. Pushing away any apprehension. "Thank you!"

chapter thirteen

That Saturday, Nora and I hiked the path near Grant's Tomb, a mausoleum in Riverside Park, then hiked south to the Hippo Playground on Ninety-First Street. The trees had erupted in yellow and red, and the ground was flooded with color.

"What are you going to *do*?" she asked.

"I applied to be a barista at Starbucks."

At my job interview, the store manager, who was at least five years younger than me, like most of the staff, had appeared stern as she read my CV. "Personality is more important than skills. We're really looking for friendly multitaskers."

Did articles on eco-anxiety render me unfriendly?

"Of course," I'd said, holding her gaze. "I'm a people person."

"I was accepted into the training program," I reported to Nora.

Nora halted and stared at me. "That's minimum wage."

"It's fourteen bucks an hour and health benefits."

"You're kidding, right?"

"Look, I can't deal with more pressure." I felt wiped out yet wired, as if I'd pulled the last all-nighter senior year of college. Everything was over. Everyone would soon disperse.

"This is a shitty time to bring this up, but Oni decided she wants to stay in New York for good."

Oni, the woman who would be subletting my bedroom, was a

web designer at a digital marketing firm, sleek and tall and a whiz in the kitchen, having spent a year at a culinary institute before college. She and her cookware were moving in at the end of October. Nora had found her in two days—through a friend of a colleague—which was impressive even for this high-speed rail of a city. It was supposed to be a temporary arrangement, not an official sublet, until I could save enough money to return. Oni had professed to being in an in-between situation; her lease was up, but she was staying in New York until the end of the year.

"I thought she was leaving after the holidays, that she was engaged," I said.

"She broke it off."

We were walking again, me kicking the leaves like a child.

"Wow. What about the new job in Atlanta?" I asked.

"Turned it down. She asked if she could cosign."

Our lease was up for renewal in December.

"We agreed to keep it month to month," I said.

Nora handed me her thermos. "She wants a more permanent situation."

I swigged down the mint lemonade. "You said Oni's great. Do what you have to do."

"I'm just so worried about you. I can't imagine how you're even processing everything."

The word "processing" grated. My best friend didn't understand that I no longer had the time or funds for much self-reflection. "I'll find something on SpareRoom at some point, as soon as I can afford it."

"I feel like I'm abandoning you."

"You're not. Just don't judge me for staying with Drew."

Nora had protested when I'd mentioned his offer and my acceptance—to move into his extra room. "That's totally unrealistic. Doesn't he think you're his girlfriend?"

"We don't label what's going on with us."

"Okay," she said. "If it works for you guys."

"It does. We're keeping it open, casual."

Temporary. For me, anyway.

"Actually," Nora said, "I started seeing someone and it's been kind of a whirlwind, too."

I stopped and reached for her. "You did?"

"Don't sound so shocked!"

It had been a while since she'd dated anyone seriously. And since Nora wasn't a fan of open relationships, she'd been "in a sexual desert" for over a year. "Like monogamous?"

Nora straightened her back and neck as if about to stretch into a pose. "You know how I am."

"Yes. Dumb question." Only I had changed, not Nora. "How did you meet this guy? How long has this been going on, and why didn't you tell me?"

"A few weeks. Matthew. He's a student in my restorative class. He's a physical therapist at a hospital. And I didn't say anything because you're going through so much shit."

"You're blushing!"

"I'm not," she said, touching her face as if to stop color from suffusing through the skin.

"How did I miss this?"

"We haven't stayed over at each other's places yet. Let's not talk about him until more time has passed. Could be nothing."

"It's not nothing. It's definitely something. You are the most sensible person I know," I said, meaning it as a compliment.

"Thank you. Makes me feel like Elinor Dashwood."

"And look who she ended up with!"

"Hugh Grant!"

We both broke out in laughter.

"So, as the sensible one," she said, "let me ask you: Are you going to tell your parents that you'll be living with Drew?"

"No. But don't worry. They won't call you to check on me. They're a mess."

"Oh, God. Isn't the new medication helping?"

"Not much. My mom sleeps most of the day."

"Shit." Nora inhaled sharply.

For a few minutes, we didn't speak. I glanced at my friend's profile, her upturned, small nose, the tip of her ear sticking out under the cap with the nonprofit's logo on it, the new piercing in her eyebrow.

"Look," she said, "why don't we do this: you can crash on the couch any time you want so you don't have to feel like you're with Drew out of desperation."

"That's very generous of you. But I'm pretty sure Oni won't be onboard. It would be too crowded."

"I'll make that the condition of her cosigning."

There was no way Nora could legally enforce this arrangement, but I shrugged. "I'll get those boxes out of the closet soon."

On this evening at the coffee shop, I was "killing it," according to DeeDee, who was instructing me. After wiping the wand, I poured the 2% into the paper cup. DeeDee, at the register, handed me the next order. Kids were dressed for Halloween, as Disney princesses and superheroes, dinosaurs. Their parents pushed them in strollers, and held their gooey, candy-coated hands. The mothers cleaned their fingers with wipes they kept in the baby bags or their pocketbooks. The dads scooped them up when they cried.

I smiled at the customer, a man with scraggly hair and a vacant expression, an infant wrapped in some complicated bandage-like carrier on his chest.

"Adorable," I crooned, although I could only see the light fuzz on the top of the baby's head. It took talent, this ever-ready cheerfulness, something I needed to acquire.

For however long it lasted—ten minutes, an hour—I lost track of my thoughts, the screw inside of me loosened. I pumped the vanilla syrup for the caramel macchiato latte, prepared a S'mores Frappuccino Blend for a skinny blonde, toweled off the counter.

Then the beep and blare and riot of sirens. The fire trucks zoomed past the store, lighting up the street.

"Hey, Ellie, you okay?" a woman asked. I couldn't remember her name. "You okay, honey? You're sweating. Let me do that for you."

How long had I been standing there with the receipt in my hand? I stared at it: *ten-p vanilla, ten-p caramel, extra drizzle, add whip*. The word "drizzle" lay on my tongue, like a hard stone.

"Not many trick-or-treaters," Nora said, joining me in the living room at close to midnight.

"Same as last year."

A few children with their parents, then the usual stragglers of teens roaming the hallways wearing zombie and Trump masks.

Nora switched on the dim overhead light, then scrunched beside me on the couch. "Not good to sit in the dark."

"I'll be out of the shower by seven thirty tomorrow morning."

"Oni isn't bringing her stuff until *after* work."

"Ah," I said. We hadn't discussed the details.

"Come sleep with me," she said.

I smiled at my friend. "That's a tempting offer. But I think it would only confuse me further."

She plunked her head against mine. "What are you most confused about?"

"Quantum physics. String theory."

"Understandable. Anything else?"

"Only six in ten Americans see climate change as a threat. Party affiliation outranks scientific knowledge in determining whether someone believes human activity is to blame for it."

"That *is* worrisome. You should write about it."

"Ha. Good one," I said, the tart taste in my mouth.

"Anything more personal?"

Like the panic attack I had at my low-key new job? No, I didn't want to share that, didn't want to hear the purr of pity, followed by the cluck of concern. I twisted away, sat up straight. "Nope."

"You really think you'll stay in Drew's extra room?"

"Dunno. What's the difference? I'm not drilling you about Matthew." When she didn't lower her gaze, I added, "You never did this when I was with Sam."

"You were happy with Sam."

"I was in college. Everyone is happy in college, even if they don't realize it until they have to deal with the shitty job market and their student loans." I lowered my voice, as if suddenly in a library—or a house of worship. "Josh was alive."

"I know, honey. It's just, I saw how you were around Sam, how you were together." Those few weekends she'd driven from Connecticut to Ithaca in her used Jetta that died our senior year. "That glow didn't come from Ecocriticism in the Humanities."

"What was I supposed to do? Follow him across the country so that when we broke up, I was three thousand miles from everyone else I cared about? We wanted different things."

Nora gathered a sliver of her hair and twirled it around her finger. "And Drew, do you guys want the same thing?"

"Open relationship, closed." I shrugged. "Fine by me."

"This isn't *you*. Just going along with what a guy wants. You should find a therapist. Let me help; I'll do some research."

"Are you kidding? How would I pay for that?"

"We'll figure it out, I promise. You need to forgive yourself, stop blowing up your life."

"Being with Drew isn't blowing up my life!" I cried, edging further away from her. "What do you have against him?"

"Nothing personal. I barely know him. But he's Josh's best friend, which has to be . . . significant."

"Stop being my faux shrink."

She bobbed her head. "You're making huge changes without giving yourself time."

"What choice do I have, realistically, huh?"

"You have to forgive yourself about Josh. And all of it, Anna Nuñez."

"This doesn't have anything to do with her," I said, thinking of Anna's Facebook posts referencing her flawed appearance. I'd complained to Nora: She should focus on other things. She was still pretty. Didn't she have any interests outside of herself?

But Anna's self-preoccupation didn't absolve me of my actions that day.

Nora squinted as if trying to see an image that was far out on the horizon. "You've talked about Anna, what happened, her scars, for thirteen years."

"Let's drop this. I had a hard day."

"Okay, honey. Hope you get some rest."

"Yep."

After a while, I trudged to the bathroom to wash up. My door was ajar and the blinds up. I stopped to stare at the bright lights of the bridge.

The whole "living together as friends, free to see other people" scenario lasted for two nights. The first one, I made up the futon with my sheet and blanket, freshly washed in Drew's in-unit laundry machines, and lay in the dark for hours. The room was dark, even in daylight, as it had only one small window, which faced an air shaft. It felt like a performance, how Drew and I politely greeted each other like pals when we passed each other in the hall or met up at the fridge.

The third night, he offered to pick up Thai food and chocolate babka from my favorite Israeli bakery. We ate in the living room, off of his grandmother's lacquered floral trays, while streaming *Vertigo* (my choice). We drank sparkling wine, the bubbles gurgling in my belly. When it was over, the duplicitous Kim Novak dead, Drew said, "So, did she fall or jump?"

"Debatable."

He wiped a flake of chocolate off his upper lip. "Maybe we should have gone for something a little lighter, *His Girl Friday*?"

I felt seized in a chokehold. That was the film Audrey and Josh used to watch in our living room, her favorite. Didn't Drew know? Quickly, I sprang up and ran to the bathroom. Then the terrible retching, my stomach being pulled through my throat.

"Jeez, Ellie, what happened?" he asked from behind the closed door.

"Be right out."

"Can I do anything for you?"

"Just a minute." I turned on the faucet so he wouldn't hear, and to provide the illusion of privacy. After the nausea had passed, after the shaking, after rinsing twice with mouthwash, I said, "Must be food poisoning."

"Does that come on so suddenly?"

"Not sure." I soaped the vomit out of the edges of my hair and cleaned my face and hands. For the first time in months, I was confident sleep would come without any assistance—if I was able to fall into bed without an analysis of what had transpired.

"Want me to get your Klonnie?" he asked.

"I'll be okay without one."

The bottle was in the office; I followed him into his bedroom instead. We lay together without a discussion, Drew's arms wrapped around me.

"I never had sympathy for Josh taking those drugs," I said. "And now, I'm chugging them every other day."

"Totally different. He took them to excel, to live up to your parents' expectations. And to your example."

His words pricked like a blood test needle into my vein. "What are you talking about? I had no expectations of him."

"The example you set." He kissed my forehead, as if to soothe a child. "You were his brilliant older sister. He felt so much pressure, all the time."

"He told you that?"

"Ellie, he didn't have to."

I pulled out of his embrace, rolled over to face him. "Why are you saying this? Are you trying to hurt me?"

"Course not," he grimaced. "Families are complicated and fucked up, even the best of them. But Josh's choices weren't your fault."

"He went to college on a sports scholarship, no loans to repay, adored by my parents and by his loyal, beautiful girlfriend. A frat boy, popular on campus." It swam in me—the familiar bitterness, a slow poison, sickened my spirit.

"That scholarship wasn't guaranteed. He had to play well and maintain his academics."

"What, like a B average? It's not like he had to work two jobs at the same time."

Drew was quiet, his gaze a gentle rebuke, as if to say: *See, such high standards?*

I chewed on the inside of my cheek, the bumpy, wet flesh. "I only worked one," I admitted. "Is that why he stopped confiding in me?"

"He didn't talk about you or your parents that much, not for years. Mostly about Audrey, first how to have a long-distance relationship, then how not to lose her." Drew stretched out, his arms above his head. "The irony was, Audrey was high a lot herself. At one point, Josh thought she was smoking weed every day."

"Recently?"

"Less so since college graduation. She got her act together, he said, and was really critical of him, his addiction, that he didn't have a steady job."

"Maybe Josh's issues became too much for her. People break up all the time for less."

"What more could you or *any* of us have done?"

"Go to sleep. You have work in the morning."

Another kiss, on the lips now, as if to seal us together. Then Drew flopped over onto his stomach, his hands scrunching the pillow under his head. After a few minutes, his breathing grew deeper.

She was smoking every day.

What if she came to see Josh that night, having driven the sus-pected silver car? It could have been the used one she purchased or her mom's. The police might have gathered this information.

I blinked in the dark, building an argument the way I'd outline an article, using bullet points, cutting and pasting, deleting and adding. Okay, so Audrey could have gotten high, which made it hard for her to remember what happened. She was traumatized. Anyone could have acted impulsively in that position. What if she had a fight with Josh, she lit up, and . . .

I visualized Audrey flinging a joint onto the living room rug in that Rosalind Russell, *His Girl Friday* comedic gesture. *No.*

What if they were both stoned and drunk (weed, beer, Ativan) and the furniture caught on fire? *No.*

They rescued Josh from his room on the third floor.

They argued upstairs and when the fire started, Audrey ran out, terrified. She believed he'd follow. Maybe she called 911. Had there been two emergency calls?

My eyes ached from strain, as if they were in charge of calculat-ing the possibilities. I closed them. Why was I searching for a sce-nario in which Audrey's negligence caused the fire, which caused my brother's injuries, which led to his death—other than to exonerate myself? The chalky yellow pill appealed, but I didn't allow myself that relief.

Drew moaned, a dirge-like cry.

I shook him when he did it again. "You're having a nightmare."

He sighed loudly but didn't wake.

The red neon numbers on Drew's digital clock clicked to 12:53. More time passed in which I must have dozed. The clock read: 6:48.

Drew was seated at his desk, computer light dimmed.

"Hey," I said.

He smiled at me. "What are you doing up? I can work in the other room."

"That's okay."

"Go back to sleep."

"Can't," I said. "I have to get to the store."

In the shower, I held onto the handle of the sliding door in case the nausea came on again without warning. I dressed in the same outfit I'd worn yesterday other than my underwear. Most of my clothes were still tucked away in a cardboard box.

"Early emails sent," Drew said when I returned to the bedroom.

The sun was a white stamp in a pinkish orange-and-blue sky. The clouds resembled flames.

"You were crying out in your sleep. Did you have nightmares?" I asked.

Drew squinted. "The same one, over and over. Josh was trapped in your house. I couldn't get to him."

"Me either." My body didn't move.

"He's my best friend. I should have been there. I knew he was fighting with Audrey."

Finally, there was something I could give, someone I could help. "I'm the one responsible. I was so sick of my parents' obsession with Josh. I never even wondered what he was going through, why he'd become addicted to drugs. If I'd had more compassion, I would have stayed in the house, and he'd be alive."

Drew smiled sadly. "Guess we're made for each other."

Were both our moral compasses broken? "Yeah," I said.

This was love then.

chapter fourteen

"These damn headaches aren't going away," my mother said. She was sitting up in bed, a pillow wedged behind her back. The rain was battering the windows. "Dad thinks the dehumidifier he bought will help. Of course, it won't. The medication is causing them."

The first two antidepressants had made her too queasy to eat and hadn't elevated her mood enough to continue on them. This one, my father had reported, was more effective, had curbed the constant rumination. "Are there things the doctor can do to help with side effects?"

"They can pump me up with all kinds of crap, knock themselves out."

"The meds can take a few weeks to even out." I offered the standard line, the one my father had been quoting me each time the psychiatrist tried another drug. "Maybe you'll feel better soon."

"I'll never feel better," she snapped. "You're old enough to realize that."

"Sorry."

There was nothing more to say. *We'll get through this together. We're still a family. You have me*—were all hollow offerings. Insufficient, even cruel.

She stared straight ahead, as if mesmerized by a phantom visible only to her eye.

"Go spend some time with your father. It will be good for him. He's had to put up with Aunt Celeste, and you know how she gets on his nerves."

"Yeah." A burp of a laugh. "Get some rest."

My father was standing in the living room, talking on the phone. "Thanks, thanks again, for everything. Of course. I'll tell her."

He fixed his gaze on me, bloodshot pink. His arms, peeking out of his rolled-up sweater, looked too long and bony, like the tall extraterrestrial in *Close Encounters*. As kids, we'd watched the movie alone. Josh, at eight years old, had been frightened by these creatures, while I'd been fascinated.

"That was Richard Garvey," he said. The professor who'd taken over his classes for the semester. "How did Mom seem?"

"She has a headache."

"It's all this rain."

My skull felt tight, in sync with my mother's. "She says it's this new prescription. But they do seem to be helping a little. She has more energy."

"There's only so much they can do," he said. "They're not happy pills."

That phrase "not happy pills" had become his mantra, as if needing to convince himself, not me. I was the outlier in this story. It was just the two of them and Aunt Celeste, under a dome of mourning. I'd asked over and over what I could do to be of use. Since there was no answer, I desperately needed to piece together the events that led to the fire. My form of atonement.

"The thing to watch out for," he said, "is that the medication doesn't activate her."

I pictured an explosive device, attached to a timer. "What does that mean?"

"To hurt herself."

"God, Dad. What kind of bullshit is that?"

"Don't worry, Elle. Do you want me to order an early dinner?"

It wasn't yet four thirty. As soon as I got to Drew's, I'd research dangerous side effects of SSRIs. "No, thanks. I should get back to the city."

"Okay. Be careful driving in this weather."

"I will."

"About Thanksgiving. Obviously, we're not going to be up for anything. Celeste asked me to pass on an invitation to join them."

"Um, no, thanks."

He nodded, solemnly. "I understand. It's regrettable you aren't closer with Jake and Aaron."

My six-foot-four cousins with their gigantic feet, raucous laughs, and obsession with *Game of Thrones*—tidbits my mother had shared with me over the last few years. The older one was majoring in engineering, following his stern, silent father's example. The younger fancied himself a budding filmmaker. I saw them so infrequently that if I passed them on a busy NYC street, I might not recognize them.

"Maybe you can go to Nora's."

"Maybe," I echoed, having no intention of asking.

"It would be good for you, to be among supportive people. You don't want to be isolated."

Words of advice most likely garnered from Dr. Weissman.

"Don't worry. I won't be."

I didn't want to be with anyone.

"Speaking of support"—I turned to the condolence cards lined up on the credenza—"you guys have a lot."

"There's a bagful of others in the closet. Mom didn't want to put any out here since we have to move eventually." It was a month-to-month rental, a situation that would need to be addressed by the end of the year. "But Celeste convinced her to choose some, thinking it would make her feel better to see them displayed."

"Has she met Mom?"

"Your aunt is trying, Ellie."

"Yeah," I said, perusing the cards. There were a few from my father's male colleagues, but most were from women: neighbors, realtors with whom my mother worked, a few of her longtime friends. Only one was addressed solely to my parents, excluding my name. When I read the signature, my hands curled until they cramped.

"Why did Mom get one from Beatriz Nuñez?"

Anna's mother.

My father swallowed hard, his Adam's apple bobbing. "No idea. I've barely looked at those."

"That woman hates me!"

"No one hates you, Ellie."

If only he'd hug me, so I could lay my head on his chest and catch a hint of tobacco and spearmint gum. But he tucked his phone in his pants pocket and said, "You should say goodbye to Mom before you get going."

"K." I bent my head and rushed up the stairs.

I swung open the door gently, in case she was sleeping. My mother was on her side, curled around her pillow. She turned around, peering at me, like a coyote frozen in her tracks.

"Sorry," I said. "I didn't mean to wake you."

"You didn't."

"I'm leaving in a minute."

"Can you switch on the lamp?"

I did as she asked, then stood before her, like a chambermaid. Not sure what to do next, I twirled the chain of the necklace Drew had given me around my finger. It held two double-plated, silver-and-gold circles.

"Where'd you get that? It looks expensive." She eased herself up against the headboard.

"Sam gave it to me." My face felt hot from the lie.

"I've never seen you wear it before." She lifted her hand to reach for the charm. "I thought Sam had been living off college loans."

"He saved for this, for my birthday. It was a long time ago."

"Sam." Her tone was wistful, as if it were she who'd lost him. "Lovely boy. I'd always thought you acted too hastily, giving up on him."

"That's not what happened."

"Never mind, none of my business. I apologize."

"Thanks."

"I tried so hard to protect Josh," she said, in the same melancholy voice. "From the time he was a little boy."

"Mom, Josh was happy, popular."

"He was vulnerable; there were things he was scared of."

I thought of my recurrent dream, my brother in his footsie pajamas, showing up in my room because my air conditioner didn't buzz and whir like his did. In this nightmare, he'd catch on fire. But in reality, he'd lain quietly under his blankets until his breathing was steady puffs of air, as if from a toy steam engine. I could have reported this habit of his to my parents; they would have bought Josh a better unit, one that didn't frighten him. But I never did. He'd asked me not to say anything. I could tell he was ashamed. My mother coddled him yet modeled a stoic, can-do attitude, which must have confused him. Not catered to, I never had to decipher her mixed messages.

"All kids are scared of things," I said.

"It is a matter of degree. You were always so strong and independent. I didn't worry about you. With Josh, there were things you didn't see."

"I saw them."

"Then why didn't you take our warning more seriously?"

There was the verdict: I'd killed her boy.

My life's a mess, I could say.

At least you have a life, she'd counter.

My eyes and nose filled up so quickly, my face was aching. "Bea Nuñez sent a card."

"Yes."

"I don't understand. Are you friends?" I asked.

"We've stayed in touch."

My anger had a rhythm, a bongo beat. "Why would you do that?"

"I felt for her, for both of them. Anna was seriously scarred."

"Mom, I know. But it was an accident," I argued. "I'd never do that on purpose, and I did everything to make up for it. I saw Dr. Elliot, I . . ."

"You can't compare your suffering to what they went through."

The urge to keep protesting, to lobby on my behalf, surged up, along with my tears. But her gimlet glare, her sunken cheeks, deterred me. "I'm sorry."

"I'm sure you are. I don't have the energy or desire to discuss this, Ellie. It was just a card."

"I didn't start the fire in our house, Mom. I didn't cause Josh's addiction."

"Of course," she said, kindness creeping in, too late. "No one is accusing you of either of those things."

"You are," I mumbled too quietly to be heard.

I drove in the opposite direction of my destination, a few blocks away from the shell of our scorched house. Growing up, I'd found the McAllister's home to be an antidote to my mother's tasteful, minimalist decor. It was stuffed to the brim with cookery—a pot of stew or soup always simmering on a low flame—family photos framed and hanging on the walls in most rooms, and an assortment of pets: their cocker spaniel, Rupert, now ancient and deaf in one ear, their overfed tabby cat, Lotus, with his sag of a belly, and, when we were younger, numerous hamsters and gerbils. I'd imagined Nora's mom as part of the joyful menagerie, with her elegant, giraffe-long neck, ginger fly-away hair, and large eyes fringed with straight, light lashes that she never bothered to adorn with mascara.

Since middle school, I'd spent Christmas Day with this big, boisterous family: three siblings, eight aunts and uncles, and a multitude of cousins. Mrs. McAllister greeted me the same way each time: "It's lovely to see you, Ellie."

To which Nora would respond, "She practically lives with us, Ma!"

Even during college breaks, I'd frequent their kitchen, den, and Nora's room, traipsing around in my socks and sweats like the rest of the clan.

"Well, it's lovely whenever I do."

"God, Ma."

"Thanks, Mrs. McAllister," I'd say.

"Oh, for gosh sake, call me Vivian."

But I never could bring myself to do it. None of my friends referred to my mom as Peri, and she never suggested it.

I adored Mrs. McAllister. Now, I was idling outside her Victorian, as if hoping for a glimpse of her. After twenty minutes, she emerged with Rupert on a leash. With her beanie of a hat and her rubber boots on, she looked young, carefree.

I sat up straight, as if catching sight of a celebrity or a romantic interest. My face in the rearview mirror was sallow, my eyes liquid, the circles underneath more dramatic than usual. I willed myself to press on the accelerator. Mrs. McAllister, Vivian, rushed toward me, squinting in the twilight. The rain had stopped. She was waving and calling out. My name, I assumed.

Be my mother.

But then I was gone.

As I sped away, heat flooded my body, the way it did, sometimes, the first day of my period. That wasn't the case now.

I was crying silently. Weeping for myself, not for my brother. I wanted to be cradled in Mrs. McAllister's arms, like a child, like an innocent. I wouldn't be spending the holiday with them this season, not for the lack of an invitation. Of course this year, more than any other, they would welcome me with love and compassion. Yet I couldn't do that to them. I'd be a golem at their celebration, an inanimate lump of clay, a creature of pity.

Listening to Billie E sing about how she needed a place to hide, I wondered what I hoped to find. And how it would work. Audrey's mother lived in another neighborhood across town. The sun had set, and there would be no lights on the Findleys' cul-de-sac. What if the car was parked inside the garage? Even if it was in the driveway, I'd have to shine my phone's light to discern the color, then snap photos. And for what purpose? Why bring them to the police when they would have obtained this information for themselves?

For me. Just for me. For my peace of mind. No, not that. For absolution.

I slowed down once I'd turned onto the street, which was narrow and quiet. There was no one arriving with groceries or briefcases or children, no dog walkers here. There was a sheen to the black sky from the rain earlier in the evening, and most of the front lights were dim. I couldn't make out many of the house numbers, but the few I could indicated that they were increasing as I got closer to the end of the block. Fear banged through my body like Josh's ball, how he kicked it over and over.

A normal person doesn't do this. A normal person leaves crime-solving to the police.

The Findleys' ranch was the second to last, a tricky spot from which to make a fast escape. I drove around again and parked across the street, facing the avenue. The porch light was off and it was dark inside. Audrey was an only child of a single mother who worked full-time. Clearly, I hadn't thought through the timing of my investigation. There were no cars in the driveway, which should have been incentive to give up, go back to the city. For a moment, I was comforted by that notion, imagining myself in the apartment with Nora.

Sorrow swelled in me when I remembered and, with it, a renewed determination. I turned off the engine and dug my cell phone from my bag. From my vantage point, I couldn't make out any figures in nearby windows. It was a liminal moment between the activities of the day: life in the world and that in the home. I had to hurry.

I darted toward the Findleys'; if anyone noticed me, I'd seem suspicious. But it wasn't like watching a fire. I was just a visitor. Instead of heading for the pathway, I strode toward the garage. The wind had picked up, was crackling in my ears, like a warning. I didn't dare to look for witnesses. All that mattered was spying inside the cloudy windows. All that mattered was detecting if there was another car inside and, if so, its color.

There was. Metallic gray.

chapter fifteen

I told no one, said nothing. It felt like too big a secret to share without official police validation, too inflammatory to even whisper aloud. In another way, it seemed like gossip, an insignificant coincidence. There was no indication that Audrey was in town that night or that she'd driven the car back to her apartment in Brooklyn. The color matched or was close enough. But how many grayish-silver cars were there on the streets of our town, hundreds?

My mind picked at these thoughts as if they were itchy scabs.

A few times, I was tempted to disclose my discovery to Nora, but our relationship had become more distant since I'd moved out. She was busy with Matthew, the boyfriend I'd met only once: a muscular guy with a thick tuft of hair and a narrow chin. When he looked at Nora, sliding his arm easily over her shoulder, I imagined hearts lining up in a slot machine. My friend was too cool to gush, but clearly, they were smitten with each other. My own behavior around Drew was questionable on our double date, my squirmy gestures when he mimicked the arm-over-the-shoulder action and my nervous chatter to cover my discomfort with his public display of affection.

Nora wasn't keeping track of the investigation, and it felt easier that way. I considered confiding in Drew. I imagined him zeroing in on this information, mulling it over, doubling down on his suspicions about Audrey but not going so far as to accuse her of arson. That day in the hospital cafeteria he'd defended her, doubted her capable of such a terrible deed, even an accidental one. That *I* was capable was a proven fact.

What to do about what I'd learned? I contemplated calling the sergeant. "I remembered," I'd say, "Audrey has a gray car. Or maybe it's her mother's." He might ask what had jogged my memory. "Oh, spying on her." Obviously not. "It just came back to me."

But I didn't contact him. I'd caused enough damage in my life: Anna Nuñez by my impulsive act, Josh by my abandonment. I wouldn't do that to Audrey. I decided to wait for Abbott and Volpe to do their jobs.

On Thanksgiving, I spent the morning hours grinding beans and steaming milk for the stragglers of fellow shopworkers and foreign students who'd remained on campus over the break. It was just me and DeeDee and Tracey, a college kid from Charleston, whose parents were divorced. "To avoid my mom's hideous boyfriend and my dad's schadenfreude," Tracey said when DeeDee asked why she hadn't flown home. "I hate turkey anyway. Inferior-tasting bird." DeeDee would join her boyfriend's family in Queens later, and I'd lied about my plans, when asked, claiming to be headed to my aunt's house. It sounded less pathetic than "chicken with mixed veggies and *Orange Is the New Black.*"

After wishing my coworkers a happy holiday, I left with an almond croissant, so oily it stained the paper bag. Szechuan West was half filled with undergrads and a couple of Chinese families. The hostess retrieved my order without comment, which buoyed me. Such indifference would be difficult to find in my hometown, where I'd face looks of either pity or, worse, suspicion.

Entering the empty apartment, my mood lifted. For the next twenty-four hours, the place was mine. I could exhale, weep, binge-watch, polish off the desserts. What I did, instead, was change into my jogger pants and long-sleeved T-shirt, and ate my dinner straight out of its planet-killing, plastic container. I didn't stream the show about prison inmates, sticking with network TV and switching channels for a while. The night slipped by with me finally self-medicating on a reality series about oddly paired couples—misfits and wannabee celebrities—and half a bottle of Drew's Cloudy Bay sauvignon blanc.

It was nearly 10 p.m. when my phone beeped. *Can I come up?*

Nora. I tugged on a circle of my necklace. Only bad news could bring her here.

Sure.

Waiting for her arrival up the elevator, I oscillated between her possible announcements: my mother's collapse and hospitalization from depression, news of Audrey's arrest, a police warrant issued for *my* arrest.

"Hi," Nora said when I opened the door. She was flush with the cold night air. The silver loop in her eyebrow was gone, her only piercings two discrete stars in each ear. She was wearing a wool hat with a faux-fur pom-pom. She looked like herself again.

"Hi. What are you doing here?" My stomach spasmed as it did so often now.

"I brought you pie." She jerked up her arm, showcasing the jute bag with a Whole Foods logo on it. "My mom's apple crumble."

"I love her apple crumble."

Nora grinned. "I know."

"Come in."

She did, sweeping by me. "Where's the kitchen?"

I pointed and then led the way. The floor under my gaze was

fairly gross: scuff marks, dust, a few flakes of cereal shoved into the wood crevices. It wasn't my job to clean the common spaces, although I picked up the slack when Drew was too busy. Ty took out the garbage if asked, but otherwise was useless. Living here felt as though I'd slipped back in time, to the years in a college suite, only without the optimism.

"Did something happen? Did you stop at my parents'?"

"No." She plunked the bag down on the counter. "Are they okay?"

I caressed my belly to signal: no bad news. "They're the same," I said. "My mom's a little better. She seems to be able to deal with this third medication. At least she's not sleeping all day."

Nora's eyes glistened. "That must be so rough."

"It's hardest on my dad."

"Ellie, I'm sorry about *everything*. Judging you, pressuring you."

"Thanks. It's all worked out. How's Oni?"

"Good." She leaned in closer, close enough to touch me. But she didn't. "She's not you, though."

Heartsick. A warm ache in my chest. "You guys get along and the place looks amazing."

I'd visited once when Oni was out and peeked into my former bedroom. There was a silky tank-and-shorts set lying across the carefully made bed. Her furniture was pine, and the ivory blinds were down, blocking the view. The air smelled faintly of lavender and lemon. No traces of me anywhere.

As for the rest of the apartment, it had been spruced up, too. Oni had brought her alpaca throw for the couch, her handwoven Indian rug, her stainless-steel cookware, and her Japanese knives.

Nora said, "We got a kitten. Raphael."

"Wow," I said, the ache spreading to my torso.

Nora and I were dog people, always had been. We'd discussed

how we wished the building would change its policy and allow us to adopt one. I was partial to retrievers of all kinds. Nora was a sucker for any large dog, but especially ones with goofy walks and corkscrew fur. She showed me a picture of this tiny animal with striped paws and enormous green eyes. It was adorable, but a cat.

"Come meet him; he's really friendly. Stay over. You're always welcome to stay."

Welcome. Such a formal word, used when speaking to distant cousins, flying in from overseas. "That sounds fun, but there isn't enough space."

"Oni is in Atlanta over Christmas for a week."

"I'll think about it." I wouldn't. "How'd you know where I was if you didn't talk to my parents?"

"Drew texted me."

"He did?" Again, my thoughts flew to misfortune. I was too much for him to handle, and he'd turned to my friend for help. That was why Nora had mentioned my staying with her, a temporary solution until a permanent one could be found. "Why?"

"Because he cares about you. 'Cause you're alone on a holiday, and I should have invited you to our house."

"That's okay. I wouldn't have come anyway. It's easier this way."

"I want to apologize. I was wrong about Drew and about you living here with him."

I nodded slowly. So, he hadn't complained. I'd misunderstood again.

"Do you want anything to drink?" I asked. "A piece of your mom's pie?"

Nora patted her belly. "Already had one and all the other health food. I'm so stuffed."

"Yeah."

"Ellie, are *you* sure you're okay? Of course, you're in mourning. That's not what I mean. You just seem so worried. Is it your parents?"

"Yeah. Also, the police. You know."

"They still haven't closed the investigation?"

"I haven't heard anything since they interviewed me again."

I was so tired of hiding; I relayed what I'd done, my own amateur detective work. I waited for Nora to admonish me: *It's not safe. You're not really Jessica Jones.*

"That does seem coincidental," she said instead, scrunching her face in concern. "What did Drew say?"

"I haven't talked to him about it."

"Why not? You trust him, right?"

"It's not that. He doesn't think Audrey's capable of such a terrible thing."

"Do you?"

"She's distraught over Josh. That much I believe." I shrugged. "I just don't want to make another mistake and fuck up another person's life."

Nora reached out, gave me a quick hug. "Maybe you should stay away from her, at least until the police figure out who was driving the car."

Or get closer to her. Figure it out yourself.

During the holiday season, awaiting the gravestone-gray days of January, I didn't contact Audrey. I was in some kind of stupor, a malaise, although those words were too gentle. My mind kept dissecting my mood and sense of identity, a relentless but futile exploration. I didn't feel a connection to the girl who'd set fire to Anna Nuñez's sweater, whose lit cigarette possibly scorched her brother to death. I was some amorphous person, unfathomable to myself. Was this depression, then?

Drew reached across the kitchen table for my hand. "There is no pressure at my aunt's place on Christmas. Everyone is already miserable."

"That *does* sound tempting." I laughed.

"It's kind of relaxing not to have to make an effort since nothing intellectually challenging is ever discussed."

I waited a beat to withdraw my hand from his, to wrap it around my mug of peppermint tea.

"Just for the record: they are old-world Republicans."

"Hard to resist, but no."

"Elle, you need to be around family. Mine. Nora's. Just not alone."

When I shook my head, he sighed. "At least let's do Christmas Eve."

"Sure." I wasn't certain what that entailed. "You don't mean midnight mass, do you?"

He smiled. "We're lapsed Presbyterians, which means we get to rule the world without worrying about attending services. I haven't been inside a church since my grandmother's funeral, fifteen years ago."

"Nice gig, white boy," I said.

"I know. It's unfair. Instead of midnight mass, I can book us dinner at Twelve Metro West. Ty will be in Austin. We can come back afterward, have the place to ourselves."

To fuck.

We did that almost every night anyway. What was so festive about that? God, I was such a bitch. It wasn't like I didn't use sex to my advantage, to chase away anxiety.

"Twelve Metro West might be a little too . . . celebratory," I said, "considering."

Drew's cheeks reddened. "I'm sorry. You're right. We'll eat here, maybe watch a movie. We can exchange gifts."

"Oh," I said, startled. The gift idea hadn't entered my mind.

"Rather, I'll give you *my* present. Don't worry about buying me anything."

"Of course I'll get you something. Otherwise it's not exchanging."

"Get us a bottle of prosecco."

"I can do better than that."

"No, please. I don't need anything else."

What does that feel like?

I awoke to a Listerine-lavender sky on Christmas Eve morning. I'd made it through the night without jarring dreams or head-splitting hours staring at my phone. I was on my way to the bathroom when Drew appeared in the hallway, one of those lacquered trays resting on his arms. There was a glass cake cover over the plate of toast and scrambled eggs, and a cup of tea with the string hanging over the side. It reminded me of a tampon, that string. I had an aversion to most teas with their mossy green or astringent taste. But Drew had insisted this was a healing regime. Before the fire, coffee with whipped cream, chocolate, and bread always appealed. But increasingly, eating had become a necessary nuisance. Since the summer, I'd lost eight pounds.

I'd eat the breakfast Drew had prepared.

There was also a small gift on the tray, wrapped in blue satin paper with a bow of silver ribbon.

My body shuddered. It couldn't be *that.*

"What are you doing up so early?" I asked. Since starting at the coffee shop, I was always up by 5 a.m.

"I was too excited to sleep."

I stared at the box. "Let's eat in the kitchen. Be right there."

While brushing my teeth, I noticed a red blister on my gums. I'd been too rough with the toothbrush lately, or maybe it was some kind of stress response. I spit the blood in the sink.

"Eat first," Drew said when I emerged.

Even though my mouth was sore, I managed to finish one slice of the sourdough toast after a few bites of the cold eggs. He'd even buttered the bread for me, which was annoying but sweet.

Time to face the box. "So," I said, shaking it to hear the rattle.

"It's a car." He smiled.

Gray? "I hope it's a Tesla."

He shook his head.

"Prius?"

"Ha. Close but not exactly."

"Close?" The fear of a ring flew out of my head. "I don't need a new car, especially not in the city."

My Hyundai was secondhand but still functioned respectably. I complained about the impact it had on the environment but never expected Drew to remedy that situation.

"I was kidding. Just open it!"

I untied the ribbon and tore open the shiny paper. Inside, lying on top of a cotton square, was a brass key.

A sly smile spread, as if he hadn't so much tricked me as pulled off his surprise.

I gazed down at what was left of the lumpy eggs as if to discern the answer to his riddle in them. "I'm going to make some coffee."

"Don't you want to know what it's for?" he asked, jovially.

Don't say, "It's the key to my heart." I opened the jar of ground beans on the counter, my back to Drew. "Yes, of course."

"It's to the new apartment."

I swung around. "You're moving?"

"*We.* That's the point."

"Why? Are we being kicked out?"

His grin could light up the seventy-seven-foot, fourteen-ton Rockefeller Center Christmas tree. "The lease is up here on January fifteenth. I rented a new place."

"With Ty?"

"No. He can get a new roommate in five minutes."

A screw tightened in my gut. "Does Ty know?"

"Not yet. I'll tell him this week. Why are you so worried about him?"

I wasn't. Ty was hardly around. Mostly what I saw of him was the back of his head, his sweep of sandy hair. The question was a cover-up. It was me I was worried about.

"I'm not. Maybe he'll move in with Ruby."

His girlfriend since the Halloween party where he claimed she was one of the few women not dressed as Ruth Bader Ginsburg. Ruby came as Isadora Duncan in a Greek tunic with a huge scarf draped around her neck.

"Or another friend."

Meaning he would land no matter what, unlike me, who was free-falling.

"Elle," Drew said. "It will be our place, *your* place. I'll cover the rent, though, same as now."

"How can you afford that? You're still doing your internship."

"My mother. But I inherit the money from the trust fund my grandfather left me when I turn twenty-five."

"Wow, Drew. That's soon."

I was tempted to ask how much, but somehow discussing his wealth felt more intimate than discussing sex or, even, our grief over

Josh's death. There was a privacy around money, at least among the rich people I'd known in college, that rendered it a taboo subject to converse about outside of their inner circle.

"And your mom just . . . like . . . agreed?"

"Yeah. I sent her the photos and information, told her I'd stay there once I was working full-time. For now, my mother's the guarantor on the lease. But next year, it's another story."

Where do I fit into this equation? Kept woman? Mistress? Don't be so dramatic. You're the girlfriend.

"I haven't even seen this place," I said.

"I know. I just went to this open house, like on a whim." He was speaking quickly, not meeting my eyes. "There was a huge crowd at the showing. I got it by agreeing to pay above asking price."

That was either presumptuous or generous of him. I couldn't decide which one.

"Was this the only open house you went to?"

He shrugged, noncommittal. So, it wasn't a whim.

"It's on Riverside, quiet, two bedrooms," he said. "I can arrange for us to go check it out any time."

The noose was tightening.

Who is Isadora Duncan now?

I poured the half-and-half into my mug and considered my reaction. Drew was a good boyfriend, even if he'd made this decision without consulting me. He certainly was the most devoted one I'd ever had. Yes, I'd loved Sam, maybe I still did—at least in a nostalgic way. What difference did that make? Our relationship had been over for ages. I hadn't agreed to go with him to California; Sam hadn't fought for me to, either. He never mentioned moving in together. I wouldn't have risked relocating to the other side of the country even if he'd offered. But Drew *was* offering.

"Does your mother know I'll be living with you?" I asked.

"Of course not, because you didn't want your parents to find out. I'll tell her when you're ready. You can cosign if we renew next year. You should have a sense of security."

"That's too far in the future for me."

"Look," he said. "You've been through hell. If it's easier, just consider this as everything being the same between us, only in a much nicer place, without Ty's dishes piled in the sink and his recyclable bags of beer bottles hanging around for weeks."

There is nothing wrong with saying yes. You're not hurting anyone by giving yourself a break.

"Okay," I said.

"Yes, you want to see it?"

"Yes," I said, "to all of it."

He jumped up and ran to my side, giddy with laughter. "Woo-hoo! Put down that coffee so I can hug you!"

Maybe I do love him.

chapter sixteen

T he apartment was a dream or a trap, depending on how I
chose to view it. As stated on the website, the building was
designed by a "renowned 1920s architect," with all the lovely
flourishes, like the sculpted wings above the front door and the wain-
scoted entranceway with marble floors. Full-time doorman, roof deck,
fitness center, resident superintendent, laundry room: all the amenities
a girl could want, if only she didn't feel like a princess trapped in a
refurbished castle.

The beginning of the month fell on a Tuesday, and by Sunday
half of the 1,400 square feet was furnished with the items Drew had
casually charged from Crate & Barrel and West Elm. The decor was
shades of neutral: polished pine and oatmeal, ivory, and soft gray. My
mother would have approved if she ever saw the place. Which she
wouldn't. My parents still believed I was living with Nora, although
the subject never came up on my brief calls to my father, my visits
home.

Drew suggested we have a few people over for a mid-afternoon
housewarming party the following weekend, serve pizza, sushi, beer,
wine, and dessert from the Hungarian Pastry Shop. I brought up
inviting Audrey.

Drew glanced up from the laptop balanced on his thigh. We were
sitting up in bed, late Sunday morning, and he was composing the list

that had grown from ten to eighteen people in minutes. "Why Auds?" he asked. He cocked his head, but his voice was measured. "Won't that be hard on you? This is supposed to be fun."

"Fun might still be above my pay grade."

"I meant, we should only have people over we're comfortable with."

I smoothed my bangs down over my eyes; they were long as a shawl. "I'm okay with Audrey."

This actually was true. I thought of how she'd checked on me at my parents' place after the funeral, how it demonstrated an innate kindness. And she was one of the only people around whom I didn't have to fake cheer. Even with Drew, there were limits. No one wanted to be with someone who alternated between numbness and mourning, whose life had exploded and whose anguish had no expiration date. Other than my parents, no one was affected as keenly as I was, except, perhaps, Audrey.

Also, I needed to spend more time with her, to observe her more closely. She could be a stellar liar who'd killed my brother in a moment of insanity. This woman I liked and with whom I felt a kinship, with the metallic gray car in her mother's garage.

"If you want to, of course, let's ask her," he said.

"I'll text her."

"This place is amazing!" Nora gushed as soon as she entered. Of course I'd invited Matthew. But he was visiting his family in Colorado until the end of the week. "Can I live here, too?"

"Absolutely!" I said.

If only.

"Does a grand tour come with my visit?"

I swept Nora along. "The dining room is over here. Drew liked this layout, where it was separated from the living room by a hall rather than next to each other. He's not a fan of open concept."

Nora smiled at me, in that half-laughing way. It was a look of bewildered amusement she wore when around her affluent college friends, the ones whose parents were venture capitalists or hedge fund managers, who grew up with homes on both coasts, a staff of domestic help, art collections, and a travel itinerary that included resorts in Ibiza, Sardinia, the Maldives, Aspen, Lake Tahoe.

"That sounded obnoxious," I said, lowering my voice. "This has nothing to do with me."

"What do you mean?" She ran her hand over the cast-iron frame of the leather chair, one of six to accommodate dinner guests. "It came pre-furnished?"

"No, it's what I told you. Drew picked this place without me."

"Yeah, and it's fantastic! Better than living with some random person you found on SpareRoom, right?"

It was the trick question on the pop quiz. "Of course."

"Did he decorate, too?"

"No." I shrugged, with a freeloader's lack of agency. "We looked at stuff online, and he bought what we liked."

"How is everything else going?"

"Nothing new to report." Not since we'd been in touch a couple of nights ago.

She nodded, her eyes crinkled at the sides.

"Let me show you the bedrooms."

Ty and his girlfriend, Ruby, were in the second one—my work-space—and my first instinct was to say, "Don't touch anything." No need. Ruby's arm was looped in his, and her other hand was fiddling with a turquoise earring that had come loose. Ty's hands were tucked into his pants pockets. He smiled with his California-cuteness, a dimple on the left side of his mouth and a perpetual tan, as if the Los Angeles sun had baked itself into his skin.

"Nice digs," he said. "A real step up."

Ruby, with her cat woman eyeglasses and dyed black brows, frowned. "I *like* our place."

Meaning: *our* old apartment or, rather, Ty and Drew's.

"Yeah," Ty said. "It's fine."

"You guys should have something to eat!" I exclaimed. "Check it out!"

"We saw." Ruby tightened her grip on Ty.

No one is trying to steal him away.

I knew I looked faded and sad in my jeans and polyester sweater. I hadn't the money to spring for a new outfit, and I certainly wasn't going to ask Drew to fork over more cash. I'd applied a hastily purchased lipstick in Russian Red to add some cheer to my face. Having not sampled the color at the store, I'd glared at the effect. Rather than sexy or even pretty, I resembled Cruella. I'd wiped it off, applied mascara and a glittery blush instead.

It must have been Nora that Ruby perceived as the threat. Nora: so cool in her high-top sneakers, not a stitch of makeup on her fresh face, her plank-strong arms peeping out from a rolled-up fleece sweatshirt. My friend, the badass.

"We have a ton of food," I said.

"Nothing for me." Ruby patted her belly. "The holidays have not been kind."

"There's sushi. Practically non-caloric," I said.

"I might be the only Gen Zer who hates raw fish."

"She seems pleasant," Nora said, once we'd scurried out into the hall.

"Yeah, I think she felt you were after Ty."

Nora smirked. "Please." But then, distracted, she pointed to Audrey—who was approaching with a furry face peering out of her canvas bag. "Who is that? Can I pet him? Her? They?"

Audrey said with a shy smile, "She/her. Sure, go ahead. She's a sweetie."

When Nora touched the black-and-white head, the puppy squinted in response. "What kind of dog?"

"Collie mix. She's a rescue. Glinda."

"Good name." Nora stroked Glinda's ears. "I'm going to get a beer. Anyone want one?"

"No, thanks," Audrey said. "She was up to pee at two a.m. and, for the day, at six. I'm living on lattes."

"Poor you!" I said.

Once Nora was out of view, I asked, "How you *really* doing?"

She stared at the puppy. I realized she viewed Glinda as a therapy animal whose job was to cheer up broken people. Maybe Audrey had brought her along for both our sakes. "Good days and bad. Mostly bad."

"Me too." I caressed the dog's soft head, and she made a sound like a sigh. "It must be weird for you, my living here with Drew."

"Yeah, I *was* surprised."

"Bet Josh would be, too."

Audrey's cheeks blotted coral. "He would be."

"Because it's so awkward, his sister with his best friend. Kind of incestuous?"

For one long moment, she looked directly at me. "He'd say Drew's not as loyal as you think."

"That's ridiculous," I snapped. *What about the gray car, Auds? What would he say about that?* "Whatever went on between you and Drew, he was great to Josh. He was there for him more than anyone, even you, after the addiction started."

"I'm sorry. I didn't mean to insult anyone." She wilted, her head bowed.

"It sure came out that way."

"It's just, there were things . . . No point talking about it now. Anyway, if Drew makes you happy, Josh would be glad. He idolized you."

I grunted a laugh. "That's ridiculous."

"He was too proud to let on. He was trying forever to live up to your mother's standards—and yours."

"I had no standards for Josh!"

"For yourself," she said. "It was much harder for him to keep up his grades and hold up his end for the team, both in high school and college. To keep his scholarship, he had to function at the top of his game. You were always at the top."

"Not anymore."

"Everything is fucked up now," she said softly. "You'll get back on your feet."

"Josh could have told someone how bad the pressure got."

"He did. *Me.* And like you said, Drew. Until he started floundering after college, he was worried about disappointing your parents. He didn't want to involve them."

I swallowed hard. "He was blaming them for his drug problem?"

"It was complicated. He'd wanted to quit the team without letting anyone down, including himself."

"I can't imagine Josh not playing soccer. It was his life."

Audrey stared at me as if I were a bad abstract painting, a splattering of colors thrown on a canvas without intention or deeper meaning. As if Josh had misjudged my complexity. "No, it wasn't. He couldn't stand having to perform on that level."

"That wasn't the way I saw him."

"*Intentionally.* Do you think it was so wonderful to have your parents investing so much energy into him his whole life? He had no idea what he would do once he graduated."

"A professional career, then coaching."

Audrey's neck was long and tight, the muscles pronounced. "The chances are like one in thirteen hundred, maybe less."

"But that's why he went to UVA. MLS recruits from there," I said, parroting my mother. "If he hadn't messed up with the drugs, he could have gone pro."

"He didn't want that even if he could, hadn't for a long time. He wanted to be like you, the one with the great future."

"But he was the golden child." The conversation had gotten away from me. I hadn't wanted to dissect our childhoods. I'd only hoped to establish if Audrey had been at our house that night.

"What happens when that child grows up?" she nearly hissed. "It's like being in movies as a kid but not making it as an adult, not even wanting to."

My mother, rushing my brother out the door in his cleats and number "1" shirt, his kit bag in hand. "Where's your water bottle, Joshie? We don't want to be late for practice." Even at ten years old, he was a maestro of discipline, his body an exquisite instrument. How much had I missed, caught up as I was in jealousy?

"He would have traded places with you in a minute. You had a career path. He had no clue what to do with himself; he didn't know what his interests were outside of sports. You were the lucky one."

"Auds," I said, "you don't think he was suicidal, do you? Do you think he lit the fire?"

Her expression crumpled, the pink spilling into her neck.

"I'm sorry." I touched her wrist. *Was it your car in our driveway? What did you do—or see him do?*

"He texted me before bed, said his life was fucked. But I didn't think he'd do *that*." Her eyes were full of tears. "I can't talk about that anymore . . . How are your parents? I miss them."

I'd been visiting every couple of weekends, watching my mother struggle to stay out of the hospital. She'd force herself to shower, to sip a few spoonfuls of soup, to walk up and down the block, even though her legs felt as if they were bound by steel braces. My father was a wisp of his former self.

"They need answers. The police haven't finished the investigation," I said. "They called me in again. What about you?"

"No. Only once, a while ago. What did they want?"

"To ask about a car, not mine. A neighbor reported one in our driveway—that turned and pulled away, right before the fire."

Fear flickered in her eyes. "Whose?"

"They don't know. They didn't say. They probably won't ask you in—since you weren't there. Right?"

"Of course I wasn't. Why are you asking me again?" The puppy, awake now, whined and pawed the satchel. "I better get going."

"No! I'm sorry. Have something to eat. I'll make another pot of coffee. I brought a ton from work."

"Okay, I'll stay for a little bit." She smiled weakly. "I, um, actually wanted to invite *you* to something."

"Sure."

"I have an art show coming up."

"Wow. That's amazing." And an incredible accomplishment for someone whose beloved boyfriend recently died. "What do you do, exactly?"

"Paint. Some drawing. You'll see if you come."

"I'd love to."

Another opportunity to gain insight into my brother's girlfriend, the one who might have set him ablaze.

⟜—·•·—⟞

I arrived alone, unclear if my invitation extended to others.

It hit me immediately: Audrey's paintings were remarkable, bursting with color and energy, portraits of people in motion and in pain. A man leaping with his arms extended above him, grimacing, his eyes a pop of blue. A woman, her hands clutching her knees, her bowed head sprouting a waterfall of chestnut tresses with bold, burgundy streaks. There were joyful ones, too: a couple outside on a windy day, their hair flapping around their faces like flags, a girl strumming a guitar, her fingers a flurry of action, guys racing on the soccer field, long legged, their muscles golden, glistening. I knew nothing whatsoever about visual art, had never taken a course in the subject, and rarely frequented museums—other than planetariums, for fun. But even I could tell that these canvasses pulsated like heartbeats. Students and instructors leaned into the work, then backed away to glean other perspectives.

I scanned the room and found Audrey, holding a glass of champagne, surrounded by a group of students, a collection of tight black pants and oversized jackets. I waved to her, and she returned the gesture. "Congratulations," I mouthed, and she smiled shyly.

I returned to studying her canvases. Hanging in the center of one clean, white wall was the most striking piece. A woman lying on a bed with her pants crumpled around her ankles, her chest and face blocked by the male figure lying on top of her. His arms splayed out in an expansive wingspan, his jeans gathered at his knees, his flesh a whorl of brown, yellow, and apricot-colored movement. His upper body was covered by a navy-blue sweatshirt with a blurred number on the back, the hood covering his hair.

On a small plaque below was the title: *Rape.*

A taste of blood from where I'd chewed the inside of my cheek. Audrey had claimed to be unconscious. Queasy, I crouched forward to examine the work more closely, the mix of broad and delicate brushstrokes. The violence depicted was graphic, while the identity of victim and attacker was hidden from view. Something gnawed at me, some eerie sense of recognition: *a soccer player volleying for the ball.* His head was turned sideways, the facial features indistinguishable. The hoodie might be leading me astray. They were ubiquitous, not just worn by athletes. Still, I thought, this man wasn't a stranger.

"Excuse me," I said, pushing my way through her circle of admirers. "I need to talk to Audrey a minute."

The girl next to her bristled. "We're in the middle of a conversation."

"Rude." Another one shook her head.

"It's okay," Audrey said. "This is Ellie, a friend from home."

"I promise, it will only take a second," I said.

Audrey stepped away and I grabbed her wrist, the one free of the drink. "You're amazing."

"Thanks. I wish Josh were here." Tears reached her cheeks.

I marveled at what easy access she had to her emotions. In comparison, my feelings were a frozen pond with a few cracks signaling danger if traversed.

"The one of the assault was so brave. And powerful."

"Thanks. I wasn't going to include it because of my parents. But I decided not to invite them. My dad wouldn't have come anyway."

I'd overheard Josh talking to my mother once about how Audrey's father was some kind of corporate recruiter who lived in Philly and occasionally visited for the weekend. He'd stay in a hotel and take her to lunch with his new wife, a former-restaurant-hostess-turned-life-coach. Her parents had divorced before Audrey had turned three, so she had no real attachment to her dad and loathed these awkward meals where his wife would pontificate about "self-care."

I could understand excluding her father and stepmother. But I asked, "Your mom doesn't know about this?"

Audrey shook her head. "I'm not ready."

"Does she realize how good you are?"

Audrey shrugged. "Doesn't matter. It's a point of contention, in terms of a career choice."

A conversation for another time. "Auds, the soccer sweatshirt. Do you think it was someone on the team?"

She squinted, as if considering the question. A small fleck of her brown mascara adorned the edge of her eye, like a beauty mark. "No. Every guy in town has that hoodie."

"True. Anyway, I love all of them. Your pieces are great."

Then I noticed, across the room, a smaller one. Even from this vantage point, I could see: a house on fire. Not ours. This one was longer and lower, a ranch style, the flames spurting straight out of the windows like exhaust from a car.

Audrey's house was a ranch, I thought, the heat rising up from my collarbones. Was this her form of camouflage, a way of exorcising herself of that night without exposing that she'd been involved? Or, having not experienced it firsthand, was she trying to come to terms with this catastrophe by imagining it had happened to her own home?

Audrey was studying me; her face shimmered from a glittery peach blush. That the makeup wasn't quite blended into her skin made me like her even more. "I knew that one would upset you; I'm sorry. This is the only way to get it out of my system."

"Don't worry. You deserve to enjoy yourself today," I said. "You should be very proud."

Her face lit up.

The apartment was empty, which was a relief. I tore off my coat and sank onto the couch, mulling over what I'd witnessed in that rape scene. There was rage in her brushstrokes, and hatred. And there was something else: the way the attacker flayed himself over her body, as if he wanted to smother her with his weight. I wasn't supposed to discuss the rape with anyone, but Audrey did that herself, through her painting. The attacker was wearing a hoodie and, while everyone dressed that way, even the non-athletes, the guys at the party were years out of high school. It seemed unlikely that many would show up in those sweatshirts.

And about the fire: it felt wild and sad, not like a confession. There was no relief on the horizon, not for me. The regret for leaving Josh and my role in his death would be a burden I'd carry, like a millstone, for the rest of my life. Like what I'd done to Anna Nuñez. I resolved, then, that I'd never mention her to the police as a possible suspect. I owed her that much, at least.

I rushed to the bedroom, on unsteady legs. In the top drawer of the nightstand was my pill bottle. I hadn't taken a Klonopin in a couple of days. I jammed one down my throat, where it sat until I drank water to aid its passage.

Solitude was one thing to be grateful for. Drew was at a study group that evening. I'd bought a sandwich at a neighborhood deli. Dinner and a Netflix show would be all I could manage. Halfway through the second episode of a British procedural, my cell rang.

"Hey," Audrey said. "Sorry I was so rushed today. It was so cool of you to come so far. The trains suck on the weekend."

"It wasn't too bad." An hour and twenty minutes. "Anyway, I loved the show."

"There's something else." She sounded winded. "I couldn't talk about it there, but I wanted to tell you. My therapist suggested hypnosis to try and retrieve my memories."

"Wow. You up for that?"

"Yeah, maybe. Today proved I'm stronger than I thought."

"Sounds worth a try."

"If you want, I'll let you know what happens," she said, more a question than a statement.

"Definitely." We were in this together now.

"This is probably none of my business, but . . . if it works and doesn't, like, flip me out, maybe you could go."

I stared at the paused action on the screen in front of me, the police officers hunched over a desk, glaring at a computer, at some piece of evidence, the fake identity of a killer on the run. "Why?"

"If you could reconstruct that night while under hypnosis, you might feel better."

There was no possibility that going into a trance would rid me of this guilt—even if I wanted that.

"Let's see how it goes for you. I'll think about it," I said, knowing I never would.

chapter seventeen

My first New Year's resolution was to find out who started the fire. It was a big ask. The other one was to discover what career I could tolerate now that climate calamity triggered anxiety in me. Once a day, I checked out my LinkedIn profile as if to prove my qualifications hadn't changed. I hadn't updated it since I'd quit my job, and the earnest smile—actually showing teeth, as Nora would exclaim—was a rarity for me now. The bangs that fell just below my eyebrows had since grown in. The Urban Decay eyeliner had dried up, been tossed and not replaced. There was color in those cheeks and confidence in that face—both gone.

Resolution number two was the problem of where I would live once the turbulence and shock abated. It wasn't with Drew, not long-term; I knew that. He was starting to sense it, too, my restlessness, my inability to fully relax around him—as much as I tried. I longed to be alone.

The last time we'd had sex, we began as we often did, with me on top, his palms on my breasts. But once we'd reached the part where Drew was covering my body with his, he must have felt me wander off. "Are you here with me?" he asked.

"Of course," I said, lifting my pelvis up, tightening myself around him.

Everything had turned fluid and warm as we moved together.

But afterward, Drew at my side, his breath slowing, the thought had drifted into my mind: *I'm not here. I'm not anywhere.*

The third resolution was the simplest: not to drive unless there was no public transportation available. But what was best for the environment was problematic for me. Grief for my brother emerged in bizarre ways. I couldn't bear to be confined in a subway where there were no escape hatches.

I have something to tell you, Audrey's message read.

We shared a mission as well as a deep remorse, a sense that we'd forsaken Josh. In our own ways, we'd both contributed to my brother's death. What I'd yet to determine was whether Audrey had been in our house that night and, if so, what she'd done or witnessed that she wasn't revealing. Despite my suspicions, I liked her.

On the way to meet her for our walk in Prospect Park, I listened to music on the train, trying not to indulge my imagination. A gunman would appear, wielding an assault rifle, or the brakes would fail, or a biological weapon would be unleashed. As soon as I hit the cloudy, much-too-warm-for-winter air, my cantering pulse slowed.

We met by Grand Army Plaza, Glinda tucked into Audrey's canvas sack. She'd layered a long wool cardigan over a tight T-shirt. Earbuds hung from a wire around her neck.

"Hey," she said.

"Hey." I smiled, observing how we'd transformed, how we were no longer on the defensive around each other.

We hit the Long Meadow, crowded with couples and families, bikers and toddlers strapped into strollers.

"Aren't you going to let Glinda out?" I asked.

"She hasn't gotten all her shots. She's not allowed to be around other dogs until three months." On one side of our path, a terrier was running off-leash. On the other, two Labradors were chasing a ball.

"Poor pup." Glinda was yelping at the sight of possible playmates. "Sounds like a lot of work."

"It's a ton. I love her, though. She's such a blessing now." Auds caressed Glinda, who licked her hand in return. "My roommates complain she whines whenever I'm away. She's in her crate, so they don't have to take care of her. But the noise drives them crazy."

"What are you going to do?"

"Look for a studio after the semester is over, if I can find one I can afford, up my hours teaching to make rent." Her mouth tightened. "It will be a distraction, at least, working so much."

"Can't you stay put until Glinda grows out of it?"

"I'm on the lease, so yeah. But my roommates can make my life miserable." She glanced down. "More miserable."

"Do they know what you've been through?"

"They're not my friends."

"I meant about Josh, not . . ."

"Yes," she said curtly. "The other thing—that's between you, me, and my shrink. And Dr. Morris, the hypnotist."

My arm reached for hers. "Is that what you wanted to talk about?" When she nodded, I asked, "Did you remember who the guy was?"

"No. I still can't see his face." She scrunched up her own. "He wore this black bracelet. It was black, leather maybe, with a silver pendant in the middle, a symbol of some sort. It looked like a bug."

"That's good, really specific!"

"Except, I started to hallucinate before I passed out again. I was being eaten alive by some giant insect."

"Oh, my God."

"Yeah. I definitely saw the bracelet, though. It was real."

A breeze cut across the path. Dried-out brown leaves flew up, and Glinda barked as a few whizzed by. She tried to catch one by biting the air. We both laughed.

"It's okay, sweetie," Audrey cooed to the puppy.

We stayed silent for a moment. Glinda stood up and clawed at the side of the satchel, whimpering.

"Can I hold her?" I asked.

Audrey nodded her consent.

The puppy felt warm and heavy in my arms. "It's okay. Everything is okay." She stuck her tongue out as if to lick me but peed on my hands instead. "Oh!"

"I'm sorry! Glinda, no!" Audrey took the dog from me and eased her back into the canvas sack, despite her kicking in protest. "I have some paper towels and wipes. See why my roommates want me out?"

"Doesn't bother me. She could pee on me anytime."

We giggled as I wiped the urine off my hands, then searched for a garbage can. After we threw out the dirty wipes, Audrey fastened her gaze on me. Her eyes shone, a malachite green, and the constellation of freckles on her cheeks stood out in the sunlight. "Before hypnosis, my body was processing what happened to me, but my mind wasn't. Does that make sense?"

"Shit, I'm like that most of the time. Has hypnosis helped?"

"Yeah. My brain has started to catch up." She shook her head, those auburn waves. "It's hard . . . When I try to picture the guy, it's as if those drugs are still in my system. I reimagine that giant insect on top of me."

"Maybe you should stop, then. Maybe suppressing stuff isn't so bad."

I was talking about myself, too.

"I need to keep going now that I've started. It's just really expensive, all this therapy. My mom's paying for the hypnotist, Dr. Morris, *and* Jane, the shrink. Mom is on my case to get certified to teach in public school so that, eventually, I'll land a full-time job. We're not rich."

"Is that something you want to do?"

"Ugh, no. Kids are adorable but not what I had in mind. I'm getting the MFA so I can teach college students. But I have to be realistic about my prospects. Most academics end up as adjuncts for poverty wages . . ."

"Did you tell your mom what happened to you yet?"

Audrey was so pale, like dappled parchment. She dug into her tote bag for a sketchpad and black-tipped pencil. "Do you mind if we stop for a while so I can draw the trees? It's calming."

"Course not."

"My mom thinks all this treatment is to deal with losing Josh."

I didn't want to push her, to ask why she hadn't been forthcoming with her mother. Would I have been with mine, in her place? Doubtful. "Since your punch was spiked, how much of your memories will even be clear ones?"

Her hand was making swift circular movements on the page. "Dr. Morris wants me to try and access stuff from before I drank the punch. 'Reconstruct the evening,' he said."

"To see if anyone was, like, stalking you?"

"To start to . . . *heal*." She whispered that last word as if it offended her. "Dr. Morris is four hundred dollars an hour; Jane is two twenty-five. I have to *heal* more quickly, or my mom will go bankrupt. I mean, she's also helping me with rent."

I wondered about her dad but didn't ask. "Four hundred an hour is insane."

"Yeah. Maybe I should do that for a living."

"Me too. I could use a lucrative profession."

We grinned at each other, comrades in our foolish choices.

"Jane says I need to learn to self-soothe."

"You could purchase a vibrator on Amazon. Much cheaper."

Her hand stopped moving, mid-stroke, and she slapped my arm lightly.

"What about Dr. Morris? What does he say?"

"His whole focus is on helping me remember. Hypnosis is a relaxation technique, so that if things come back to me, I won't freak out."

"Do you think it's effective?"

"Yeah, maybe. I have this sense of the guy who did it."

"What kind of sense?"

"That it was personal."

"Auds, of course. He raped you."

Her face filled with color so quickly, it was like titrating an acid, turning water pink. "Ellie, what if the guy thought I wanted to have sex?"

"You weren't sober enough to consent."

"Do men know that?"

"The good ones do," I asserted, with more confidence than I felt.

Her fingers were back at work, as if they had minds of their own, like these girls in college who knitted before exams. "Dr. M said I might confuse suggestions for memories. I think someone *did* give me my glass of punch. The whole bowl couldn't have been spiked. No one has said or posted anything about it. Whether this guy thought I wanted to have sex with him or not, I'm pretty sure he chose me for a reason."

"What kind of reason?"

"That's what I'm trying to work out," she said, pressing so hard she made a slight tear in the paper. "There were so many girls there that night. So, why me?"

I stroked her shoulder, unable to answer her question.

"Tall flat white and one of those," a beaker-thin guy said, pointing to the raspberry walnut and oat nut square in the glass case a couple of days later.

Tracey handed me the paper cup with *GFW* in black ink before retrieving the pastry. Even at this in-between hour of 11:20, there was the din of impassioned chatter among the buzzy students. I caught: "bloviators" and "seminar assholes" and "socialized to believe that crap" and "Mexico City was so cool" and "Nuan is worried about her parents in Shanghai."

While pouring the double shots into the cup, I heard a smug male voice say, "I thought that shit was in Wuhan, which is like ten hours away."

"Beckett," a girl said, "it's a *virus*. Did you even take basic bio?"

A shiver ran through me, a sense of déjà vu. What moment was I reliving? I couldn't pinpoint one.

"Sure. Skipped AP."

"How'd you get in here?"

"His dad donated a building." A higher-pitched girl.

"Fuck you, Gabby!" A guffaw. "It was only a wing."

"The Chinese locked down the city a few days ago," bio girl declared. "My dad is friendly with a bigwig who used to work in the CDC. He says this is like a new kind of SARS, only they're predicting a much bigger outbreak than the last one."

While adding frothed milk, the reporter in me awoke to the clarion call of my heart: *Text Rashad!*

I looked up to assess the source. The threesome stood behind a bedraggled mother, with a squealing child tugging on her arm, placing her order. Beckett was between the two young women, grinning an off-center, scared grin, his teeth bright and even.

Gabby, dark-eyed with a small dove tattoo on her neck, said, "It came from a bat or something at an animal market, like Ebola."

"SARS, not Ebola," said bio girl, violet-streaked curls under a puffy pink hat. "We're encroaching on animal habitats. I read about that in my environmental systems class, how this is linked to climate change."

"That sounds really sketchy," Beckett said. "Like unrelated."

"It's not," I pronounced. "It's logical."

The three of them stared at me, the barista. Gabby cocked her head as if considering: maybe I was a student, a really old one, in grad school. When it was her turn to order, she addressed my coworker Tracey, "I'll have a grande honey oat milk latte."

My phone vibrated in my pocket, but there were four cups to fill and more orders on the way. Even with the help of the third barista, Jerod, it would be a while before I could glance at the text.

"I got this. Take a sec," Jerod said with a new-hire smile.

"Thanks," I said.

It was Audrey: *Can you talk?*

At work. Tonight?

K. Text you after my class.

This connection between us was a balm, an unexpected gift. But for the first time in months, my thoughts were focused elsewhere, on a problem to crack that was unrelated to my life.

꒰────•●────꒱

Inside my building, I nodded at Jerry, the barrel-bellied doorman who greeted me with a "Good evening, Miss Stone."

Was his nose always this pink and moist, or was he getting sick?

Stillness upon my arrival. Drew wasn't here. These were the only moments that afforded me any peace these days: alone in this luxurious space, like a guest in a lovely B&B. I changed into leggings and a T-shirt, poured myself a glass of wine, then settled on the living room couch with my laptop. The urge to work, even just to research an emerging disease, was a thrill. After a while of jumping from one report to another, I texted Nora: *Where the fuck have I been? How did I miss this?*

I sent a woman-with-hand-over-her-eyes emoji because there was no ideogram for my feelings: a crack in my despair, a tingling excitement over a possible public health emergency. How fucked up was I?

Nora responded: *What?*

Possible pandemic.

Huh? That's mostly in Asia.

It was here, too, lurking. I changed the topic, so as not to scare my friend, and we made tentative plans to grab coffee later in the week.

Drew messaged me to say he'd bring home dinner by eight; work was running late. *Thai? The usual?*

Sure, I agreed, even though, after my early morning shift, I'd be half asleep when he came home.

Another ding. It was Audrey.

This a good time?

Yep.

Can I call you in a few?

Yes.

I returned to my Google search, obsessively pulling up information and eagerly speed-reading until my phone rang.

"Hey," Audrey said in a small voice. "I had another memory of . . . the guy."

"A hallucination?"

"No. This was from before I passed out. I was trying to resist. But I was dizzy and out of my body. It wasn't even like being drunk or stoned. I'd never felt this out of control before."

"Those drugs, I heard they are really powerful. But you remember resisting. That's good, Auds!"

"Yeah, I didn't consent. There's something more." Her breathing was jagged. "He held my arms over my head and squeezed down on my wrists. He held me so tight, it hurt."

A rustling inside me, like a squirrel in the eaves of a house. "Auds, his face, his eyes? Can you picture those?"

"No. Just what I felt and this sense . . ."

"Of what?"

"Like he'd conquered something. Like he'd conquered me."

chapter eighteen

I t was different. It was. Drew was never rough or overpowering.
I'd never subjugated myself to his will. And yet that position, my
arms raised, his hands clamped down like manacles—could that
be a coincidence?

I was seized with the instinct to run, to bolt out the door and
into the elevator. I could crash on Nora's couch or sleep on Audrey's
floor. But I didn't do either of those things. Since Josh's death, I'd
abdicated control over my own life. I'd forsaken my ambition, my
sense of autonomy, my belief in a future. Now, at least I could revert
to an old habit: research. I scanned Facebook, Twitter, Instagram,
LinkedIn, and TikTok for images and videos that might reveal the
black bracelet with the silver pendant.

On my boyfriend's wrist.

Drew's smile was broad and bright on LinkedIn. You could make
out a dress shirt and jacket, no tie, in his profile picture—the same
one he used on Twitter. His Instagram account was private. I'd never
thought to limit who could gain access to mine; then again, I rarely
posted. Most of my images were from college and, following that,
snapshots of articles about the environment that I, or other science
writers, had published. After graduation, the purpose of the app had
become career-driven, to build readership. Unlike Audrey (I'd

checked after Josh's death), I hadn't commemorated my brother's life with throwback, happy photos.

I could send Drew a follow request for IG and, of course, he'd grant it. But the timing might strike him as strange, or at least that's what the humming in my head was warning. Truth was, he wouldn't care. Once I surveyed his albums on FB, it struck me that Drew might not want people at work to view some of these "rich-boy" vacation shots of him: in a bathing suit and neon-green baseball hat on Ipanema Beach in Rio; standing on the Pont des Amours bridge overlooking the lake in Annecy, France; on a mountaintop in Yosemite, in his suede biker jacket, next to a couple of guys I didn't recognize.

No bug bracelet. No jewelry at all, in fact.

Maybe it was a coincidence. Maybe Audrey's recollection had nothing to do with Drew. Yet I couldn't shake the feeling of his hands clasping my wrists as he moved above me, his watchful eyes on me until the last moment, when he'd look away.

Drew burst into the apartment with the bag of takeout, and I startled. "Hey, hi," I said.

"Hey, hi yourself. What's going on?"

"I was deep into Google."

"Ugh. Don't read the news. Come eat while it's still hot."

All I craved was the pineapple, bathed in sauce. The chunk was sweet, more like candy than fruit.

"Don't you want your chicken?"

"Just sugar."

He grinned. "That's what I'm here for."

I fought the urge to recoil. "Yeah, well, there's this thing I've been thinking about. There's something I wanted to ask you."

"Course."

"It's about . . . sex." I glanced down, not out of shyness but to mask my deception. "The way you hold me down, you know, with my arms above my head."

Drew shot up in his seat, as if called upon to answer a difficult exam question. "Does that bother you? I'll stop. I thought you kind of liked it."

He'd never forced me to splay out, so vulnerable, my body long and exposed. I'd never protested. I hadn't minded the lack of intimacy in this position. It had served a purpose for me: passion without intimacy.

"I wondered how come you do it," I said.

"Oh, well, that's kind of embarrassing."

"You can tell me. Was it something another girlfriend wanted you to do?"

"No one has complained." He laughed, blushing, a tendril of hair hanging over his forehead. "God, this was years ago. Josh had some guys over after a game, and I was there, too. They watched this movie. Twice."

He named a film that was famous for graphic sex scenes, one of the couples going at it in a bathroom stall in some beautiful Parisian restaurant. I'd never viewed the whole thing but had caught snippets on some station: HBO or Showtime.

"The main character, he did that with his hands and Simone Larson"—an actress with big breasts and even bigger lips—"seemed really turned on. A couple of the soccer guys boasted that they'd tried that before and that their girlfriends seemed to like it."

A wave of relief sloshed over me. The rapist could have been any of the soccer players. "Which guys on the team?"

Drew tapped the side of his beer glass. "God, this is really weird, Elle. Why do you want to know?"

"Humor me, okay?"

"Yeah, sure. Well, definitely, Archie Dunmore was there."

The center back, the most popular kid on the team with his jeweled blue eyes, sculpted cheeks and chin, elegant long legs. Everyone in our town had heard about him, even me.

"Yeah, he was going out with some cool girl," I said, reaching back in my memory. These were not my friends, not my crowd. I was in college at the time and only saw these boys when home, over breaks.

"Tatiana Rey. And then this other obnoxious kid. He bragged that it worked for him, too. I don't know if I believed him. He didn't have a girlfriend but claimed he was hooking up with a few of the freshmen. So, I figured it was worth a try."

"What was this guy's name?"

"Rory."

"Rory Martin?" I asked, wheezy voiced.

"Yeah." Drew took a sip of his beer. That elastic band appeared above his brows. "What's wrong?"

My thoughts were scrambled: what to share, what not to, issues of confidentiality vying for the value in disclosure. "The night before the fire, Audrey went to a party. It was at Rory Martin's house."

"Yeah, I know. That's why Josh didn't want to go with her. Josh hated Rory. I don't get what these questions have to do with us."

I ran my index finger over my top lip, the spot where Drew's foam mustache lay. He wiped it off with his napkin, which he then crumpled in his hand, as if it were a pest.

"Audrey confessed something to me, the other day. You have to promise not to say a word about this."

"Of course."

"She thinks someone drugged her punch that night. Did Josh talk about that part?"

"No way." Drew shook his head. "She thinks Rory drugged her?"

"It was his house, so probably," I hedged.

"God, that's awful. I'm just surprised she told you. Are you guys friends now?"

"Not close ones. Audrey feels burdened, responsible for Josh's death in some way. Guess we have that in common."

He nodded. "So, not to be crude, but what does it have to do with us?"

"Getting to that. Audrey thinks she might have fooled around with Rory," I lied.

"Wow, no wonder Josh was furious. And Josh knew this?"

I was in too deep now. "Yeah. They fought about it when I was home that day. Audrey said she was super drunk or drugged. I don't think it was full-on sex." Where did this fabrication come from, and why did it even matter? A half-truth didn't vindicate breaking my promise to Audrey to not share her secret. "She mentioned he pinned her down. So, I just wondered . . ."

"What?" Drew's irises turned a darker brown, a magic trick. "You think it could have been me?"

"No. I'm sorry! I didn't realize this was some tribal bro-move."

"Yeah. I get why you'd freak out." His smile was false, as if forced for the camera. "We were idiotic young guys trying to figure shit out, what turned girls on."

"What about Rory, what was he like?"

"He was loud, friendly with a bunch of guys on the football team. Used to glom onto them and their girlfriends." Drew raised his bottle of beer. "Like me, right?"

"You weren't that loud," I said, confident now he was innocent, that I'd been right to confide in him.

"Ha. Thanks. The difference was Josh really *was* my best friend. I glommed onto him, it's true. In my defense, I was a nerd with low self-esteem."

"Ah, yes, the nerd defense."

"I was aware of my lowly position in the pecking order. Rory wasn't clever or funny, yet found himself hysterical. Thought he was cool because he was popular-adjacent."

"The worst!"

"Why would Audrey cheat on Josh with a guy like that?" he asked.

I gazed down at my chicken, drowned in oily sauce. I thought of how this bird was inhumanely slaughtered, its beak cut off, fed grain filled with antibiotics, doused with chemicals.

"She thinks her punch was drugged; she was really out of it and can't remember any details."

Drew frowned and stared at the bottle in his hand. "Did she say if other people at the party were drugged, too?"

"No. That night is kind of a blur for her."

"Convenient."

I felt his response squeeze me around the middle. "That's callous." When he murmured an apology, I asked, "Was Rory jealous of Josh?"

"Sure, I mean back in high school. Tons of people were."

"Do you know if Rory liked Audrey?"

Drew's eyes slid over mine. "Probably. There were a lot of kids who had crushes on Audrey. But she was Josh's girlfriend. I can't imagine anyone hooking up with her, even if they were drunk and even if she was willing."

"Josh wasn't this big deal anymore. I mean, it was years ago, and he was fucked up by this point. Rory could have thought she was fair game."

"Dunno. I'm not an expert on Rory Martin."

"Yeah."

"It's upsetting, that's all," Drew said slowly, as if dropping beads on a string. "If that happened, it's so fucking disrespectful on both their parts."

"Not if Audrey didn't consent!"

"Okay, true. So you believe her story?"

"Yeah, I do. You can't ever say a word of this to her. She told me in confidence and . . . I trusted you."

"Of course I won't. But I have to ask," he said, steady, with a nugget of anger in his voice. "Did you think *I* had sex with her?"

"It crossed my mind."

"Josh was my *best* friend."

"I know."

"I've been trying my best to take care of you. How can I do that if you won't, at least, start to let go?" he asked, mournful, extending his hand to mine. "Not of Josh's death—I don't mean that. No one can expect you to get over that. But you can't trust me? Are you unhappy with me?"

"It's not you." I dropped his hand. "I'm unhappy with everything. I get it if you're fed up."

"I'm not, Elle. I'm wondering if anything will help."

"Knowing who started the fire would. I keep piecing it together in my head." My mind snagged on another possibility. "Josh could have acted impulsively—after finding out that Audrey . . . what happened."

"You mean *suicide*?"

"The sergeant who interviewed me mentioned that as a possibility."

"That's crazy."

"That's what I said. The sergeant said it's not unheard of. He said people act impulsively when really stressed out. He asked me if anything unusually upsetting had occurred that day. I didn't know, then, about Audrey—just that they'd been arguing."

"Josh wouldn't do that to himself. He loved her, sure. But he wasn't some insane romantic poet."

"No," I said, "he wasn't."

"Audrey having sex with Rory Martin wouldn't make him burn down your house." Drew sounded tired. His long day of taxing work showed on his face, which suddenly looked a greenish yellow behind his tan. He glanced down at his half-eaten meal, then stood up and took his plate and beer bottle to the sink.

"Josh *was* taking drugs," I pushed. "He'd been drinking, too, which could have made him act irrationally."

"I guess he could have—accidentally—started the fire. If he was preoccupied and stoned," Drew agreed, his back to me.

Had I offended Drew by implying his best friend had killed himself? This was my brother we were discussing—yet Drew seemed more upset than I was about that possibility. Had I become heartless in my quest for absolution?

"The police haven't closed the investigation, though."

"I wonder why," Drew said, stacking his tableware into the dishwasher.

It lay like a pebble in my mouth, salty and hard, the news about the silver car. I wanted to discuss this development, to poke at it, to analyze and ponder what it meant with Drew. More now than ever before. But doing so would lead to my divulging that I'd tracked down either Audrey or her mother's vehicle, and that the color matched the one that our neighbor had seen. And I couldn't do that. I couldn't sacrifice Audrey again, not after incriminating her in such a flagrantly self-serving way.

"It's so hard on my parents," I said instead. "My mom is obsessed with finding out."

Drew turned toward me, his head bowed. "Poor thing. How's your dad holding up?"

"He's consumed by worry about my mother. That's what he talks to me about, not about the police."

I'd stopped asking my dad if he'd heard anything new a few weeks ago. The last time, he'd made this noise over the phone: a sigh, followed by a groan, as if suffering a moment of excruciating pain. And I'd apologized for inquiring, promised not to mention the investigation again.

"I need to keep going, Elle," he'd said, by way of explanation, "to get Mom well and then, after the summer, to return to teaching. I can't take another semester off."

The university had been generous, not that my dad hadn't earned this last-minute sabbatical. Few people were in such a position: to be paid while not working. Still, money was tight for my parents without a second salary. *At least they won't have to pay for Josh's rehab.* The thought was forbidden, blasphemy, a sign of my immorality. *Despicable.*

"Will Mom be able to go back?" I'd asked. I was unable to envision her ever again showing homes to prospective buyers, shepherding them through the rooms, pointing out how the space was perfect for their young children. "Ever?"

"This isn't the time to talk about that," my father had said.

It was a soft rebuke. My mother's loss was incalculable. She was cocooned in a husk of grief from which she might never emerge.

My dad hadn't asked me about my own situation, not in that conversation. He'd been doing so less and less often. If Josh were alive, he'd have realized that I couldn't pay rent at what was now Nora and Oni's place on a barista's salary. I'd been scraping by as a journalist. He'd have wondered how I was managing to pay off my student loans.

Drew asked, "You think the police are still considering it an act of revenge by someone who Josh owed money to?"

"No idea," I said, which was the truth. "People shoot people everywhere in this country, malls, churches, nightclubs, elementary schools. So, I guess burning down a house because you are owed money makes a certain sense. Fewer victims than most violent crime."

Drew's forehead crinkled. "You're exhausted."

"Always."

I'd been exhausted for so long, I couldn't discern if this state had worsened.

"Why don't we zone out, watch TV?"

"I was going to do some more research. For freelance work," I said.

"Tomorrow," he said.

"And tomorrow," I answered. Drew looked at me quizzically. "Sorry, yes."

It had been a routine Nora and I fell into during high school, quoting from *Macbeth*. In tenth-grade honors English, our teacher read this soliloquy aloud with her chin high and her eyes focused on the bulletin board—filled with notices about sports events and auditions for *Urinetown*—across the room. "To the last syllable of recorded time," Nora would mimic, adding her version of a Scottish accent.

Now, I thought, *The last syllable is coming soon.*

With climate change, there would be no one around to record anything. I had to hurry to help solve the planet's problems while I still could. Problem was, I couldn't even solve my own.

The next morning at 5 a.m., I woke up to get ready for my shift and found a late-night text message from Audrey: *He said, I'll be gentle.*

chapter nineteen

anic had a taste. Vomit. I reached the bathroom in time to release the contents of my gut into the toilet. Quickly, I locked the door afterward—even though Drew was asleep—then washed my face, used the mouthwash.

It was impossible to count how often Drew had pinned me down during sex. Only that once he'd whispered, "I'll be gentle." Right before he'd declared he loved me for the first time.

In the shower, I held onto the chrome door handle, feeling unsteady. My brain and body craved a respite, a chance to reassess, after months of ping-ponging between dissection and avoidance, numbness and hypervigilance. The decisions to quit my job and to move in with Drew had drained me of personal agency, had rendered me dependent and weak. My close inner circle—the people with whom I used to check in daily—had diminished from Nora, work friends, and my father, to Drew. Only Drew.

The rapist and liar.

Why had I allowed myself to fall so far?

There wasn't the opportunity for rest or analysis.

In the bedroom, wrapped only in a towel, I walked on the balls of my feet. The floors didn't creak in this renovated dream of an apartment—I was careful, nevertheless. Quickly and quietly, I slid open my dresser drawers, grabbing underwear, a bra, socks, jeans.

My sweaters hung in the closet, so I tiptoed across the room, realizing how ridiculous, how comic my movements must have looked. Drew's breathing was soft, measured puffs.

I decided to leave before he woke up, call in sick from the street, wait for him to go to his internship, then spend the day searching the apartment. The commonplace hoodie wouldn't be confirmation. Only the bracelet would count as evidence.

I bought my coffee and a scone at a nearby Starbucks and sat at the one outside table, even though winter had returned as February drew to a close. I averted my gaze to the sidewalk, grimy and gray. There was a dull quarter and a stiff wad of gum nearby. I picked the blueberries out of the dough and tried to ascertain the clues I'd missed about my boyfriend.

That term, *boyfriend*, momentarily cut off my breathing, as if I'd been seized around the neck. I sipped on my coffee; any liquid would do.

Face it, the only guy you've ever loved was Sam.

It had been hard to pinpoint exactly why, what was missing with Drew since the circumstances surrounding our relationships had been so remarkably different. I was another person then, a striver, clinging to my future with teeth and nails, pessimistic about the planet yet optimistic about my ability to fight for it—and for myself. Always, with Sam, I felt a sense of comfort, umbrellaed in his presence. He was at ease with himself and the world in a way that was a rarity among our twitchy, cerebral peers. He calmed me like a weighted blanket.

Trauma changed me in ways I still couldn't ascertain, perhaps on the cellular level. But it was also true that, with Drew—as he so aptly claimed—I couldn't relax. I realized, as I shoved the scone into the paper bag, that I was more at ease when alone.

Alone wasn't possible, not financially. Somewhere in this city there was a room where I could close the door to outsiders—even roommates. This was the plan that bloomed as I strode back to Drew's building. For it was never my home. Every place had been temporary—even my haven with Nora—since leaving my childhood house, and now that was gone, too.

"Hi, Anthony," I said to the daytime doorman who was close to my age but—with a receding hairline and shaved-too-thin mustache—looked older. "Did you happen to see Drew leave for work this morning?"

"Yes, Ms. Stone, Mr. Colins left"—he glanced at his wristwatch—"about ten minutes ago."

My interactions with Anthony embarrassed me more so than with Jerry, who was middle-aged, less formal, seemingly at ease with his years of service. There was a sense of pageantry with Anthony, as if he were acting out a part in *Downton Abbey*, where the servants recognized their place in the pecking order—not all without resentment. The irony was that, low as his salary was, Anthony earned more money than I did.

"Thanks so much. Hoped to catch him with this," I said, holding out the bag with the half-eaten pastry hidden inside. Proof that I'd dashed out to get breakfast for us. "Guess I'll see him tonight."

As if he cares.

I could hear Nora's voice in my head: "Covering your tracks, Jessica Jones?"

There's nothing to hide.

"Other than rummaging through his private things?"

Couples searched for proof of a suspected affair all the time—perfectly legal—so hunting for clues of rape seemed fair to me.

I didn't bother to switch on the lights, even though there were no rays pouring in from the windows today. I threw the bag out in the kitchen garbage and tore off my jacket. The second bedroom, which was slotted to be my workspace when I was ready to pursue freelance writing and editing, currently was being used to store Drew's grad school books and papers. He'd purchased one of the ever-popular mid-century wood desks, which was slick and stylish with only three slim drawers. Inside the middle one were several business cards of managing directors, a senior analyst, two vice-presidents, and a data scientist at the investment bank where Drew was hoping to secure a full-time position. I had no idea what any of these people actually did—other than toil eighty hours a week to eventually be rewarded with one-percenter status. Drew's goals conflicted with my values, as most of the global banks were funneling huge funds into fossil fuel industries.

I'd known this all along. Of course I had. But I'd been in flight mode, making choices no longer based on my former self, my past decisions, or my moral standards. I was, in effect, a stranger to myself. Drew, quite possibly, was a stranger to me, too.

I turned to "our" bookcase, the one divided by row. Mine were the top ones and held a few hardbacks from school with my notes scribbled inside, essay collections by both science writers and a few millennials whose observations about pop culture had taken off, plus a handful of novels. Drew's consisted of titles with the words "corporate," "managerial," and "finance" in them. He also was a fan of Erik Larson, Dennis Lehane, and Kazuo Ishiguro. When we were setting up this new apartment, I'd paid fleeting attention to his favorite authors, who he explained dealt with topics that captivated his attention: history, true and fictional crime stories, and artificial intelligence. An eclectic mix that signaled a traditional male combination of interests, nothing sinister. That's what I thought then.

Now, I wondered about the tier devoted to depravity or, at least, illegal deeds.

There was nothing incriminating in the office, though, not even anything revelatory about the man with whom I lived.

Walking into the bedroom, I felt like an interloper, not the person whose pajama bottoms were tucked under one of the pillows with Sam's T-shirt, the one I'd given him originally, after our visit to the Museum of Natural History. At the gift shop, I bought him a tee that read, "I Wear This Shirt," above the printed periodic table of elements and the word "Periodically." He'd gotten me blue socks with green T. rexes on them that looked menacing in a colorful way. "Shockingly," he'd said, as we combed through the souvenirs, "there are no melting ice caps underwear."

"No wildfires?"

"Nope," he'd said.

"Guess no one wants a burning bush near their vagina."

Drew, having no idea that my nightwear had once belonged to my ex, found it "cute."

I gazed at the room, which lacked personality. There was no artwork on the walls even though I'd urged Drew to hang up his travel photos, ones he'd purchased, not taken. He insisted we buy prints we both liked—an activity that I'd delayed. It struck me as too romantic, denoting a permanency for which I wasn't ready. The kind of knick-knacks I'd kept at my old place—the Capricorn candleholder and Sam's snow globe—were buried with my underwear rather than showcased on top of my wardrobe. I'd left the glass vase with the dried lavender sticks at Nora's; most likely, Oni had thrown it out.

Drew's acacia wood dresser was next to mine, a matching pair he'd ordered for us. I dug through his clothes, the ones that were not neatly hung up in the closet, pushing aside polo shirts and jeans, socks and briefs, T-shirts and thick wool sweaters. There was no bracelet hidden in any folds or pockets, and the only sweatshirt was a pullover with the Columbia logo embroidered on it.

The closet was mostly his stuff. Mine consisted of two black dresses, footwear—high-top sneakers, two pairs of boots, sandals, and ballet flats—and an oversized cashmere cardigan, the kind I liked, a present from my mother. There was an overhead shelf with two cardboard containers pushed to the back. They belonged to Drew, were taped shut and labeled in red flair pen: "High School" and "College." I'd seen him stack them in here when we'd first moved, and I'd never questioned their contents.

I dragged a chair from the living room to use as my stepladder. Even then I had to stand on my toes to reach them as they were positioned, tucked tightly into the corner, like carry-on luggage Drew didn't want to get jostled mid-flight. I chose the bottom one, marked "High School." I tried my best not to tear the thick tape keeping the cover tightly secured. But I ripped the white paper on one side; there was no way to conceal that it had been tampered with. Once, I'd done something similar with Sam. I'd found what looked like a journal atop a pile of notebooks on his floor. He'd been in the shower, and, without a second thought, I'd opened the leather-bound diary to find it filled with doodles and questions about coursework, reminders of appointments, and random musings about his future—all career related. My name didn't appear once on the pages I'd surveyed. Mortified that I'd invaded his privacy, I vowed never to do such a thing again.

Yet here I was, flipping through cards from Drew's friends, invitations to birthday parties, recognition of achievements: a printed version of his SAT scores (excellent), National Merit Scholarship—a ping of jealousy—letters of acceptance to several elite universities.

He'd been a bigger nerd than I was! But, curious and competitive, I was wasting time.

What mattered were the two small jewelry cases. I should have opened them first, yet delayed out of fear. There were photographs scattered among the papers. The majority were of Drew with Josh, from childhood (maybe nine or ten years old) to the two of them in their graduation gowns and hats, grinning like golden retrievers begging for treats. Then there were the ones of Audrey and Josh—which I rifled through quickly at first, driven to see if any were of Auds alone. There weren't any. The ones here of my brother and his girlfriend weren't posed pictures. Some were intimate, not explicitly sexual but candid and alluring. In one, Audrey's mouth was open slightly, her tongue touching her front tooth. In another, she was resting her head on Josh's shoulder; her eyes were gazing up at him and his down at her. From these pictures, it seemed as though Drew had a crush on this subject—which was both of them.

I had hours before Drew's workday ended. I could take a break, pace myself. I didn't. My stomach muscles were cramped, my body demanding answers. I unclenched the brown box, the top attached by a spring. Inside, seated on a plastic-molded structure was an expensive-looking watch with a round clock face and a beige leather band. I heard myself exhale. I'd never seen Drew wear this and wondered, for a second, why something so handsome was confined to the closet. When I opened the second case, my guts spasmed, worse than before.

It was as Audrey had described: black leather with a silver pendant in the shape of what looked like a water beetle. Something clicked in my brain, from the mythology course I'd taken freshman year. This was a symbol of the Egyptian god whose name now eluded me. He represented creation.

I glanced up, as if caught. Of course, there was no one else in the apartment. The only sounds were coming from upstairs, the news blaring from the neighbor's TV, words indistinguishable, tone dire. I returned the contents to the box, all but the bracelet. Having not figured out what action to take next, I restored the box to the closet and the chair to the other room.

My next instinct was to flee. I stopped myself when I reached the kitchen, decided to make peppermint tea to settle my stomach, and evaluate my options in a rational way. Never mind that my heart was a hammer, my vision slightly blurry, my head heavy, as if stuffed with mud. I had to fight my body, will myself to behave as if this were the hardest exam of my life, one I needed to ace.

As I heated up the mug full of water in the microwave above the oven, I noticed my hand quivering. Bottom line: I couldn't live here anymore. Where would I go and how would I afford it? I knew from securing my apartment with Nora that landlords would ask me to submit assets: bank statements, retirement accounts, or the signature of a guarantor. I'd saved what I'd made for a few months; it only amounted to a little over four thousand dollars. I could pay a couple months' rent—but who would let me sign a lease and where? No one and no place. Not on my pathetic salary. March was a few days away, which meant that I was looking at a mid-month or April situation. I needed to find a share with some stranger looking for a roommate.

"Jesus, I'm so fucked," I blurted out to no one. I had the urge to call Jae at Terrafeed, to hear her say in her playful way, "*Maintenant quoi?*"

"Oh, just catastrophe," I'd answer, and she'd come back with, "*C'est la fin des temps.*"

How I missed her! How I wished I could attend the next editorial meeting. Anticipating the dystopian fallout to come caused a crazy adrenaline rush in me, the way going into battle zones must be for war correspondents.

Not now! Concentrate!

I had to address my current problem, not pine for my past.

At the kitchen table, I let the tea cool and went to retrieve my laptop. Then I scanned two websites, requesting info and sending messages into the void, responding to listings in Harlem, Bushwick, Crown Heights, Bed-Stuy, and the Lower East Side. By lunchtime, I was ready to bolt again and had to talk myself through the next steps. I texted Nora: *Can I stay on your couch tonight?*

Instead of staring at my screen, I attempted to make myself a Monterey Jack sandwich—since bread and cheese were two items Drew always kept stocked, along with Hawaiian Kona coffee, almond milk, a bottle of Cloudy Bay, and a couple of German beers.

"Just take a bite, one bite," I said softly to myself, as if prompting a child.

Normally, I'd tear into this sourdough loaf, dip it into the tub of butter when Drew wasn't around to see. Even though my appetite had waned since Josh's death, bread and butter still soothed me. I nibbled now and watched for my phone to light up.

Finally: *Sure. What's going on?*

Will explain later. Do you have to check with Oni?

No. We have an "open" relationship.

Ha! What's a good time?

7:30?

Yes. Thank you! Also, can you ask your friend Jasmine about that tutoring service? Need to make money.

Of course. You sound motivated!

Yep. More later.

I checked my messages; nothing yet from potential roommates. I thought about Jae again, with whom I'd shared drinks on a couple of occasions. We'd been on our way to becoming work friends when I'd quit. Then there were some of my college friends, with whom I'd lost touch after the fire. I simply couldn't bear to discuss my situation with them. It was incredible how easy it was to disengage from group texts and even private messages, especially since people were spread out across the country. The digital world allowed for disappearance, as if one could vanish into a parallel universe or be sucked into a wormhole. A lonely but discrete existence.

The rest of the afternoon, I walked around the Upper West Side—to Central Park West, past the museum, into the park and the forested Ramble. On a path in this wooded area, I wondered if the birds' loud cries were customary for winter or if there had been a change in migratory patterns as the season had warmed. The birds might be nomads; so was I.

By evening, I'd headed back uptown, stopping to get take-out chicken pho to bring to Nora's. I could have chosen to eat at a table like another young woman with only her phone for company. She was staring at it and texting frantically, while tears rolled down her cheeks. Chatter from other couples' conversations filled the restaurant; a waiter repeated an order, and the front door swung open and let in the cool, damp air. Rain threatened.

Even with her roommate there, it would be calmer at Nora's. I hadn't prepared my excuse for staying over yet. I'd reconciled that full disclosure wasn't the best path. Nora would freak out. She'd insist on my staying on the couch indefinitely, which would cause issues between her and her roommate. Plus, I'd be divulging Audrey's secret.

"We had an argument. I just wanted a break," I said when she opened the door.

"Sorry. You want to talk about it?"

Nora looked different, her eyes bigger and her skin glowing from some creamy new blush. I realized she was wearing mascara, which she never had before. A decision shaped by her job? It seemed unlikely that a nonprofit in the arts would require longer, darker lashes.

Oni's influence.

"Not really. Just needed a break. I brought dinner with me, if you don't mind." I should have ordered a dish for her. "I'm sorry. I didn't even ask if you wanted anything."

"I have vegetable quiche Oni made yesterday."

I glanced around the living room from the doorway, as if both the dish and the chef would surface suddenly from the shadowy hall.

"Come in before Raphie tries to escape."

Once in her kitchen, I asked, "Where is that little beast?"

"On Oni's bed. She went out for drinks after work. Raphie likes the light, so she keeps the blinds up for him."

Even at night, the lights from the bridge shone into the room. "I liked that, too."

Nora picked at the flaky crust with her fork. "Want to try some?" Her voice was forlorn. Did she miss me or just feel pity?

"No thanks. This is fine." I pointed my spoon at the plastic bowl of soup. The pinging sound had started a moment ago. I could hear it, although my iPhone was inside the pocket of my backpack. "I should just check this."

Nora nodded and I retrieved my cell. Drew's message read: *Hey, did I forget you were doing something tonight? I brought Chinese.*

Not coming back. I know what you did.

What??

To Audrey.

I didn't do anything to her!

She told me about what happened at Rory Martin's party. You were there. You lied to me.

I glared at the message bubble while Nora chewed discretely in the background.

Drew's response appeared: *Why do you think that?*

That's not the right answer. I found your bracelet.

I petted the pocket of my backpack where it lay in its box. Of course, I'd snatched it. Who wouldn't have?

What are you talking about?

I typed: *Rape.* Then deleted the word before sending. Foolish to antagonize someone capable of such violence—and such forethought: drugging Audrey's drink.

Instead, I wrote: *It wasn't Rory. You did it.*

"Fucker," I mumbled.

"Ellie," Nora said. "What's going on?"

"Hold on," I said to her.

I'm calling you, Drew texted.

No, don't.

My phone rang and I waited for it to stop. Four times and the call went to voicemail. Then it rang again. I couldn't ignore it anymore. After two rings, I picked up.

"First of all, it was the worst mistake of our lives," Drew said, his voice thick, as if he had a cold.

"Our?" I whispered.

"Yeah, look, we messed up big time. But I feel worse about lying to you. Just come home and I'll explain what happened."

Home? I thought, and lifted my gaze to Nora's face.

chapter twenty

I silenced notifications on my phone. Oni came home soon after, tearing off her long wool coat. "Well, Grendel passed on my design for the Windham account, just as I thought," she announced. She stopped and smiled when she saw me, a smile that showcased the deep dimples at the sides of her mouth but wasn't reflected in her eyes. "Sorry," she said. "I didn't realize you were visiting." She ran her hand over her hair, pulled into a tight ponytail that ended with a mass of black curls.

"Ellie is staying over," Nora said. "Sorry about Grendel."

"No. No problem. We can talk about it tomorrow." She addressed me, "Everything okay?"

I nodded and Nora said, "Man trouble, ya know."

"Certainly do, my friend!"

I wasn't sure if Oni was referring to me or Nora as her "friend." The reference to Drew ended further conversation. Oni went into the bedroom to change her clothes and Nora said, "Sorry. Just slipped out."

"It's okay. Why else would I be here?"

The three of us hung out in the kitchen for a while, discussing Nora's and Oni's job pressures. I, of course, had nothing to add, other than, "I have the early shift." A signal that sent them scattering to their bedrooms before 9 p.m. Oni scooped up the cat, and it lay in her arms like a furry infant.

Even though I turned out the lights early, I was acutely aware of the night sounds—heat pumping through the pipes, and the slosh of the cars outside in the rain. The couch was soft and too narrow. My mind was focused on that one word: "our."

It was close to midnight when I called Drew. He answered after one ring. "Ellie, I'm so glad—"

"What did you mean by 'our'? You mean you and Audrey?"

"Yeah, what happened between us at the party."

I clung onto the thin cotton blanket draped over me, balled a corner of it in my fist. "The rape."

"What are you talking about? Who said anything about rape?"

"Audrey did."

"That's ridiculous. You said so yourself, she had sex with Rory. I thought she didn't want you to know it was me. I didn't, either."

"She doesn't remember the guy. She remembers the bracelet, your bracelet. I have it here."

I heard him suck in his breath, that deliberate pause, then the crack in his voice, like ice breaking underfoot. "You went through my things?"

As if *that* were the crime, as if trespassing surpassed sexual assault.

"I never saw this on you. Took me a while to put two and two together."

"It was a present from my dad for my graduation from college. I barely ever wear it."

"You did that night, though. It was hidden away with pictures you took of Audrey and Josh. Pretty fucking voyeuristic."

"Jesus, Ellie. Is this an investigation? I don't go sniffing through *your* stuff. Look, those were from years ago. And yes, I was jealous of Josh."

Obsessed.

"Why did you say she had sex with Rory?" he asked.

"We were talking about pinning women down, and that just slipped out. Audrey isn't clear about who did it to her."

Now his voice was lifted, high and angry. "We had sex. No one *did* anything to her."

"You lied to me."

"We all lied!"

His accusation stung like a nettle in the finger. He was right. And wrong. "Audrey didn't; that was me, not wanting to expose her secret." I had anyway. "What's your excuse?"

"I panicked. I was afraid you'd break up with me." He was speaking so quickly now, almost stuttering. "You said Audrey cheated with Rory. I figured she didn't want you to know the truth."

"You were *protecting* Audrey? That's bullshit." Disdain had a taste, like bitter tea.

"And myself, obviously. I was very drunk. We both were. We behaved really badly."

"She had a beer and a cup of punch. That doesn't mean she deserved to be raped."

"Of course not! Stop saying that."

"You claimed you couldn't imagine anyone hooking up with Josh's girlfriend even if she were willing."

"I was ashamed. I *am* ashamed."

I pulled the blanket up to my chin. A vision came to mind: of Josh, as a little boy, lying on my bedroom floor, draping a sheet up to his eyes. I shook my head as if that would rid myself of the memory. I needed to focus on the present. "How did this happen?"

"Why would you want the details?"

"So I can believe you."

Which I won't. I imagined Drew on top of me, his eyes clamped shut, willing himself not to finish too quickly. *I'm sorry, Joshie.*

"Audrey came over to me at the party." He'd slowed down. "She'd been texting me for a while, telling me she was fed up with Josh. She'd been flirting with me. I mean, it had been obvious for a while; she wanted to sleep with me."

"Oh, yeah. 'Cause this woman who'd been with my brother for years suddenly wanted to fuck his best friend?"

"Elle, she's not this angelic person she appears to be. She's been disloyal to him before."

"Really? How? And how do you know this?"

"Look," he said, "that night, she asked me how I could stand it anymore, the drugs, living with your parents, not working. She kept saying how admirable I was for sticking by him. She went on and on about how disgusted she was."

"Doesn't sound very sexy to me."

"It wasn't. She was acting weird and uninhibited."

"Uninhibited how?"

"Just loose and loud and touching me. She was coming on to me, Elle. She said I'd changed; I looked great, was making something of myself, that the roles were reversed, and Josh should see *me* as a role model now. Audrey . . . she's . . ."

"Beautiful."

"Unattainable—or always had been. I'd never been the kind of guy unattainable girls went after." Coyly, he added, "Girls like you."

"I'm just ordinary."

"Not to me. You're brilliant. You're Josh's brilliant older sister. Anyway, I was flattered by Audrey's attention. And turned on. I admit it. I wasn't seeing anyone."

"Oh, well, that makes it all right. 'Cause Audrey was with your best friend."

"She swore she planned on breaking up with Josh. That doesn't justify my actions. We had this history, this yin-yang thing. Then, when she'd started confiding in me, it was like this fucked-up aphrodisiac. I swear, Elle, that's the truth."

Despite my misgivings, this narrative made sense. I pictured the fat, goofy, immature Drew who was once Josh's sidekick, desperate for my brother's life. There were instances when he tried to dress like Josh, talk like him, imitating his cadence—measured and with a hint of humor, unless angry—and his expressions: the side smile and the wide grin.

That version of Drew was gone, reconstructed through grit and grind. In its place was this fit, confident version of him: Drew 2.0.

"Did you spike Audrey's drink?" I asked.

"Of course not!"

"Who did?"

"Ellie, I didn't even realize it was spiked. Are you certain it was? Maybe she was just embarrassed that she drank so much."

"Audrey has PTSD," I skirted the question. *Gray car. Rape accusation.* Not the same thing, I admonished myself. *Can't justify assault because a woman's intoxicated, however it happened.* "You should apologize to her."

"I swear, I thought we were both into it. I'll do whatever you think is right."

"For her sake or mine?"

"Both. I don't want to lose you."

I couldn't see the lights from the bridge, my former beacon, not from my vantage point. There was no one and nothing helping me navigate my life, so I had to rely on my instincts.

"Were you so desperate to be like Josh, is that why you chose me?"

And I realized, in my increasingly weary state, that maybe I'd chosen Drew for the same reason. Not that I coveted Josh's situation—

his incapacity to move forward, his addiction. It was his place in the order of things: not just the son, but the sun.

Drew released a sob. "Ellie, that makes no sense. He wasn't your boyfriend. I'd never deliberately harm you."

Like whiplash: the pain radiating down my neck, the onslaught of fatigue. "I need time to process things. And sleep."

"Will you be home tomorrow?"

"Maybe."

When I hung up, I thought, *Where else would I go?*

Predawn, Nora appeared outside the bathroom door. I'd just showered, dressed in the steamy small space between the tub and sink, and was rushing to get to the shop.

"What is it, Ellie? What's going on?" she asked.

"I want to break up with Drew."

And I recognized then that I did. Desperately.

"Did he hurt you?"

"Physically?" I leapt to an extreme—a tell. "Of course not."

Nora moved closer, so close I had to stare at the floor not to cry. "In any way, treated you badly?"

"I just want to be on my own."

"I get that. You just seem kind of alarmed."

"Yeah, like everyone. Gotta run, Nor. I'll call you later."

At work, my thoughts flitted around the room like canaries. One alighted on the shoulders of a woman with a fierce, wet cough: *Is she infected? Stay out of the store!* Onto the braids of a girl with purple glitter on her cheekbones: *Keep away from the cougher.* Another on a man with a satchel full of groceries, cucumbers and tomatoes peeking out: *Buy dry goods on the way home.*

"Hey, Ellie. Get this guy his drink?" DeeDee called out to me.

"Coming up!" I said, staring at the order—triple, venti, soy, no foam latte—hoping muscle memory would kick in, pulling my T-shirt up over my nose and mouth.

"What's with the burka look?" Tracey asked.

"Coming down with a cold." I glanced at her, admiring the recent addition of blue-streaked bangs in her dark hair, how they brought out her eye color. "Steer clear of that customer." I nodded toward the one hacking into her fist.

"Hi. When you get a minute, can we talk?" It was Drew's voice, filled with gravel and anguish. I was on the other side of the counter from him, my machine facing that direction. But I refused to face him.

My hand shook as I poured in the second shot of espresso. There was too much to process: self-protection from both illness and my boyfriend.

"I'm busy," I said. He was so close, I could smell his body lotion, some mixture of black pepper, wood, and lemon.

"I have time," he said.

"No break for a while."

"I have the whole day."

"Is your office closing?" I asked in surprise, finally looking at him.

"No. You aren't going to tell me to stock up on toilet paper, are you?" He smiled.

"Dried food. Canned beans."

"Need me to take over for a minute?" Tracey asked. "What kind of dried food you talking about, like apricots?"

"I'll make you a list. He can wait. You have two capps to make."

A half an hour later, I told DeeDee I needed to get some air for five minutes. "Max."

She shot Drew a wary glance and nodded.

I kept my distance, not wanting us to touch. "Why are you here?" I asked him as soon as we reached the street.

"I couldn't go in. I barely slept," he said.

"Yeah, well, I haven't slept in months."

"You think I'm one of those #MeToo guys." His voice was scratchy and sad.

"My feelings aren't a political statement."

"Yes, they are. Every white guy with money isn't the same. I never wanted to join a fraternity. I'm not one of the bros at work. I never saw sex as something I was entitled to."

"Other than this one time."

"Not entitled. No more than a woman is." He reached for me; I flinched, and he withdrew. "Why do you trust Audrey, who you barely know, over me?"

"I believe she was assaulted." Drew might have convinced himself that what happened wasn't rape. Or, maybe, both of them were at fault, were misremembering or stretching the truth.

"You're breaking up with me, right? 'Cause of Audrey." He corrected himself, "I mean, the two of us, her and me."

I was shivering in my cotton shirt and apron, without my coat. The dress code prohibited most sweaters, and I'd forgotten to take the one I wore most days to Nora's. "Did Josh know about the two of you? Did he set fire to the house because of it?"

Drew winced. "No, Ellie, no."

"We rushed into this for the wrong reasons."

"Not for me."

He sounded so forlorn that, for just a second, I had the urge to comfort him.

"You're freezing," he said, and slid one arm out of his leather jacket. "Take this."

"I have one in the store. Thanks. I have to get back in there."

Although I wondered: How was the ventilation in there? Had the cougher spread her viral particles? What surfaces had she touched while I was too busy to watch her?

He held his coat out to me and it hung there between us, a handsome, empty vessel. "Elle, just come home later. We can hash this out."

"I was thinking of staying with Nora for a while."

"There's no space at Nora's. If it makes you more comfortable, I'll sleep in the second bedroom."

"We tried that."

"It's the rational thing to do."

"Thanks for mansplaining."

"Sorry." He grinned an *I'm just your average clueless guy—trying hard to change* grin. "Guess I'm still learning the ropes of being a good boyfriend."

"You have been," I said, a reflex but not a false statement.

There was the conflict. No one had offered more support than Drew. No one had been kinder or more available or more patient.

"Why would Audrey lie?" I asked. The question was directed at me as much as at him.

He shook his head. "Maybe she's not. Maybe her drink *was* drugged, and she had a bad experience. And I was a pig and didn't notice how out of it she was. Maybe we're both right and wrong and there's no one way to tell the story."

"You did this to—"

He interrupted, "To Josh. Not to you. Not to Audrey. Josh was the victim."

"Okay. Why would you do that to him?"

"It was a terrible, impulsive thing," he repeated his argument.

"If you'd like us to go to a counselor to talk this through, I'll do it. I believe there's hope for us as a couple."

"I appreciate the offer," was all I said.

"If you're going to move out, take your time. I can't stop you. I won't even try."

"Be honest with me. Did you want to hurt Josh?"

"Never." His mouth quivered, and he pressed the heel of his hand into his temple. "Never in a million years. He was my best friend. I loved him."

"Did Audrey want to hurt him?"

"You'd have to ask her that."

My mind switched to the night in her mother's driveway, peeking into that garage. The metallic gray car. Why hadn't the police closed the investigation yet?

"I will," I said. "See you later. At home."

The light turned on in Drew's eyes. I had the urge to curl my body against his chest.

chapter twenty-one

Turned out moving was not an option, not now, as February folded into March. I'd stocked the apartment with beans, brown rice, oatmeal, peanut and almond butter, whole wheat crackers, frozen strawberries, paper goods, and bags of coffee. Drew shook his head and laughed when I returned from the store with these items. I'd worn one of the surgical masks I'd ordered online a couple of weeks before and had gotten either nervous or puzzled stares in the supermarket. I ignored the instructions coming from the White House response team and modeled my behavior on the public's behavior in China. My hands did tremble as I touched each item on the shelves; once done, I doused them with sanitizer.

The second Sunday of the month, the governor issued a statement in which, among other things, he assured us that the risk remained low in New York. Drew watched intently, his breathing slowed. Not mine. The governor could reassure us with all his mighty certainty, but I knew better.

Monday morning, I put on the news first thing upon waking. As I suspected, the number of cases in New York was steadily rising—and those were only the ones accounted for. Yet a meditative calm suffused through me, as if I were a skier soaring down a mountain without fear of tripping, tumbling, or crashing.

"You should work from home," I said to Drew.

"I can't." He stood there in his towel and underwear, fresh from his shower.

"Things are going to get worse."

In his sly, sweet voice: "I'm glad you still care about me."

He ran his fingers through his blow-dried hair. I felt the pull of desire for him—my odd response to crisis. We'd gone from having sex almost every day to a week without as much as a kiss. Drew hadn't pressured me, although we'd shared the bed. He'd apologized about his "huge, asshole mistake" with Audrey several times. "I hope you can forgive me, eventually," was the last mention.

Had I? No. But the barricade I'd built between us was breaking down.

"When does your shift start?" he asked.

"Eleven."

"*You* calling in sick?"

"Can't afford to."

"We'll be okay. We're young and healthy. We're the lucky ones."

"Probably. In general, plagues tended to affect the more vulnerable. But the Spanish Flu killed more young people than old."

"Oh, yeah, Ms. Google?" he asked, his jaw set. "Why?"

"They were mostly poor immigrants, living and working in crowded conditions."

"See? We *are* lucky."

"No one knows enough about this one yet, the scope of it, the magnitude." The last word reverberated in my ears.

"Let's wait and see."

There was no point debating. Smart as Drew was, this was not his area of expertise. I was no virologist, but I *was* a science geek.

In the coffee shop, there was an extra buzz of tension. Less chatter, no laughter, customers grim-faced in a stoic procession, caffeinating themselves to get on with their daily grind. It was Jerod, Tracey, and me, hustling to fill orders. The foreboding feeling trailed like a sick, wheezing dog, sensing its imminent demise. I regarded the atmosphere with an outsider's curiosity: yes, worse was coming. Yet having adapted to tragedy, I could adjust to this, too.

A couple of hours into my shift, my phone pinged. After I finished making a soy latte, I read the message from Audrey: *Haven't heard from you in a while. You ok?*

Yeah. Sorry.

Thought you were ghosting me.

I *had* been avoiding my conflicted feelings about her. I wanted to believe Drew wasn't deceiving me, which would mean Audrey was either duplicitous or confused.

Any new breakthroughs in hypnosis?

I took the receipt for my next order.

Audrey: *Dr. M thinks memory loss is from drug or traumatic amnesia.*

Maybe it's better to have amnesia now, with everything going on. I added a frowning-face emoji.

The bubbles on my screen bobbed like otter heads, in and out of view as I made an espresso macchiato. *My roommates are going back to Indiana and Vermont.*

Great! No more probs with Glinda.

Dr. Morris is taking some time off out of "caution." I'm freaking out.

Frown emoji. *Really sorry, Auds. But gotta work. Customers. I'll call u.*

I knew I wouldn't.

I had to choose a side. By staying with Drew, I'd chosen his.

By mid-month, we were watching the run-up to a tsunami that was certain to level the land. Only we weren't running from it; when not at work, we were sheltering in place. Drew no longer doubted my reactions, such as scanning news sites targeted for public health officials, or ordering nonperishables from Amazon before they ran short. I felt empowered, capable of taking on this giant.

"You seem better," he noted, "just when everyone else is falling apart."

"I feel . . ." I searched for the word as I wiped down the kitchen cabinet with sanitizer, "equipped."

The outside world mirrored my inner one, energizing me.

Drew consulted me before responding to his mother's panicked phone calls. "Look, Mom," he said, strung out after an intense workday, followed by his last in-person evening seminar, "if it comes to that, I'll go to the house on the Cape, if Danny isn't using it."

"What was that about?" I asked once he'd hung up. We were sitting at the kitchen table, Drew still in his work clothes, me in my sweats. I'd made us peppermint tea, which was still too hot to sip. "What house on the Cape? Who is Danny?"

"My grandparents' place in Woods Hole. We share it with my uncle's family, split up the summer. Danny's my cousin who sometimes crashes there on school breaks. But my mom said he's doing a semester in New Zealand. They shut down their borders, so he's staying there through August."

"Nice to have that option."

His family's money was a shimmering overcoat that could protect them, not just from rain but from viral droplets.

"Well, I don't. I have to finish my internship," Drew said.

"My dad thinks I should come back to New Jersey."

"When did he say this?"

I blew on the tea, stared at the pale green liquid. "He called me the other day. I promised I'd get back to him."

"Did you?"

"I left a message, said I was worried about them, to stay put in the house as much as possible."

If my dad got ill, I'd crumble. Yet keeping my distance from them was an imperative. I couldn't allow myself to be pulled into the undertow of my mother's depression.

Drew frowned. "Elle, you have to talk to them, after everything they've been through."

"I told him I need to be here, definitely for the health insurance through work—which is true, especially now."

"He's worried about you. Just reassure him you're all right. Of course you can't move there."

"He thinks I'm still at Nora's."

Drew nodded in encouragement. "That's okay. It doesn't matter."

"I'll do it now." I pushed the favorite star on my phone, and my dad answered after two rings. "Hi," I said. "What's going on there? How's Mom? She's staying home, right?"

"Yes. She was starting to get better, sleeping less, eating more."

"That's great!"

"It *was*. She's had a setback; she's frightened by this . . . whatever the hell it is."

"Of course she is. Everyone is," I said, with some of my old, star-student conviction. "You have to protect yourself, for Mom's sake."

And mine.

"She loves your guy."

Drew? "What guy?"

"Your governor. She wishes Josh's doctor had had his confidence, that he'd been more on top of things."

My governor was not on top of things; he's just a better actor than Lawrence Olivier. But better not to scare her more. "That's her depression talking."

"Yeah. Hey, Ellie, the law school is switching to online for the rest of the semester—and the instructions are confusing. Could use some help."

I laughed in relief. "That's so good to hear. We can FaceTime and I'll explain."

The coffee shop closed temporarily, and we were paid for thirty days. I doubted any of us would be returning this spring, so I hugged Tracey and Jerod goodbye. I tried to tamp down my terror over losing my benefits.

"Upside is Gracie can relax now that schools are closing," Jerod said. His family lived in Miami, forty minutes from the massacre in Parkland. His fifteen-year-old sister, Gracie, had been struggling with anxiety attacks ever since: startling during thunderstorms or when a door slammed shut, sticking close to the walls when she walked from one class to the other, avoiding trips to the mall or the movies.

"You going back to Florida?" Tracey asked him that last afternoon.

"Hell no," he said. "I'll take my chances here in my crappy, overcrowded dorm."

We set ourselves up in the spacious apartment. Drew was using the second bedroom as his office, dressed in his ironed cotton shirt and shorts for his video conferences. I sat cross-legged on the stripped mattress—laundry to do later—and stared at a graph comparing the

United States to Italy's viral trajectory on my laptop. The caseload was soaring here, at the epicenter of the country.

I called Nora from my bed. "Do you have a minute?"

"A couple," she said. "I have to deal with this Zoom shit with my team. We tried it yesterday. This one guy was bouncing around like he was in a space capsule. Great view of his nose hair."

"Lovely! So, obviously, I need a new gig, one I can do from home. I have to make at least enough to pay for Obamacare. I figured with schools closed, parents might be willing to hire more tutors to help them cope."

"Did Jasmine get in touch with you? She promised she would."

"No. I'm sure she's dealing with a lot. Should I try her again?"

"Definitely. You have to. Elle," she said, her voice dropping, "I'm getting scared. People are dying from this thing."

"Yes, but you won't. Be careful."

"How?"

"Order masks online and wear them when you're outside the apartment. Do it today, if Amazon still has them in stock."

"I must have missed that latest piece of advice."

"It's *my* advice. The authorities are behind, either in keeping track or reporting," I said boldly, and straightened my back. I might not have been an epidemiologist, but I could make accurate predictions from the statistics as they became available. "Look to Singapore and Hong Kong."

"Is this as bad as SARS?"

Worse.

"I don't know what's going to happen."

Actually, I had a good idea. The city had been reduced to a subway train whose brakes had failed while the engineers fought over how to stop the crash.

"New York is in big trouble," I'd announced to Drew last night, in detached, research mode. In my element, again, at last.

Drew cracked the knuckle of his index finger with his thumb. Then moved onto the next finger, then the next. "We should go to the Cape until this thing passes."

Those words—*this thing passes*—caused my neck to shrink down into my shoulders. There was no way to gauge the length of time the crisis would last. I'd be alone with Drew, possibly for months. Could I stand such confinement? Hard enough if I trusted my companion without question, if his presence were a safe haven. But, I reasoned, it was here, in this smaller space, or further from contagion, in a larger one.

It would mean disclosing the situation to my parents. Unless I presented the plan as a group sojourn. "Could Nora come?"

"Sure."

Nora's voice caught when I spoke to her. "When do the locusts appear?"

"Leave the city with us. Drew's family has a house in the country. You could stay with us."

"He has a country house?"

"Nora, he's rich."

"Clearly. You like that about him. I get it."

As opposed to Matthew, who was tired of having a roommate at thirty-one years old. He found it infantilizing.

"It does make things easier."

I thought of that day in Anna Nuñez's garage, the Burberry coat, the lacquered lighter, the recognition that her trust fund would pave the way to her smooth future, not just the money but the connections. I might not have made the leap between designer clothes and social contacts with bigwigs like the science editors at the *New York Times* or the *Washington Post*, not at sixteen years old, when I hadn't even considered what my career path would be. But I knew I was smarter and more disciplined and a harder worker than Anna and that it wouldn't matter one whit.

"I'd never realized how loaded Drew was," I said. "Josh didn't seem to notice the differences in their circumstances. Maybe because Josh could get a scholarship; sports are rewarded more than grades. Anyone can get good grades."

"Not anyone," Nora said.

"It never occurred to me that if Josh wasn't trying so hard to get and keep his soccer scholarship, he wouldn't have become an addict. He could have escaped the fire. Maybe there would never have been one."

"Oh, Ellie. Let's not backtrack."

"You're right." The city was going to be full of Joshes soon, dead by infection from another source. My attention would be turned away from myself.

"Shit, I have to Zoom. Let me text you later?"

"Text me anytime."

"All day long."

We laughed. She was my best friend, after all.

By April 1, Drew and I had been holed up in the apartment without outside contact for twelve days. At first we'd picked up our deliveries, but now we were ordering food through Grubhub—when there was availability—and Amazon, which was frequently out of toilet paper and other necessities. The streets were empty and still, like a diorama of a long-lost city from an ancient time. The only reminders that living beings still inhabited Manhattan were the screams of the ambulance sirens and the 7 p.m. gathering at our open windows, when people clapped and cheered and hollered for the first responders as they made their way home after their grueling shifts. Refrigerated trailers were parked outside a few hospitals, and white tents set up near another. "Surreal," Drew muttered when he read the report online.

Living through a global crisis, I'd imagined, would be a blitz of noise and commotion. This was the opposite. The honks and squeaks and din of car traffic had all but vanished. The annoyances of civilization were muted, as if by an act of biological warfare. Yet the buildings remained, monuments of dignity, unfazed. I felt much like these edifices, preternaturally calm. After Josh had died, the world had continued. Now, the world had stopped, in shock and heartsick. This mass isolation and grief felt like company, like comfort.

Every evening, after Drew and I applauded, we walked down the stairs—avoiding the elevators—wearing our surgical masks, a container of hand sanitizer in each of our pockets. We went for a walk in Riverside Park, making sure to keep our distance from the few other outliers who dared to decamp from their apartments. They hurried past us with numb or frightened expressions. No one smiled. There was the occasional head shaker who'd meet our gaze. Dogs pulled on their leashes to greet us. Their owners restrained them with tugs and firm commands. I longed to touch these animals, with their open-mouthed grins and frantic tails, to feel their warm bodies against mine. Each one reminded me of Glinda and my guilt over Audrey.

But I didn't text her. I didn't call. I held onto what I had, having to salvage my situation. Drew and I were a couple again, having sex almost every night. For me, it was like opening a valve to release trapped air. I couldn't allow myself doubts about him.

I had to focus on employment. Parents were scrambling to cope with school closures and online classes. Yet even with Drew's influence—he was friendly with a student whose father operated a tutoring service—no one was hiring new tutors. "Jerry thinks things will pick up closer to the end of the term with finals and papers due." Jerry: the man who ran the business.

"Okay," I said, "I hope it's soon."

While researching employment opportunities, I had TV news on in the background. I tried to discern the truth in the Tower of Babel that made up national and local leadership.

I read aloud the statistics to Drew at breakfast. "Which means it will double in two weeks."

"Time to leave."

"It's a long ride. What about bathroom breaks?" I asked. A new wrinkle.

"We'll pee outside."

I pictured myself squatting on the grass along the highway. "I can't do that."

"I'll stand guard."

"I'll hold it in if I can."

"Let's go Saturday so I can air out the house on Sunday and we can set ourselves up."

I nodded. "I need to tell my parents. And see if Nora wants to come."

"Oh, right," Drew said, a hint of disappointment in his voice.

I called my father. He said, "Honey, we're so concerned about you."

"I'm going away." I gave my prepared statement: a few of us were driving to the Cape to stay in a friend's house. He wouldn't ask for specifics: Which friends? Whose house? Where exactly? My mother was the one who used to keep track of the details.

"You can reach me on my cell, and I'll let you know when we get there."

"What if you don't feel well?" he asked. "It makes more sense for you to come here."

"Dad, I'll be okay. It's isolated—which is good—but there are hospitals and medical facilities. I checked. Anyway, that's not going to matter. I'll be fine."

"You'll be so far from us."

"Do you guys need help?" I asked, stretching my legs on the bed, pointing my toes until they ached. *Please say no.*

"We're okay. Mom can't see Dr. Weissman in person anymore, but that seems to be fine with her. She's just frustrated with the investigation."

Good. The Same. "Have they given up?"

"Not officially, because of Josh's . . . because it involved loss of life. They're facing department shortages."

"Are they delaying it?"

"That's the official word. I think they've reached the end of the line. Nothing suspicious was found at the scene—which they determined months ago—and there's no evidence of foul play."

"What about the silver car in the driveway?"

My father sighed. "It could have been a fluke. Or a mistake in timing on the neighbor's part. There is just no new evidence of anything. Mom feels they are giving up. Hold on. She wants to talk to you."

I bent my body forward. If I could touch the tip of my big toe without strain, my mother wouldn't be angry with me.

"Ellie?" she said, in a flat voice.

I snapped back up. "Hi, Mom. How you feeling?"

"Sergeant Abbott isn't answering my calls anymore."

"He must have a lot to deal with."

"We all do."

I murmured agreement.

"You're going to the Colinses' house in Woods Hole?"

I inhaled sharply. "Have you spoken to Drew's mom?" He'd promised me that he hadn't mentioned my name. If he'd lied, I could never trust him again.

"No. Not in months. I assumed."

"Oh, well, it's me and Drew and Nora and her friend. He's the only person with . . . the resources."

"Good," she said, not warning me like my father had.

But I wasn't upset. My mother and I were the same in this respect. Already bereaved, we weren't deterred by the unraveling of the ordinary world.

chapter twenty-two

It was such a relief to see Nora in Riverside Park that I lurched toward her for a hug before hanging back and nearly stumbling over a rock. Touching wasn't allowed, of course—was potentially treacherous.

Nora greeted me, her hand covering her mouth, "Is there any way to weaponize the bird flu?"

"Someone doesn't have to weaponize the bird flu." I smiled. "The birds are doing that."

These were quotes from the movie *Contagion*, which we'd watched obsessively in high school. For the adrenaline rush and the horror, and to witness Gwyneth Paltrow seize and foam at the mouth. It had been entertainment and fascinating to me. We'd rewind to the brain dissection and grasp each other's arms.

"I miss you," I said.

"Same."

We walked toward the river, standing far enough away from each other that we had to raise our voices to be heard. The early evening air was cool, the sky a collage of dusty-gray clouds with slivers of white and pale-blue background peeking through. I watched a plane overhead and wondered who was on it, if they were fleeing, refugees from our metropolis.

"How's Matthew holding up?" I asked.

"Same."

Every few days, he'd relay that supplies like new N-95 masks still hadn't arrived at the hospital. Nora tried to reassure him. Earlier in the week, she'd checked with me to see if I had any news about shipments, as if I worked for the CDC. Which made me feel strong, affirmed, a survivalist who could serve as a role model. Matthew's colleagues were increasingly agitated, snapping at each other, hollow eyed, straggly haired, and gray faced. Everyone appeared the same to him, no matter their race or gender: waxy, bloodless, and exhausted.

He was unwilling to meet with Nora, even outside. They connected, after his shifts, on the phone. Sometimes he fell asleep while Nora spoke. When she heard his gentle snores, she coaxed him awake by repeating his name and then insisted he go to bed.

"I need to see him," she said, "in person."

"He's just trying to protect you."

"Yeah." She stared at the river. "I don't think I can come with you to the Cape."

"Why not?" I glanced at my friend. The weather had rendered her slightly wild: her feather earrings fluttered in the wind; her hair curled around her face. But the fear on her face—her lips a tight band and her nostrils flared—were not from a dip in temperature. "Doesn't Matthew think it will be safer for you there?"

"It's not about him. I just don't want to leave. And there's Oni. She shouldn't be alone."

"She can come, too."

"Drew won't mind?"

"I'm sure it'll be fine."

Better than fine. I'd pay more attention to him if Oni accompanied my best friend. A wave of regret flushed through me for extending the invitation. I wanted Nora to myself.

"That's really generous. But we can go to my folks' if it gets too bad here."

"You still don't like Drew, do you?"

Nora dug the heel of her hand against her temple, as if I were giving her a headache. "I'm literally losing sleep over the fact that my boyfriend could get this horrible plague and that's what you care about, if I like Drew?"

"I'm sorry." I slapped my hands over my face. What a pig I was! "You're right. That was really selfish of me."

"Yeah. Plus, you're projecting."

"You think *I* don't like Drew?"

"You were miserable the night you came over."

"Couples fight."

"Do *you* like him enough to be in this much of a committed situation?"

"For now," I said, quickly. "Considering that it's just been the two of us in the middle of a shit show, we're getting along well."

She nodded slightly, as if even this slight movement was hard-won.

We'd reached the Hudson River, passing the magnolia trees on the way. I loved their cotton candy–colored blossoms, and how they reminded me of fancy British hats worn at weddings.

I gazed out at the water, which rippled serenely. "It's so eerie, the quiet."

"Everyone but you is losing it, which is pretty ironic," Nora said. She glanced around and I followed her gaze. The buildings across the river were squat and unevenly spaced, like rotten teeth.

"There's something I haven't told you," I said.

"*You* aren't sick, are you?"

"No! It's about Drew and . . . Audrey. She confided in me. I'm not sure if I should even share this with you."

Nora looked askance. "Don't, then."

"Am I driving you nuts?"

"It's okay, a distraction."

"This has just been bothering me for a while. I need a sounding board."

She raised her chin, still proud of her status as excellent secret-keeper. "I won't say anything to anyone."

I nodded. "The night I stayed over, we fought about it."

"You and Audrey?"

"Me and Drew."

Nora stopped short. "Back up. I'm confused. I thought Audrey and Drew hated each other."

"Apparently not. Misconception on Josh's part."

"Is this about Josh and the fire?"

"Not directly. I mean, no. Drew had nothing to do with that. If you don't hate Drew yet, you will now." I took in a deep breath and said, "They slept together. It was just the once. At a party. They were drunk."

Slept together. According to Drew.

"Jesus," Nora exclaimed. "Did Josh find out?"

"On the day of the fire. From Audrey. Well, not exactly the details, but yeah."

She rushed toward me, and I extended my arm, as if in a salute, so she'd keep her distance. There was not a soul nearby to witness her misstep.

"What are you doing, Elle?"

"We can't get too close."

"Not that. Why are you staying with Drew?"

"He promised me. It was just the once. He feels horrible about it."

"Did he confess this to you before you moved in?" Her eyes were lit up with rage.

I studied the ground, the tufts of grass and scattered twigs. "Only after Audrey told me about her talk with Josh."

"Wow, so brave of him. What you said before—you're no longer projecting. I *don't* like Drew. And I don't like you being with him, how it's changed you. The world is imploding and here you are, defending him. What I don't get is why Audrey came to you."

Because she believes she was raped.

"It's complicated."

"Um, yeah." Nora's laugh rattled. "Audrey thinks Josh burnt down your house, doesn't she? He was already depressed before she hooked up with his best friend."

Guilt draped over me like a hood. For lying about Audrey's "version" of what transpired at the party, for selfishly confiding in Nora when she had her own worries. "We don't know. We, uh, both feel responsible."

"It's not the same thing, Elle. Stop taking it out on yourself and get angry at the right people."

"I keep wondering about this other thing." I quickly explained the missing piece in the police investigation. Nora's mouth opened in astonishment as she listened. "I went to Audrey's house a while ago and saw a silver car there, in her garage."

"Oh, my God! This is all so fucked up! Was she there? Do you think *she* burned down your house?"

"No idea. I just want to forgive Drew. This situation is messing with my head."

"Because it's twisted and sick. You can't go to the Cape with him."

"He didn't hurt Josh on purpose. And he and Audrey, it was one night."

"That makes what they did okay?"

I turned to observe the river, again, unable to deal with Nora's scrutiny. "No. It's not okay. But he's a good guy who made a mistake."

"Listen to yourself, Elle. To your hyper-cerebral self, not the one able to cope during a plague, this other shadow self who has taken over your brilliant mind in Drew-related matters."

"There's nothing wrong with my mind. Not brilliant, but it's fine. My circumstances suck."

"You need to get away from him."

"I'm basically unemployed, broke, and dependent on Drew right now. It's him or my parents, and the thought of living with him doesn't make me feel hopeless."

Nora stared at me. "I'm seriously concerned about you."

"I can handle this crisis."

"What about handling Drew?"

"He's temporary." Wasn't everyone?

Nora said, "I just hope he realizes that."

After we parted ways, I checked my phone. There were texts from CVS, informing me that my refill of clonazepam (the generic form of Klonopin) was ready and to view delivery eligibility, and one from Audrey. She wrote: *My hypnotist died! His office left a message.*

Good, I thought. *Now you'll stop searching for answers, leave well enough alone.*

What a vile person I'd become, my response to a man's death so merciless, so selfish.

You didn't wish the doctor dead, I reminded myself. I stood in front of my/Drew's apartment building, far enough away from the awning so that Anthony, the daytime doorman, wouldn't notice me, and wrote quickly.

I'm really sorry to hear.

I can't handle being alone anymore. My mom wants me to come home. Are you going to your parents'?

My windpipe closed. I grabbed the water out of my backpack and guzzled some down. Then I screwed the top back on the box. I couldn't divulge my exit plan to her for fear that she'd ask to come along. That is, if she honestly didn't remember having sex with Drew. *If* it had been consensual and not assault. If—I had to shut down ruminations, which would get me nowhere.

No. Staying put for now.

I still dream about the rape. Sometimes about the fire.

You should tell your therapist about that.

Meaning: not me.

She wrote back: *I know you're going through a lot.*

You too.

Can we keep talking?

No, I thought. *I need a break.*

Yeah. Of course.

We ate leftover Chinese takeout, mostly brown rice, dumplings, and some soggy broccoli. Drew didn't have much of an appetite; he pushed all but the rice aside, even the few pieces of straw mushrooms, which he usually loved. I nabbed them, with his permission. Everything had disagreed with my stomach for months, yet now I was starving. I also was sleeping better, as if hibernation were healing.

Drew, on the other hand, woke up several times each night, as he would report the following day. Bad dreams would disrupt his rest, and he had resorted to drinking more coffee to keep up with work. He was increasingly short-tempered and then apologetic for his moodiness. When I asked him about his nightmares, he'd murmur that they were about Josh and I wouldn't push him further. Better to be spared the details, to accept the respite from my personal sorrow that this plague had afforded me.

We'd accepted how glued we'd become to our phones and laptops, even during meals. Drew was finishing up a project, and I was reading an article on what seemed like an overly optimistic endgame for the pandemic—*I could pitch a better piece*—when a text arrived.

It was another one from Audrey. *I'm on my way home, to my mom's. You should come back, too.*

Irritation fluttered through me. Why was she bothering me again? *I'm okay.*

I have a bad feeling about you being there.

The muscles in my neck seized up with anticipation. She was referring to Drew, not the city. Her memory must have been restored. Or she'd been lying to me all along and was ready to admit that rape was a cover story. And what about the silver car in our driveway? Was it hers, and if so, why had she shown up at our house that night? To confess? To plead her case? Audrey was like a crossword puzzle I couldn't solve. As soon as one answer fit, it canceled another one.

I laid the phone down gingerly, as if handling it was perilous.

Drew asked, "What's up? More terrible statistics?"

"Yeah."

When he returned to his screen, I wrote: *What do you mean?*

Scared for you. Your parents have already lost Josh. You should leave.

So, not about Drew. *What does your shrink say?*

I was gaslighting Audrey, turning her anxiety into a pathology rather than a reaction to a terrible event. Her messages didn't read like pretense, a scheme to hide her one-night stand with my boyfriend. But, I reassured myself, she could have blocked out her role in sleeping with Drew after she drank the spiked punch. The fault probably lay with a third party, the person who drugged her. Drew wasn't culpable in any of these scenarios—which is what mattered most to me.

She sent: *PTSD. Having flashbacks.*

Any more clues who the guy was?

Still blurry. And no more hypnosis.

Trauma had become tedious: hers and mine. I'd felt frayed, leaked of empathy, reduced to my survival instincts for months. Now, as the world was beginning to implode, people crumbling, I was coping.

I don't know what to say, Auds.

Get out.

"Elle," Drew said, his impatient gaze on me. "Who was that?"

"Audrey. She's a mess today."

"What does she want *now*?"

"She went to her mom's. She's bugging me about going back to New Jersey."

"What's with her obsession with *you*?"

We clicked. We liked each other. We formed a bond over our loss, one that excluded you. Why, you'll ask, and the answer would involve sex and declarations of love and the obligations these things created.

I said, "Substitute for Josh, maybe."

"No, that's not it. She's upset you're still with me after what happened between us."

"She doesn't remember who did . . . who the man was."

"You haven't told her?" Blood rushed into his face.

"It's not my place to say anything."

He shook his head hard, like an animal with a bug stuck in his ear. "We have to clear things up. It would be better for all of us to get this out in the open."

"That's not your decision."

"If it's not mine and not yours, whose is it?"

"She has to come to it on her own. With her therapist."

Drew bit the knuckle of his index finger. It was Josh's habit, as a boy, which he'd outgrown by adolescence. The way he mimicked my brother's expression so effortlessly disturbed me. But I filed his gesture and my reaction under situational stress.

"Wouldn't it be better if she realized that she wasn't attacked, that she was complicit in what happened?" he asked.

"What if she doesn't see it that way?"

"This isn't a he said, she said. We've been over this."

"Let's not talk about her now."

I was selfish but, also, self-preserving. If Audrey's memory was restored, I'd be forced to justify my choice to live with the man she considered her rapist. *Now, not later—if, and when, the city healed.* I'd reached some sense of resolve. The world was heading toward a crisis; I had an advantage on others. I'd been honing the skills to survive a disaster for three seasons.

I rushed from my seat with my dinner plate. "One thing at a time."

"Just promise we'll clear the air with her soon. It will help our relationship."

"What's wrong with our relationship?"

Immediately, I regretted asking. What I craved was movement, not conversation. Skimming the surface of the frozen lake, not pounding the ice until it cracked open.

"Elle, I might be a man, but I'm not a moron. You haven't forgiven me." Before I could protest, he raised his hand. "It's on me, not you. What I did was a mistake, the sex and then hiding it from you. That's why transparency is the way to go now."

"We have to do what's right for Audrey, too. She's not up for a big confrontation. She's too fragile."

Which might or might not be true.

"What about us?" he asked, petulant.

"Let's get away, some distance. We need a break from this shit show."

"Good!" He clapped once.

I could train him into compliance if I just kept leading the way.

My phone rang. I scooped it off the table, peered at the screen, then pushed decline.

"Now what?"

"No idea. Probably spam."

"As long as it's not Audrey. Jesus."

"Nope." I read the surname again: Goldsmith. "This is so weird. I think it was my next-door neighbor."

"The one who helped you, across the street?"

"Weirder. The old woman with the dog."

"Eyelashes?" I'd told him about how the only time I'd seen her without the fake ones was the night of the fire. "What does she want?" Then he touched his hand to his heart. "I hope your parents are okay."

"They don't live near her anymore."

"Oh, right. Good."

I waited to see if she'd left a message. But when one didn't register, I called her.

She picked up immediately. "Rita Goldsmith."

"Yes, hi," I said, "this is Ellie Stone."

"Eleanor, hello."

Eleanor? How did she know my full name, the one I rarely used?

"Gayle Peterson gave me your private number when we met recently. She had it from when you babysat for her girls. Everyone's being cautious now, chatting on our lawns, what with this flu going around. We've been concerned about your poor family."

I imagined the two women, bundled in early spring sweaters,

under the Petersons' yet-to-bloom dogwood tree, cupping mugs of steaming tea. I'd never seen any indication that Mrs. Goldsmith, who was at least twenty years her senior, was friendly with Mrs. Peterson. Apparently, they were, enough that they gossiped about us.

"How are you doing, my dear?" she asked. "You poor thing, everything you've been through."

"I'm . . . okay. How are you?"

"Never mind that. Old age, not for sissies, as they say."

"Did the police get in touch with you again about what happened?"

"Not at all! I had to telephone *them* the other day after speaking with Gayle."

"You called the sergeant in charge?" I asked. Drew's face furrowed with sympathy.

"Yes, I did. I mentioned to Gayle how interested he was in my observations when he interviewed me. It turns out he spoke with her, too. *I* recognized that car," she said in a hushed tone now. "It was dark out but, with the fire, I could see quite clearly. It was the same one I'd seen many times in your driveway, over the years, while I was walking Franklin." Her basset hound.

I envisioned Mrs. Goldsmith as she appeared that night, in her lilac robe, with that silver bracelet around her ankle, setting our house ablaze. For attention, to play a role in a dramatic story. But the absurdity was too much.

"Do you know whose car it was, then?" I asked.

"No, my dear. I haven't been snooping on your guests. My husband and I frequented car shows for years, mostly of the fancier brands, just for fun. I developed an interest in automobiles and I can say for sure that the one in your driveway was silver, a four-door sedan, most likely a Toyota Corolla or a Nissan Versa."

"It wasn't mine," I snapped. "My car is blue."

"Of course not. I'm well aware that you drive a blue Hyundai Accent."

So, a snoop after all.

My shoulders fell and I unclasped my hand—the knuckles yellow, not white—the one not holding the phone. There were scratch marks on my wrist where my skin had itched since the autumn. What had I expected, that she'd accuse me of arson?

"I'm sorry, I'm not following. Why did you contact Officer Abbott again?"

"Frustration, my dear. I expected that, by now, the authorities would have gotten further along, especially since I'd provided them with a significant clue."

How many cozy mystery shows had she watched in which the village reverend or his savvy female gardener solved local murders?

"What can I do for you?" I asked.

"I thought you might be aware of the comings and goings, family and friends. It could be a comfort to your parents to know that your brother might not have had a hand in his own tragedy."

"My parents are aware of how helpful you've been. Thank you. But we're not sure whose car it was. There wasn't enough to go on."

"I understand. That really is the detectives' job to solve! I thought that young woman might have some answers, the one I noticed taking photographs of your house a few days after the fire. I assumed she was some kind of investigator, even though she didn't look the part: such—well—*sexy* clothes and too much makeup."

That raw patch on my wrist flared up, tender. I visualized Anna Nuñez in an FB photo, one of them I'd glimpsed in the burn unit: skinny black jeans, mesh crop top, strappy black sandals displaying her pedicure, and matte red lipstick to match the nail color.

"Was this someone you'd seen before, one of our friends?" I asked.

"No, dear, not that I can recall. When I mentioned her to the sergeant, he wasn't that concerned. He said that fires can attract all kinds of curious, kooky people. At this point, the investigation is bound to fall apart, unless someone steps in."

"Why?" I shoved the thought of Anna aside. There was no way to verify the voyeur had been her. And even if there was, I'd vowed not to cause Anna more pain—no matter what she might have done. "Has anything changed?"

"Haven't you heard?"

"Heard what?"

"Sergeant Abbott is on leave from the department. I spoke with a desk officer just the other day."

"Did this desk officer explain what's going on with him?"

"*That* they wouldn't say. But I have my suspicions—and my contacts over there," she bragged. "I just don't want to be a source of gossip."

"Is he sick?"

"Not confirmed yet. I thought you'd want to pass on the message to your parents. If they have the stamina for it, they should stay on top of the police, not let them drop the ball."

"I'll tell them," I said, certain I wouldn't. My mother had complained that Abbott wasn't answering her calls but hadn't been apprised of this recent development. She would be outraged that our former neighbor, who was not involved in our tragedy, had been informed.

"I'm just curious, Mrs. Goldsmith. Why are you so interested?"

"Justice, my dear. Justice." She sighed. "Stay safe from this dreadful flu."

"You too."

I didn't bother to correct her about the nature of this scourge. She'd discover for herself, soon enough, what was to come.

chapter twenty-three

We departed into the cool, damp morning, a day that would only get frostier and more humid as we headed north. Drew had directed me to pack a few heavy sweaters and a winter jacket; the weather could be unpredictable in early spring on the Cape, he claimed. Where wasn't it, anymore?

Drew insisted on driving my car since he was familiar with the route—not that it mattered. He used Waze or Google Maps, like everyone else. I was only too glad to oblige and take on the less stressful role of passenger. An hour and a half later, Drew was cursing the stop-and-go traffic, the "assholes" weaving in and out of lanes, the non-signalers. His one hand was clenched on the wheel, and the other was a fist shoved into his cheek.

Forced to decelerate, he shouted, "Fuck you!"

"Um, sorry?"

"I was talking to the dickhead in the white Lexus."

"You know he can't hear you, right?"

"Relieves my frustration."

"Is this a harbinger of things to come?" I was only half joking. As confined as we'd been in the city, there was a sense of comradery there. If absolutely necessary, I could take to the street and find others who were walking or running or biking to escape their partners. On the Cape, we'd be secluded.

He smiled wanly. "Only of being in Connecticut."

"I thought all WASPs loved it here."

"That's a cliché. It's the third-smallest state but might as well be Texas for how long it takes to get through it."

An exaggeration as we entered tiny Rhode Island within two hours, a sliver of land so quick to traverse, it lacked rest stops. Which was fine, since I'd sworn off using them. Drew put on the podcast *The Daily*.

"What a fucking mess," he said after a few minutes of listening.

"Yes."

"Music?"

"Please."

We rode peacefully over the Bourne Bridge and took the scenic route that hugged the water. I opened my window to the crisp slap of air, the rustling wind, the birdsong. Once we entered the town, I was surprised, despite the giveaway of its name, to find the place full of woodsy, twisted roads. All the pictures I'd seen of the Cape were of beaches and rectangular, shingled homes with shutters painted in nautical colors. But this was a different landscape, one that I imagined would turn a lush, deep green within a month's time, trees popping with pink, white, and lavender flowers. There was nothing open and expansive about the street that ended with Drew's family home. It sloped down a hill that led to a thicket of protected land—the Colinses' backyard.

"I'll take you to the main street later, plenty of ocean views, don't worry," Drew said.

"I'm not," I said, noting the rocks lining the pathway, the pine needles littering the ground, the shrubs and ferns and bed of green.

Although nature appealed to my senses, it also screamed disease. Up here, tick-borne ones like Lyme or even Rocky Mountain spotted fever were possibilities. Mosquitos could carry threats, like West Nile.

"We need bug repellent," I proclaimed. My voice rang in my head from stuffed ears. Allergies, I hoped. Car door ajar, a shiver ran through me from the cold. "I didn't think to bring any."

"I'm sure there's some inside."

"It'll probably be expired. Can we order stuff?"

"There's a CVS and a Walgreens. I made a list of places that do curbside pickup and those that deliver food and other stuff."

"Thanks. It just looks so remote here."

"This time of year, the town *is* pretty dead, other than the scientists and students at the Oceanographic Institute."

"Thank God for scientists."

"We can go into Falmouth if you want more action."

"What kind of action are you talking about?" Massachusetts had issued a "stay-at-home advisory"; non-essential businesses had been ordered to close.

"There's a French pastry shop there."

"Oh, good! Croissants go well with pulmonary distress."

"Exactly. You'll love it. They have cream puffs and chocolate tarts, your faves." He sprang open the trunk. "Let's lug our stuff in first."

My computer bag strapped around my shoulder, I grabbed my rolling suitcase. "God, I have to pee so bad."

"You can have your pick of bathrooms."

Set back from the road, behind a column of trees, was the contemporary-design house, consisting of floor-to-nearly-tip-of-the-triangular-roof windows. Once inside, Drew parked his luggage in the entrance and said, "This is it."

"It" was an open-plan palace with high, cathedral ceilings, living room on one side, modern kitchen on the other, plus a separate dining area, a full bathroom, and a laundry area. I scurried to the downstairs toilet, where I texted Nora: *OMG. He's so loaded. Josh never talked about that.*

My brother had to play soccer for his college scholarship, while his best friend's family could have just donated a building to his university of choice. Or, at least, a wing. Had that difference in their circumstances chafed against Josh, who'd turned to drugs to keep himself in the game?

I followed Drew through what felt like a maze to the enclosed porch, up the stairs to a quick round-up of the four bedrooms, balcony, two other baths, and open hallway with views of the floor below. There was a finished basement with a "maid's quarters."

"Want to see the pond?" he asked, as I stared at the row of large knives hanging on the magnetic bar next to a sink and small oven on this lowest level.

"You have a private pond?"

"There's one out back." He pointed to the sliding doors.

"Who *are* you?"

"It's not as big a deal as you think. There are these estates on the harbor that go for over ten million. Anyway, my mother and her brother inherited the house, not me."

"But you will someday."

"I guess, when my mother dies." He squinted at me. "Along with my cousins."

"I'd love to see your watering hole." I tried to sound jaunty, less invested.

We surveyed the pond, which shimmered in the waning sun. "It looks like pea soup in bad weather," Drew said.

Nora pinged me. *Money Honey.*

Health insurance!

Mine would run out in the third week of April. And then what would I do if infected, or worse yet, hospitalized?

You'll have to marry him for that.

Never.

Never say never.

She was joking. But how hard would it be to just slip into such an arrangement? Drew loved me and I felt attracted to, and protected by, him.

"What's up?" Drew asked, nodding in the direction of my phone. He'd started paying more attention to my notifications, jittery with anticipation or peeved at my being distracted. Or both.

"Just telling Nora we arrived."

"Good. Not Audrey." He headed back to the entranceway. "Want a beer?"

It was barely 5 p.m. We'd eaten PowerBars and trail mix for lunch, and I was hungry. Lately, Drew needed alcohol every day to unwind. "I'd love to have an early dinner."

"Give me a few minutes to chill. It was a long drive."

"I offered to split the driving."

He ignored me and rushed back outside to grab the canvas satchels I used, in the city, to grocery shop. I watched to see if his scowl disappeared once he was alone. But I couldn't tell from my viewpoint.

Drew was subdued and withdrawn that evening, after insisting that he pick up the pizza and salad from the neighboring town of Falmouth. "It's easier. We'll stick with peanut butter and beans after this," he said.

"Make sure to wash your hands afterward. Wear a mask."

"Thanks for the drill."

After we ate, he suggested we binge a Netflix show but couldn't last through the second episode. He went to bed early, and I followed him soon after into the pine-scented bedroom. The bed was king-sized with a fluffy comforter. Drew promised we'd change the sheets "tomorrow," but swore a housekeeper had cleaned the place after his cousins' last visit. "It's fine," I said. "There are no contagions here." He ignored this comment and flopped onto one side.

Despite the distance between us, I stirred several times when Drew moaned, cried out, or rolled over.

The first to awake, I faced an empty refrigerator. We'd planned to order a delivery of groceries after breakfast, so I settled for cold cereal without milk. As I munched on the dry organic flakes, Drew shuffled into the kitchen in thick boxer shorts, his Ralph Lauren navy hoodie, and thick wool socks. I was in my UNIQLO joggers and an old college sweatshirt, which didn't close; the zipper had jumped the tracks. Suddenly, I recalled the conversation in the cafeteria between Nora and me, all those years ago, when Anna and Claudia had invited us to pack up the designer garb to donate to Karen's Kloset. "I'm sick of this bargain shit my mom buys me," I'd confessed to my friend. Staring into my coffee cup, shame sluiced through me. I was no longer that kid in competition with her brother in Anna Nuñez's garage, but remnants of my former self still tugged at me. I would text Nora back: *Not marrying for money!*

"You look upset," Drew said. "Sorry I was so cranky last night."

"It's okay."

He handed me his iPad. "Let's order food. This place delivers. We can get whatever you want."

The grocery store was a high-end market with loads of prepared dishes, including quiches, casseroles, soups, fish, chicken, meat entrées, and four types of lasagna. We'd never have to turn on the oven except to heat up meals if we chose to be lazy.

"Says it will take four hours to fill," I said.

"I'm surprised it's not longer." He shrugged. "I can show you around town. It's tiny, but at least there's the view of the Vineyard, and no one is going to bump into us. The caseload isn't bad up here."

Not yet.

My phone pinged and, instinctively, I glanced down.

"What happened?" he asked when he saw my expression. "Who's sick?"

"No one. It's political."

The message from Audrey read: *Text me when you are alone, NOT with Drew.*

"I'd love to gaze upon the Vineyard."

We drove into the village and parked across from the harbor, Buzzards Bay a sparkling teal blue in the light. While strolling on Water Street, the drawbridge rose to allow fishing and sail boats to go out to sea or to return to Eel Pond, an enclosed area—that led to the aquarium—where ducks congregated near the docks. The few boats, steered by big-bellied men in sun hats, displayed American flags that flapped lazily in the breeze.

"Are they alerting the Canadians in case they wander into foreign territory?"

"Nautical tradition, probably, and colonial pride."

"Ah," I said. "Am I witnessing you in your natural element among your Puritan brethren? We Jews aren't part of that whole Mayflower deal."

"Josh was my best friend for twenty years," he said. "Suddenly, you're acting like I'm some hard-core WASP."

"Sorry, I was just trying to lighten things up. Things have been so heavy for so long."

He pinched the bridge of his nose as if to stave off a sinus headache. For a minute, no one said anything. "Yeah. I'm sorry, too."

It was too pleasant here to argue, even under a patchy sky. Sitting on a bench, on the other side of the bridge, I observed the gulls as they honked, chirped, dipped, and circled one another, in a kind of ceremonial dance. Almost seven months had passed since the fire, and my nervous system had spent most of it in a state of hypervigilance. Now, as the world was ending, I felt calmer.

"Good. You're smiling," Drew said. "I didn't mean to jump at you."

"Thanks for taking me to this cool town."

"Sure."

"You're fortunate to have grown up with this, even with all the fucked-up shit in your family."

"It's funny how we want what others have."

I noted the clouds had turned gray. "All I wanted was not to have to grind away to get somewhere in life. I worked so hard while Josh got all the praise."

"That's what I mean. You're so angry at your family, and I would have done anything to be part of it. I was so lonely. My mom tried, but she was preoccupied with her own loneliness once my dad left."

"What about your aunt and uncle and the cousins you split the house with?"

"I saw them, maybe, twice a year. My aunt barely spoke to me because I was this chubby, awkward loser. She didn't want me to rub off on Tracy and Dexter."

I whipped around and stared at him. "She named her kids after the characters in *The Philadelphia Story*?"

"See." He grinned. "That's what's so great about you. Who else would recognize a reference from an eighty-year-old movie?"

Sam. We'd watched the film together, along with *Adam's Rib* and *Bringing Up Baby*.

"I can see why you liked to hang out at my house," I said.

"You say that now. But you hated me back then. You can admit it."

"Hate is way too strong a word. You were a pest. But what was I? Certainly not a Tracy Lord."

"Josh was a Dexter Haven." He glimpsed up and raindrops fell onto his cheeks. "At least to me."

"We should go. No umbrella."

On the way back, my phone rang. I retrieved it from my canvas satchel to make sure my parents weren't calling. I'd texted my dad the night before to alert him that we'd arrived safely. He'd answered quickly: *Thanks for letting us know.* I posed my usual question: *How's Mom?* No response yet.

"Who was it?"

"No idea."

When her voicemail registered, I ignored it. Until that evening.

"Please, Ellie," she implored. "Call me when you're alone. Or when he's asleep."

Her memory is back.

I didn't wait for Drew to go to bed; he had reading to do for his seminar and was nervous because he'd fallen behind. The huge house could easily accommodate us both. He chose to work in one of the other bedrooms and, wrapped in an oversized sweater, I stood on the second-floor balcony, staring into the sable night. The backdrop befitted the tone of Audrey's message.

She picked up after the first ring. "Ellie."

"Hi."

"Is he there?"

The gust of winter caused me to shiver. I was tired, and like Drew, ready to speak directly. "Not right with me. Why?"

"This is just between you and me. I spoke to Maddie, the friend I went with to Rory's."

"Well, that's good."

"Yeah. She moved to LA in January. I hadn't been in touch for a while, so she thought I'd ghosted her. It took me a while to come clean about why. We caught up on stuff, how surreal this corona-thing is, how scared we are. It's getting bad in California. Not as bad as here yet."

Here. In the darkness, the pond was a barely discernable black eye.

"It will," I mumbled.

"So, I finally told her, and Maddie was shocked. I wish I'd done so sooner; she was really supportive. Also—get this, Ellie—she'd heard rumors about other girls being drugged at the party. A bunch of them wondered if there were roofies in their drinks."

I reached for the railing and used it as a ballast. Squatting down, I could feel the doubts clear from my mind as if a cyclone had torn them from the roots. Drew was not to blame after all.

"Wow!" I said. "Was anyone else . . . assaulted?"

"Not that she knows of. But a couple of them needed rides home to sleep it off."

"Did Maddie see who spiked your drink?"

Not Drew. What would have been his motivation?

"No. But she said Rory poured a lot of cups and put them on the table for whoever took them. Maybe he spiked, like, random ones."

I couldn't stand this anymore, keeping track of the intersecting lines of the story for months, a story that was revised in the mouth of each protagonist. Finally, there was a narrative thread that made sense. "Auds, listen, I *know.* Not what Maddie told you, not that part."

"What do you mean?"

"About you and Drew."

"What about us?" Her voice quaked.

"You guys had sex that night. He confessed. It was a mistake."

"What the fuck? I never *had sex* with him."

I pushed out the explanation. "He said you were acting very uninhibited, that you came on to him. I get that you were drugged and can't remember everything, but he didn't realize . . . he really thought you were into it."

"Is this some kind of sick joke? You're saying your boyfriend did this to me and you knew?"

I hesitated. Her distress was sincere. Her accusation would be lacerating if I didn't numb myself. But I had to argue on behalf of Drew, whose account also was credible. "He said you'd been doing that before then, that you were giving out signals you wanted to sleep with him for a while, not just at the party."

"What, like a lighthouse? Are you saying I was *asking for it*?"

"Auds, please, no. That isn't what—"

"How could you do this to me? So, all this time, you've been lying to my face!"

"I didn't know who, what, to believe."

"How could you not tell me? How could you live with him and pretend to be my friend?"

I had no good answer. "You *are* my friend. I just . . . He said you guys were into each other and—"

She screeched, like a cat whose tail had caught in a door. "Fuck you!"

chapter twenty-four

Before I could decide what to do next—call her back, text, wait—I heard Drew, his slightly slurred diction, "Why are you apologizing to Audrey?"

Rage radiated from him, yet when I swung around, he was barely visible. The lights were off in the bedroom behind the balcony.

"I was being insensitive," I said, stepping further from his shadow.

"How much can you do for her? She doesn't let up."

"Yeah. It's cold out here."

"So come in. I'll turn up the heat."

I slipped through the glass door, careful not to as much as graze his arm, my loyalties pulled in opposite directions. "It's so dark."

"That can be fixed," he said. "There is a solution to everything."

"Not everything."

"Between us. In this house. You told her, didn't you?" When I nodded, he said, "And what, she denied it?"

"She's upset that I wasn't honest with her all along."

"We should have been up front sooner." His anger was gone, like a match extinguished. "But the rest . . . she's lying." He hugged me from behind, his breath on my neck. Even from this angle, I could smell the beer. "Let's go downstairs. I could use something to drink."

"Yeah, okay."

I didn't say: *Don't. No more.* A little alcohol made Drew erratic, moody, a lot, and he became sleepy and sad. Better the latter.

In the living room, he sat in the deep-back armchair, next to the windows, his legs stretched out onto the matching ottoman. I was on the couch decorated in the same alabaster linen fabric. Every object in this room was tasteful, designed to be soothing. I was not soothed.

"You said Audrey came on to you," I said, carefully, after he'd finished another half a bottle. "She swears she didn't."

"What kind of proof do you need? She said things to me in private that I can't substantiate. But I have texts between us—from before then."

"Was there anything sexual in them?"

"She never acted the way she did at Rory's party. She wasn't that stupid when sober. She'd already been caught by Josh more than once."

Was that a dodge, an excuse for his behavior? I put my wine glass down on a coaster on the coffee table. I'd been careful to only have a few sips, to stay clearheaded. "Doing what?"

"She fucked at least two other guys," he said.

Fucked. A hard growl.

"I thought he just suspected Auds of cheating." I couldn't keep track of all the lies.

"I was trying to honor my relationship with *my friend.* I'd sworn I wouldn't say anything."

"I get that, but Josh is dead. You can talk to me."

He cocked his head, as if considering. "He spied on her, read her messages when she visited him in college. Things blew up after that. They broke up for a few months, but she begged him for another chance."

"So Josh was humiliated."

"Of course. She was sleeping around with these assholes, these faux artists that she thought were so cool. You should see these messages Josh sent me his senior year. Vicious. He was so pissed at her. I still have them. Do you want to see?"

"I believe you."

"Good." He smirked. "*Finally*. I'm going to get another beer."

Soon, he'd be too drunk to grill for information. When he loped back into the living room with a fresh bottle, I slid closer to him on the couch to secure his attention. He didn't try to cuddle.

"After they graduated, once Josh started having problems, did she do it again?" I asked.

Drew raised the bottle to his wet lips and bit the rim, as if ready to break the glass with his teeth. "Dunno for sure. I'm going to assume so. Things between them got worse once she moved on with her life, started grad school, and he just stopped functioning." A bubble of spit came out with his laugh.

"The thing I don't get is why she stayed with him."

He shrugged. "Man, I tried to warn Josh. You can't just live with your parents, take drugs, and expect a girl like that to be with you while you try to figure out your shit. Get any decent-paying job and roll with it."

A girl like that. Drew had been in love with her.

"Fake it!" His eyes were cloudy as he stared ahead of him, yelling at my brother. "God knows, I had to learn to fake it. What do you think I did most of my life?"

I clutched my arms around my rib cage, uneasy. Alcohol was not having its usual subduing effect on him. He was furious and showing a side of himself I'd never seen before. My pulse was thundering in my ear as I asked gently, "How have you faked it?"

"I can't be an obvious screw-up and have my mother adore me

and let me hide away, like yours did. My mother would have gone apeshit. She would have worried I took after my dad. I had to make this life for myself. It's not some calling I had, to be an aboveboard investment banker—one who doesn't end up involved in some illegal shit. That's the problem with people like you."

Who was he referring to: me or Josh? I tried to lock eyes with him. Even though he was looking at me, he wasn't seeing me at all.

"You have a passion: soccer or art or something that defines you from the time you're a kid. The rest of us just go to school and hope to get some decent-paying work to get by." He laughed again. "If you're smart, you become a coder or a surgeon or—a banker. If not, you find a job you can tolerate." He slapped his thigh with a thud. "God, what a waste! I loved Josh so much. I wanted to *be* him. Until he got stuck, pining away for his glory days of being a big-time athlete."

He stared straight at me, his vision clear now. "You're the same as me, Elle. We're realists who wish we could have been the chosen one. That's the thing about us, why we are so good together."

How very sad.

"We both envied Josh for so long, we didn't know how to stop. And then Josh screwed up his life so badly. How could someone who had everything do that?"

"He was going to get help."

"Addiction counseling." Drew sneered. "What about employment? What about making plans for your adult life? How come *you* weren't freeloading off your parents?"

I'm freeloading off you.

"I'm wondering about Audrey," I said, steering the conversation away from my brother, who never would be able to defend himself again. "Do you think she was there the night of the fire?"

His body was slack, his voice coated with drink. "She could have been there. I didn't see her."

Whoosh. The sensation of a knife thrown past me, tearing off strands of my hair.

"You didn't *see* her?"

Drew's mouth drooped and his eyes grew misty. "Shit. I'm wasted. I don't know what I'm saying anymore. I'm going up to bed. You coming?"

I had to stall. There was no way I was going to lie down next to him. "Yep. Soon. Just gonna call Nora. She's having some issues at work."

That was the least controversial thing I could think of. Something of no interest to him, something that wouldn't raise suspicion.

"K. See you soon."

I waited over an hour, stunned, afraid to be near him. Even this minute, I couldn't calculate how far he'd go, how dangerous he might be. Finally, I slunk up the stairs and into the room he'd commandeered as his workspace, the one with the single bed and the modular desk. His laptop was open on top, beckoning. I didn't bother sitting in the swivel chair.

Find proof he was there.

I imagined a text conversation, never erased, between him and Audrey, planning to set our house ablaze. Maybe Drew kept a digital diary in which he revealed everything, including how he'd drugged and raped Audrey. Which was an absurd and oh-so-convenient notion.

The first two attempts at decoding his password—Josh's birthday and Audrey's full name—of course failed. I typed in Josh's soccer numbers in high school and college. Nope. A few more configurations of names and numbers were equally unsuccessful. Then a memory from a couple of months ago came to me: Drew waving his arm with his new Apple Watch fastened onto his wrist. We'd been at the kitchen table, and he'd exclaimed, "Don't you want one?" I'd barely paid attention to the demonstration of this gadget's magic trick. He flipped up the lid of his laptop and the screen read: *Unlocking with Apple Watch.*

I tiptoed into the Cimmerian room, wondering how close I needed to be to get the results he'd shown me. Not very, as it turned out.

Cracking open the machine, I saw the watch was already unlocking it, as if on cue.

My heart was slamming. I retreated from the room backward, then, recognizing this mistake—in case he awoke—twisted around, hugging this precious prize without letting it slap shut.

In the second bedroom again, I felt my fingers, how they were apart from the rest of me as they worked steadily, unafraid, competent creatures.

I scanned the texts that appeared in the various chats. There were the prominent bubbles with my photo, Drew's boss's, Ty's, a couple of other work friends I'd never met. Below was one of his mother. I scrolled until I saw Josh's name and picture, his half smile, his half squint, his intact, living self. My legs weakened; my arms hung like ropes. I quickly skimmed the messages, ones from the previous year, for "vicious" attacks from my brother against Audrey. There were none. Backtracking further would be a waste of time. What mattered was plans between Drew and Audrey to meet at our house.

I did a window search for "Audrey" and "Auds" and found a stream of chats from a few months before the rape and the fire. Drew initiated their correspondence: *Hey, how you holding up?*

Audrey: *Not good.*

Must be really hard for you.

Yeah. He still hasn't forgiven me for sleeping with Freddie and Ben. It's been three years. I keep asking why he's still with me.

He really loves you, Auds.

I love him, too. But before he was unavailable and far away. Now he's so messed up.

Not your fault.

He needs a life. I've been close to breaking up with him for like a year now. What am I supposed to do, wait forever?

It went on like this, complaints from her, friendly commiseration between them. I started to skim, speed-reading. I zeroed in on the week of the party, my mind churning, hoping or not hoping—uncertain which—to discover if Drew had mentioned he was going.

See you there?

Audrey: *Yep.*

That was it, nothing more until a couple of days later, after our encounter at the hospital.

Audrey: *OMG! Why didn't you text me when you found out?*

Drew: *Sorry. I should have.*

I had to call Josh's mom like ten times. And you didn't answer my texts.

I was in shock. I didn't know how to tell you.

Audrey: *This is SO surreal.*

Yeah.

I feel SO guilty.

Drew: *Why guilty?*

I laid some heavy shit on him right before. Like, a few hours before!

Are you saying you think he did this to himself?

Audrey: *IDK.*

It was an accident. You'd have to be crazy to try and burn yourself to death.

After that exchange, Drew kept sending out messages and Audrey replied more and more infrequently. I calculated the timing in my head and discovered Drew was still contacting her once he was sleeping with me. But only for a couple of weeks—and mostly casual, just checking-in-with-you texts. Then they stopped.

I turned to emails, focusing on the ones from the time of the party.

There it was: from a car rental service dated the evening of the fire. Under vehicle information was listed: Vehicle ID Number, Make, Year, Model, Mileage, Registration Number. But the category that caused my body to turn to liquid, poured into the chair, was the color. Silver.

The roar in my skull felt like a riptide. I checked the make—a Mazda 6—then images of them online. It could have passed for the car I'd observed in Audrey's garage. Similar shade and shape. It couldn't be a coincidence that Drew had rented a car on that night. But was it a fluke that this particular one resembled the midsize sedan that Audrey drove in high school? The same make, the same color. Just as Mrs. Goldsmith had said. The same and not the same.

I stared at the computer screen as if it had frozen. But it wasn't the machine that had frozen; it was me. My brain stem wasn't discharging commands to my spinal cord. My motor neurons weren't sending impulses to my muscles. My limbic system was . . .

Move!

Pack and go or just go? Clothes I could do without. But my cell phone and laptop were in the bedroom—with Drew. I had to return his computer as well. I would have to be quick and careful, graceful and more agile than I'd ever been. Escape was a mixture of a race and a ballet, fleetingly fast and balanced on the top of my feet to avoid making noise. Josh was the athlete in the family, not me.

Oh, Joshie. Oh, God. What did he do to you?

In Drew's lair, where he lay on his side moaning softly, I decided to stuff my suitcase with whatever was nearby: MacBook and iPhone first, then shoes and hanging sweaters. Checking on Drew in the shadows—a dim light in the hall illuminated the room just enough—I noted he hadn't changed position. His breathing was deep, filled with ahs and hums. His drunken slumber rendered me brave. I slid open the dresser drawers, pulled out my underwear in bunches like small bouquets of wilting flowers. My joggers and jeans, my T-shirts and bras. Then, as I tried to hang onto too many garments, I banged my hip against the drawer.

"What are you doing?"

Drew's question was flat, without recrimination or even curiosity. He was still dazed, not fully conscious. But soon he would be.

"I have to go." I spoke in a hush.

His body hit the bed frame as he sat up. "What do you mean? Did something happen? Is it your mother?"

The savvy answer would have been yes. "Just let me go," I pleaded, my voice tremoring.

"What are you talking about?" He switched on the end table lamp. His eyes, fixed on mine, were yellow brown, the color of a tiger's. "Where?"

"Back."

"To the city?"

"Yes." Shaking, I zipped my suitcase. The truth was, where would I go, if not Drew's apartment?

"What's the matter? It's the middle of the night."

"You're right. It's my mother. She's not well."

He waited a beat, then uttered a low, animal sound. "You're lying."

Alert now, he walked toward me, clutched my wrist. "Why are you leaving?"

"I could use another glass of wine."

"Not if you're planning to drive."

"I won't have much."

Drew looked at me, a level stare, dark and empty. Then he unhooked his hand. "Sure. I'll join you."

I busied myself with filling my glass. All around us, the outside was pressing into the dark-suffused house, through the huge floor-to-ceiling windows, the sliding doors to the deck. The woods and pond, the croaking frogs and buzzing insects were our closest neighbors. There were no Mrs. Goldsmiths or Mrs. Petersons nearby, privy to the goings-on inside here. Terror spread its huge wingspan inside of me.

"So, why were you creeping out of here?" he asked again. He glanced up the stairs, then back at me. He was piecing something together, even now, as he gestured for me to give him the half-empty bottle.

I watched him do both: awash himself in liquor as he appraised the situation. What of his laptop? Had I left the emails open? I envisioned us sprinting up those open-riser stairs. Would he push me over the railing, let me tumble to—if not my death—some limb-breaking, concussed state? I didn't budge as he sauntered past me and raced up the steps. My eyes registered the empty kitchen table and I scrambled to the counter, scoured the empty canisters. Then I opened the silverware drawer, inspecting the spoons and forks, as if one would suddenly change form, like in a fairy tale. But if not on the table, my car keys were zipped away in my backpack, upstairs.

I considered slipping out of the house with none of my belongings, waiting in the backyard until Drew passed out. Maybe he'd forget to lock the door. But it was too late.

"Why were you going through my texts and emails?" Drew asked from the second floor, peering down. "How did you fucking get my password? I told you I'd share messages between me and Audrey, that we had nothing to hide." His voice was hot as blood.

I whispered, as if confessing to my own crime, "There was nothing in there that proved she was interested in you that way."

"That's a matter of interpretation."

You were in my house that night. "I should go."

"You are spying on me and now you're making no sense: running back into the epicenter of a disaster."

You are the epicenter of my life's disaster.

"What are you accusing me of, Ellie? Just spit it out. I'm not some monster."

My mouth was dry as paste. "You were there. You rented a car that night, the same color as Audrey's. You drove it to my house."

He came back down to the first floor, shifting his gaze over me. "Not for the reason you think. Give me a chance to explain."

When I didn't respond, Drew headed for the refrigerator, took out another beer, and popped off the cap on the edge of the counter.

Something flipped in my belly, something I didn't want to come up. "So, you rented a car, which looked like the one Audrey drove in high school."

"Yes, but you have to understand why."

"Was it to frame Audrey?" I shuddered.

Drew slapped the countertop. "Of course not. I knew Josh wouldn't let me in. I had to trick him to think it was Audrey. We'd had an argument."

"Why not just text him? Why come all the way to New Jersey?" My questions were a stall; all my thoughts were on exits. There was the front door and the one in the basement—too far.

"Josh called me after he'd spoken to her. He was beside himself. It just came out of my mouth, 'Of course she wasn't raped.' He asked how I could possibly know that." Drew was downing his drink now, then reaching into the fridge for another. "We'd never discussed that I went to Rory's party. What I did or didn't do was never on his mind unless he was involved. But he was pissed when he found out."

"Why did you drive out to my house?"

"Josh cursed me out and hung up. I kept calling him. He just ignored me. I had to make him speak to me."

"Why trick him into thinking you were Audrey by renting a car that looked like hers?"

Drew's eyes were gleaming, as if all the alcohol had moistened them. "If he thought it was me at the door, he wouldn't answer. My plan was to honk, and when he saw the car he'd come out. I could give him the six-pack, the vodka, and the Ativans. I knew that was the way to get through to him."

"He was trying to stay clean."

He shrugged. "There was no other way."

Drew's cold precision made me want to weep. My brother, this man whose bed I'd shared, Audrey, the woman who claimed victimhood: all three of them swirling in a brew of deceit. It felt impossible to pick out the individual ingredients, to locate the source of the poison.

"You knew I was there, that I'd see you give him all that stuff."

"Josh told me you'd left. I passed you on your street, going in the opposite direction."

I raised my index finger. "You did? Why didn't you . . . ?"

"I did! I waved. You weren't looking in my direction, never were."

"I wasn't gone long, so you couldn't have been there for even an hour."

He sighed. "Things didn't go well."

"He didn't come outside?"

"No. I honked a few times, then decided not to wake the neighborhood. Did Mrs. Goldsmith report that to the police, too?" When I shook my head, he said, "I went around the back and it was open, the sliding door to the deck. Josh was downstairs, smoking one of your cigarettes."

"What are you talking about?" I pressed my fist into my chest, my still-beating heart. "Josh didn't smoke. I never gave him my cigarettes."

"You left your pack there."

I gagged and then swallowed hard. En route to the Washington Bridge, I'd searched my bag for my laptop and wondered where my Marlboros were. "Are you saying he set the fire with them?"

For a second, Drew looked confused, as if he'd lost his bearings. "Why are you asking me all these questions? You should be on my side. Don't act like you're not part of what happened, because we all are: me, Audrey, Josh, even you."

The knob at the base of my neck throbbed. Terrible news was coming, maybe more than could be borne. "What *did* happen?"

"Josh pocketed the pills but took a couple right before he went up to bed. Once he'd calmed down, I let it slip that Audrey was untrustworthy. Somehow, it came out . . . that we'd had sex."

Why the fuck would you do that?

The answer was like a scientific theory, one I'd failed to accept until this moment: for Drew, it was essential for Josh to view him as his equal.

"Josh flipped his shit! He came at me, shoved me to the floor. There was no way his girlfriend would do that. As if I was so undesirable, so hideous, such a loser. I reminded him that she'd cheated before. He spit in my face. I'm not kidding, Ellie, in my face!"

"Maybe the idea of you and Audrey together was too much. Not that, not—you would never hurt him on purpose, right?"

"Nothing was on purpose, not in that way. My feelings for Audrey—I mean, yeah, sure, she was hot and talented and fun to be around. I wanted to be like Josh, always had. But he ruined our friendship over a woman who didn't even love him. What he said, what he threatened to do to me was unforgiveable."

"What did he say?"

"He said, 'I don't want to ever see you again. You'll pay for what you did. I'll post that you're a rapist all over social media. I'll convince Audrey to go to the police. You'll see. She'll listen to me! Just wait. I'm going to burn your life down.'"

chapter twenty-five

T he world went white and I stumbled forward. Drew was by my side, holding me by the elbow, before I could resist. He placed the beer on the counter, then led me to the couch, gingerly, the way he would an old woman. I wriggled free of him and sank onto the couch.

"Josh didn't mean that," I said. "He would never—"

"You weren't there. And what is it with you and your brother, this obsession with fire?" he asked, standing near the triangular windows now, facing the pond. His gaze was focused outward, at the milky black sky.

"He didn't mean what he said, not literally."

"He ordered that I leave, after taunting me: Audrey could go to the cops; he could go himself. Of course there wasn't anything she could pin on me since I hadn't *done* anything wrong. But you know how it is, in the moment, how you panic, right?"

"Yes," I said.

"Once Josh went upstairs, I found your cigarettes on the dining room table. I needed to unwind, to shake off the fury. And then . . . I thought of you." He turned toward me, his smile askew.

"What about me?"

"Firestarter."

This time, the knife did more than whiz by; it impaled me in the chest. "I inspired you to kill my brother?"

Drew moved to my side. "I don't think that, but others might," he said, his mouth too close, that stench of beer. "I was so fucked up. As I was leaving, I heard Josh upstairs cursing me and I took a final drag on the cigarette, and I realized I had nothing left to lose. I tossed it into a basket, that wicker one your parents kept near the back door, thinking it would just be a little flame, enough to scare people. Josh was messed up, too." He shrugged. "He might forget and think you had left that cigarette. His own sister."

There was a whistle in my ear, like the approach of a train, getting louder and louder. "Why would you want to frame me?"

"You mean like you're framing me now?"

"But I never did *anything* to you."

He gazed at me with a hint of sadistic pleasure. "You know what it's like to be dismissed. You, of all people, could understand that kind of impulsive act."

My muscles clenched. "That's not . . . that's not what happened with me and Anna."

"Wasn't it?"

"She was fighting for the lighter."

"Josh threatened me, and then I did one stupid thing, in a moment of rage. Don't you see the parallels between us?"

"Yes." I hadn't realized I was crying until my eyesight blurred. *One stupid thing—which killed my brother.* "Why did you get involved with me?"

"We made perfect sense," he said, his hand on the back of my neck now. "Josh was lost and Audrey stopped talking to me. And there you were: my boyhood crush."

"The booby prize?"

"Don't degrade yourself. I always liked you. And you were a con-nection to . . . him."

Not hot and talented and fun to be around. "You wouldn't have said anything if I hadn't found the car receipt."

He stared over my shoulder, at some faraway vision, for only a moment. "I was afraid you'd leave me, just like Josh did. I couldn't take another loss."

"Would you ever . . . hurt me?"

"It's not what I want. But I can do what your brother couldn't do to me. I can burn your life down." He grimaced, his mouth tight as a fitted bedsheet, tucked into the corners. "Just don't turn on me, Ellie."

"I won't say a word, not to anyone."

"We have to act like a couple."

"Of course. I just need time to . . . get my bearings."

"Back at our apartment?"

"Yes," I said, repulsed by the idea of returning to that place.

"What will you tell your parents and Nora?"

"Just that we were having problems, arguing from the stress of Covid and losing Josh. You know," I improvised, "like, we were deal-ing with it differently."

"What the fuck does *that* mean? That we're breaking up?"

"No," I said, rigid with fear. "I won't say that, not to anyone."

He ran his eyes over me, as if I were a deer he'd shot and he was trying to ascertain how best to lift my carcass onto the hood of his truck. "I shouldn't have told you anything. Then you wouldn't have that accusing look on your face."

"Okay, okay. I'll just say I was going stir-crazy here. At least in New York, there are a few people out on the street. You didn't feel safe there and figured better to stick to the woods. You planned on waiting until summer, then renting a car to come . . ."—the last word was hard—"home."

"Is that believable, with the infection rate so high?"

"Yes. I know how to stay healthy."

Hyperbole. Like a soldier guaranteeing she won't be shot in the back.

"You can't tell your parents," he commanded. "I'll delete the email of that receipt, even though it doesn't prove anything. You have to promise not to turn on me, Ellie."

"Don't worry. I won't say a word."

He glimpsed at me, a proprietary look. "We have to stick up for each other, like I did with Josh."

"What do you mean?"

"That day in the hospital. He was disoriented. His memory of that night was erased. He asked if you'd left a cigarette burning. I reassured him you would never do that. It was an accident, maybe electrical, no one knew yet. I protected you. That's what we do for each other."

"Thanks," I said, uncertain what was true, what I could bear.

He yawned, stretching his mouth open, exposing the cavernous maw inside, pink and red and pulpy. "Come up to bed, leave in the morning."

"I'll stay on the couch, so if I leave before you're up, I don't wake you."

"Okay, I guess. Wait here. I'll bring down your things."

Alone for a moment, I concluded it would be impossible to get any sleep here.

My suitcase thumped behind Drew on the wooden stairs. At the bottom, he delivered my phone. He hugged me close. "I'll be back in a few weeks."

"Good," I muttered.

Not long after I heard the door of his bedroom shut, I quietly gathered my things together and walked into the chill of freedom.

An hour later, I stopped at a motel chain in Plymouth, Massachusetts, and requested a room on the first floor to avoid the elevator. The young guy at reception had a crew cut and acne scars but no mask. He stared at mine for a second, then must have realized it was rude of him. He took my credit card.

"Don't worry," I said. "It's just a precaution. I'm not sick."

"No problem. There's breakfast down the hall until ten a.m.," he said when he handed me the key card.

"Thanks." I wouldn't get enough rest, but coffee and some food to go were mandatory.

In the room, I turned off the heating system and cracked open the window to let in fresh air. Then I washed my hands, sprayed them with disinfectant, set my alarm for nine, and scrambled to get into bed. It was so cold, the blankets not enough, as I dove in and out of a continuous dream. I was on a road trip with someone in the back seat, Nora, I thought, and even though I was lost and my arms jiggly, unable to steer the wheel, even though we were zigzagging all over the road, she refused to take over. The car ended up veering off a bridge. Bobbing in the water, Nora shook her head and mouthed, "I can't help you." I was trapped, drowning . . . my lungs filling, my eyes darting as if keeping sight of my friend could save me.

The light had sneaked through the fissure in the curtains, and I was short of breath. I forced myself to inhale slowly, exhale, three, four times. My body responded, as always, before my mind. But then, the recognition of what I'd learned about Josh. What I could never unlearn. I would never get out from under it; the best I could hope for was to carry this millstone around my neck, bearing the downward pull.

I rushed to shower, to dress, to brush my teeth—my gums had two new canker sores, again. I was rotting away from the inside. Dressed and masked, I rolled my suitcase to the breakfast room, where two couples were seated with their plates of eggs and toast, bowls of cereal, various juices and coffees. Pouring French roast into a paper cup, I sensed them observing me, with my nose and mouth covered. They lowered their voices, shifted in their chairs, unsettled. I chose a blueberry muffin and wrapped it in a napkin, and a container of yogurt from its bed of ice, packed both in my bag with a plastic spoon.

In my car, I hurried to eat, to sip the hot liquid. I texted my father, to make contact, to feel grounded to some tenuous sense of family.

How are you and Mom holding up?

No immediate response, so I turned on *The Daily* podcast and drove.

Closing in on Connecticut, I heard the ping and decided to pull into a rest stop. I would risk using the bathroom and buy some garbage meal from a fast-food chain. First, I read my father's message: *Mom is distraught. Sergeant Abbott died of Covid-19.*

I conjured up the sergeant's face, the puffy eyelids and broken blood vessels, in an attempt to summon compassion. None came.

I asked my dad: *The police told you?*

They'd never release that information. You remember our old neighbor, Mrs. Goldsmith?

"Now what?" I asked, aloud, staring at the half-empty parking lot. A woman held the hand of a young girl with wispy hair spouting in the wind, as they made their way toward the indoor service area. *Don't go in there! Keep your daughter safe!*

I texted: *Yes.*

She did. Turns out her nephew is an officer there.

Doubtful, I thought. Clever Mrs. G was so determined to discover who owned that car. During one of her routine "nuisance" calls to the police, she probably managed to weasel information about the sergeant out of some desk clerk.

I'm so sorry, Dad. I'll call you later.

But I wouldn't. Not on this day, or the next one or the other after that, not while still in shock over Drew's disclosure. In the bathroom, I scrubbed my hands until they were raw, then rubbed sanitizer on them. I purchased a bag of ground coffee, a gallon of milk, nuts and pretzels and a few PowerBars. Stocking up on food would be a problem once I reached city limits. Some random supermarket off the highway was a better solution. At the next exit, I wandered into a town until a Stop & Shop appeared. This would be a sprint, like a TV show where contestants competed to load up the best material before their opponents outdid them. Only there were no opponents. Just other shoppers glancing my way as I sped through the aisles, tossing cans, bottles, and boxes into my cart.

The cashier squinted at me, with my double mask, and said, "I'm out of cash."

"No problem." I swiped my credit card. "I'm not sick. Just careful."

The young woman had a blotchy face and a narrow mouth. She said nothing in response. I thanked her and bagged the items myself.

The drive was a form of self-soothing. As long as I was in this vehicle, miles away from Drew, I was free. But once I hit the West Side Highway, the millstone tugged at my neck, the sack of grain clung to my back, the corset tightened around my waist. There was no way to unshackle myself from these constraints.

Inside, I greeted Doorman Jerry with a quick wave and hurried to the elevator. In the apartment, the air was stagnant, the room like a museum diorama from another era. I'd sleep on the couch, creating whatever psychological space was possible. It was too early—only the afternoon—and time would unspool in this enclosure so slowly.

After unpacking the food, I texted Audrey: *I'm sorry. Please, forgive me. You were right all along. I was wrong about everything.*

My phone rang immediately.

"What happened?" she asked. "Did he hurt you? What did he do?"

"Not like that."

"Ellie, I think I *know*. The night of the fire. Josh texted me after I'd gone to sleep. I can't believe I never saw what he wrote. I found it, going through old messages yesterday. 'Sorry about everything. Messed up with Stoli and benzos. Talk tomorrow when my mind's clear.'"

I walked to the living room and sat upright in the armchair, questioning again. "You just saw that *yesterday*, seriously?"

"I swear on Glinda's life! The point is, there wouldn't have been that shit in your house. Josh could have gone out and bought the vodka. But benzos, no. Which means someone had to bring them to him. I figure that someone was Drew."

I hunched over, head to thighs. If I denied her allegations, she would return to them, over and over, maybe even approach the police with them, maybe endanger us both. Who could say what Drew was capable of? "Auds . . ."

"He was there, wasn't he?"

"I'm not supposed to say anything."

"You can trust me, Ellie. I'm your friend."

Was she? And if she wasn't, who else did I have to turn to?

"Okay, look, I had no idea. Drew showed up when I was driving to the city. I just found out. You have to believe me. If I'd known what he did, I never would have stayed with him."

"Of course not," she said in a thin thread of a voice.

"Drew swears it was an accident."

"Like raping me?"

"No. He didn't mean to hurt you or Josh. Just like I didn't mean to hurt Anna."

"Ellie, when are you going to get that there's no comparison? And just because his intentions weren't to destroy people's lives doesn't give him a pass."

My throat was raw, as if scraped by a scalpel. I'd never get a pass for scarring Anna or for leaving Josh alone. But Audrey was right. My misdeeds weren't like Drew's. "It's just, we have to drop this. Do you understand?"

"Yes. He's dangerous."

"We'll never prove anything, and the investigation can't drag on. For my parents' sake as well. We have to let it go."

She said calmly, "I'll never do anything to hurt them or you. You don't have to worry about that."

"Thank you, Auds."

"But where will you go now?"

I scanned the environment. Every expensive object—furniture, decorations, cookware—belonged to the owner, the man who'd killed my brother. I couldn't stay here.

"Dunno."

"Ellie," she whispered, "come live with me in Brooklyn, and we'll ride this fucking shit show out together. Or go somewhere else if you can figure out where. Just get away from him before he causes another 'accident.'"

I couldn't afford anywhere and wasn't returning to my parents'.

"We're young, which is on our side. We'll be very careful," I said. "Meet you in Brooklyn."

chapter twenty-six

Fall 2022

No one went to the police. Drew continued to harass me, even after Audrey gave me temporary shelter. Even after I took over Nora's bedroom in my old place when she moved in with Matthew. My ex wouldn't let me go; his acts of retribution I anticipated for months. The hold he had on me didn't lessen—even though his communications were filled with pleas, not bullying—until I departed from New York to Maryland for graduate school.

There I met Adam, an optimistic, unflappable man with light eyes and a gleaming smile, a man with the awestruck look of someone first discovering the Northern Lights or the Grand Canyon. I finally put it all behind me: the fires, Drew, even Audrey.

But nothing ever stayed where it belonged, in the past.

The office air-conditioning was anemic on this uncharacteristically hot morning in November. Seventy-five degrees in Baltimore. I was editing the blog for the bio department, when Professor Closkey made a gesture of wiping sweat off his brow through the glass door. I smiled and waved, one of those little British royalty waves, not too grand. Everyone on the faculty treated me with respect, but I was careful not to get too friendly, like some of the other grad students did at office parties, where the wine broke down barriers. No potential slipups for me; I needed flawless recommendations to land myself a coveted government job in DC. No longer chasing down every detail about wildfires, I was taking classes in international policies and environmental justice. The competition in my field was fierce.

When my cell phone rang, I was startled. Rarely did anyone call me here. My boyfriend, Adam—a pediatric resident in the school of medicine—was even busier than I and stuck to texting, as did the other students in my program. Nora and I spoke in the evenings when we could find the time, and my dad contacted me for brief chats to "check in" once or twice a week. Seeing my mother's name on the screen, I paused.

No more therapy revelations, please.

The last one was like a rain burst: "Josh needed so much, so much more than you, that I just gave him everything I had. I didn't have enough energy left over, and I thought you were so strong and independent; you'd be fine without me. And then, after we lost him, it was like we weren't parents anymore. Which wasn't fair to you. Poor Dad was so worried about me, you can't blame him. He was spread too thin. But we always loved you. You must know that."

No. No, I didn't. Dad, yes, but not you. I was too angry to see what you had to give, as limited as it was.

But I never communicated that to her; of course I didn't.

"Mom," I answered the phone, alert, as always, to a possible emergency. "You okay? Anything wrong?"

"I wanted you to hear it from me."

I gripped my desk, as if it were a lifeboat. "Is Dad okay?"

"Yes, he's getting by."

"Are *you*?" A trick question. She would never be okay again.

"It's Drew."

My mind jumped: Audrey reported him, finally; he was arrested for rape, but not for Josh's death. She had no evidence to link him to the fire.

"I wasn't sure if you were still in touch with him?"

"Not since Adam."

"I'm sorry to have to tell you this, Ellie," my mother said. "Drew was involved in a hit-and-run in the city."

"Oh, my God! He injured someone?"

"No, honey." Her tone softened. "*He* was the person hit. He died at the scene, before the ambulance arrived. I'm so sorry."

There was a churning noise, then a boom. As if an explosion occurred on the floor. But it was in my head. "That's . . ."

"Devastating, especially for Margaux."

They will bond over this, and Mom will never know.

"Yes," I said.

"I'm sure this will be hard for you. It's so much loss, so close to home. Is it all right, me telling you while you're at work?"

"Yes," I repeated.

"Let's talk later, when you're at your apartment." The one I shared with two other grad students who were rarely around. "Say hi to Adam for me."

I imagined her small smile. My parents adored my new boyfriend.

"I will."

After we hung up, I realized my knee hurt from banging it against the desk. I drank from the stainless-steel bottle of water and clicked on Facebook, scanning for the outcries, the bursts of shock, the throwback photos or memories. Ty's latest post read: *Can't believe this horrible news. Love you forever, Drew.*

I typed Audrey's name in "search." It had been a while since we'd been in contact. We'd drifted away from each other, as if in a coordinated effort, some form of reparation for us both. Now, I reached her voicemail. "Auds," I whispered. "Have you heard?"

Hours passed as I worked in a distracted state, my thoughts ambling. Over my lunch break, I walked through the campus on a tree-lined path, the monochrome brick buildings all around me. The familiarity was soothing, and the warm weather tricked me into expecting the burst of pink flowers. But the branches were bare.

On the way back, my phone buzzed. The text came from an unknown number and was followed by a kiss emoji.

Another silver car?

I stood very still and stared at this sentence for several minutes. Was it a morbid joke, or something more ominous?

I needed to talk to her. *Pick up, pick up.*

"Hey," she answered on the third ring.

"How'd you hear?"

"It's all over Facebook. You?"

"My mother. I'm in shock."

"Really? Accidents happen all the time. You know that, Elle."

I gasped. "What did you do?"

"He couldn't stop. Texts, calls, begging us—both of us, you and me—to give him another chance. For Josh's sake. That's what he said. Can you believe it?"

I stared up: light, Lucite-blue sky. I was stuck in some crap dystopian movie, waiting for the spacecraft to split through the sky. "What happened?"

Silence. Then: "It wasn't premeditated. Just like his defense, Josh's death."

"Oh, Audrey."

"Bye, Ellie. Take care of yourself." She ended the call.

A breeze blew, the promise of cooler days ahead. At least for now.

I erased her message.

Acknowledgments

Thank you to:

Caroline Leavitt for your excellent editing, brainstorming, and friendship. Any mistakes or miscalculations in these pages are, of course, my own.

Judy Batalion for your careful, insightful feedback, chapter after chapter, and for all your kind words.

Crystal Sershen for your diligent proofreading and for boosting my morale (and Alice Peck for sending Crystal my way).

Brooke Warner, Shannon Green, and Lauren Wise at She Writes Press for putting this book into the world.

Caitlin Hamilton Summie for your big heart and your dedication as my publicist (never mind your knockout fiction).

Sasha Troyan, Tess Callahan, Alice Feiring, Caprice Garvin, Suzanne Roth, Susan Shapiro, and Kimmi Berlin (writers all) for the friendship and encouragement over the long haul. Anne Leigh Parrish for your clear-eyed view.

The fantastic, generous, kick-ass women in my SWP 2021 cohort for tolerating my doubts, equivocations, and general ramblings, and for all the advice: Suzanne Simonetti, Leslie Rasmussen, Mary Camarillo, Deborah Shepherd, Tammy Pasterick, Valerie Taylor, Meg Nocero, Rektok Ross, and Marcie Maxfield.

Libby Jordon for your generosity and advertising savvy.

Readers of *The Happiness Thief* for your kind reception.

My sons, Noah and Spencer, for letting me interrupt your workdays with random questions rather than resorting to "the magic of Google." I'm so proud of you both.

Jay, for everything. Thank you for reading every draft without complaint and for helping me navigate the last few years in life and in fiction. I'm so lucky to have you.

About the Author

Photo credit: Jay Lindell

In addition to *Will End in Fire,* Nicole Bokat has published three novels: *Redeeming Eve* (2000), *What Matters Most* (2006), and *The Happiness Thief* (2021). *Redeeming Eve* was nominated for both the Hemingway Foundation/PEN award and the Janet Heidinger Kafka Prize for Fiction. *The Happiness Thief* was a Foreword Indie Awards finalist. Kirkus wrote about *The Happiness Thief*, "Bokat is an evocative wordsmith . . . she has crafted a sympathetic heroine as her main character. . . . A compulsively readable mystery and character study." She's also the author of a book on novelist Margaret Drabble, and has written essays for several publications, including the *New York Times*, *Parents*, and *The Forward*. She lives in Montclair, New Jersey, with her husband and dog, Ruby, and has two adult sons.

Looking for your next great read?

We can help!

Visit www.shewritespress.com/next-read
or scan the QR code below for a list
of our recommended titles.

She Writes Press is an award-winning
independent publishing company founded to
serve women writers everywhere.